"Come to view the corpse, have you, darlin'?"

The man in the bed smiled as he spoke. He turned his head and kissed the palm of her hand.

"No!" Paula jerked her hand away. "I'm here to get some answers."

Blue, blue eyes looked up at her. "Ask away, lass. Did the law let you in because you found me? For which I'm thanking you, mind. I didn't fancy lying in that dirty water for the rest of my life."

"Who put you there? Who are you?"

"My goodness, you *are* the law, aren't you?" He sighed. "Fancy that," he said in a regretful tone. "I should have figured it from the start. I've got nothing to say to you. Please go."

Paula stood up. The man was a total charmer, but he was obviously not about to cooperate ... yet.

Dear Reader,

March is traditionally the month of Spring Break, and Superromance would like to give readers a break! So look for cents-off coupons in the back pages of all Superromance novels this month, good on the purchase of your next Superromance title. Meanwhile, enjoy our March titles....

To welcome spring, Connie Bennett has penned a heart-warming story in *Single ... With Children.* Caroline Converse is terrified of Mitch Grogan's overwhelming family. But what kind of woman turns her back on a motherless brood ... and the only man she has ever loved?

Dance of Deception marks the Superromance debut of Catherine Judd, who gives us a moving, atmospheric story set on misty Vancouver Island. Shelby Rourke has put her career on hold to return to the house where she'd spent her childhood summers, in hopes of dispelling the nightmares and nameless fears that haunt her. Cullen Pierce, her longtime friend, holds the key, it seems, to mysteries her sanity won't let her contemplate....

In honor of St. Patrick's Day, ever popular Sharon Brondos has conjured up Liam Croft, a headstrong, hearty Irish hero in *Luck of the Irish.* The moment prosecuting attorney Paula Dixon stumbles across him, her world begins to unravel. He refuses to tell her how he came to be lying in a ditch with a bullet wound in his shoulder, and though his stubbornness makes her investigation difficult, resisting him becomes impossible!

Finally, Muriel Jensen has spun off her *My Valentine 1994* short story, "My Comic Valentine," into a delicious quest for revenge in *Candy Kisses.* Someone has it in for cheating lovers, patronizing bosses and sexist boors, and Detective Bill Mitchell figures Sarah Stowe is his chief suspect in the Sweet Avenger case. Unfortunately, her charms soon have him contemplating his own crimes of passion.

And don't forget to look for details in the back pages about entering our Superromantic Sweepstakes!

Marsha Zinberg
Senior Editor, Superromance

Sharon Brondos

Luck of the Irish

Harlequin Books

TORONTO • NEW YORK • LONDON
AMSTERDAM • PARIS • SYDNEY • HAMBURG
STOCKHOLM • ATHENS • TOKYO • MILAN
MADRID • WARSAW • BUDAPEST • AUCKLAND

ISBN 0-373-70588-3

LUCK OF THE IRISH

Copyright © 1994 by Sharon Brondos.

This edition published by arrangement with Harlequin Enterprises B. V.

® and TM are trademarks of the publisher. Trademarks indicated with
® are registered in the United States Patent and Trademark Office, the
Canadian Trade Marks Office and in other countries.

Printed in U.S.A.

A Note from the Author

Dear Reader:

You never can tell when the idea for a story will hit. I began this book one hot afternoon when I was doing exactly what Paula is doing in the first section—helping my Soroptimist club clean up our adopted section of the highway.

Of course, I didn't actually find a hero, but the one I imagined was Irish. Only an Irishman, I reasoned, could be as outrageously charming under pressure, marvelously passionate in love and heroically resourceful in times of danger as I needed this man to be for the story I planned to tell.

I also wanted to set the second part of the tale in Ireland, so before I wrote the book I went there.

My daughter, Pam, and I rented an apartment in Dublin, right in the area where most of *Luck of the Irish* takes place. We blended in so well that soon Irish tourists were asking us directions. Must have been the red hair! It certainly wasn't our accents. By the time we left, the story was firmly established in my mind, ready for me to put it down on paper.

Although it was hard work, it was also a magic trip. So take my hand, St. Patrick's hand and the hand of any leprechaun who cares to come along, and journey with us all to the enchanting Emerald Isle.

Sharon Brondos

To all the members of Soroptimist International of Central Wyoming, especially Debbie, Judy, Evelyn and Molly, who were with me when we cleaned up Highway 220 and this story began.

And to my daughter, Pam, who traveled to Ireland with me so that I could see how the story ended.

Thanks. No one works alone.

CHAPTER ONE

THE CROSS HAIRS of the hunting rifle sight lined up on the target perfectly. The watcher felt a thrill of anticipation. *Couldn't miss.* Not at this range, under these conditions. Like shooting fish in a barrel. A finger began to squeeze the trigger....

But let up pressure when another figure stepped in front of the target. The shot was spoiled. Couldn't take the chance of hitting the wrong one.

The watcher settled back. Well, it wasn't the end of the world. The target would wait. Better not to have it over with too soon. All good things in their own good time, Momma always said.

The watcher slipped back into the brush, covering up most of the signs of passage and presence left at the site. Momma also said that tomorrow was another day. Timing was everything. Indeed, it was.

"IF IT DISINTEGRATES or fights back, don't pick it up, ladies," the squad leader said. "But if you find goodies worth keeping, do so in a separate bag. At the end of the day, we'll give out a prize to the one who finds the best garbage treasure." The leader smiled at her troops and waved her arm, leading them on to battle. Twenty women laughed and chattered, discussing the prospects of winning the reward. Although participating in the national Adopt a Highway program was supposed to be its own reward, it didn't hurt to add a little extra incentive to get a little extra return.

However, one member of the club, Paula Dixon, groaned silently, wondering why in the world she'd agreed to join this outing. Even though it was Saturday, her job as assistant district attorney left her with plenty of paperwork to catch up on over the weekend. Volunteerism was not her style, though she agreed with the need to keep the nation's highways clean. In spite of her lifelong rebellion against adopting dainty-minded "Southern bellism," she really didn't like to get messy. It was going to be hot, dirty, filthy work, and she was used to appearing dignified no matter what the circumstance.

Paula sighed. That was part of her problem, wasn't it?

She was used to too many things. She had settled into an acceptance of it all. Her job, her house, her life. She had set her sights long ago and hadn't deviated. Ever. While she had achieved a great deal, nevertheless, she had to admit she'd been in a rut, a long straight ditch in the ground, and she had been feeling rebellious about it for some time. The same sense of rebellion that had gripped and driven her to avoid a "proper" marriage and lifestyle and become a lawyer. Worse, in her family's eyes, a prosecuting attorney.

She should be happy, but she wasn't. Not exactly unhappy, but certainly uneasy and...

Restless.

Maybe she needed a change. Something to shake up her complacency. Something she could do that had nothing to do with law or criminals.

So, in response to some visceral need to do something completely different, here she stood, bright orange bag in hand, bright orange vest on her chest, ready to collect other people's garbage. Her chapter of the women's service organization, Soroptimists International, was out to clean their "adopted highway" section. She hefted her spike-tipped broomstick and waded into the weeds.

This early on a South Carolina Low Country spring morning, it was cold enough for any snakes or other varmints to be relatively torpid, and she wore high boots and jeans, so she wasn't too worried about being bitten. Cautious, certainly. She spied an empty cigarette pack and speared it.

Zap. She zeroed in on a beer can.

"Hey, Paula," Betsy Dutton yelled from across the road, waving an empty liquor bottle. "Want to play points? One for beer, five for liquor bottles, two for soda pop, especially any plastic..."

"And twenty five for snakes?" Paula called back. "No, thanks. I'll just jab and stuff." She raised a moldy cardboard box on the end of her stick and stuck it into the sack.

"You're no fun," Betsy complained. "Where's your competitive spirit?"

"Left it in the courtroom, I guess." Paula stood straight and stretched. Lordy, she was stiff and out of shape. Thirty years old, lady, she told herself. Not old, but not young, either. *You all'd best get yourself on a regular exercise program instead of depending on your genes to keep you skinny and fit for much longer.* That was what her best friend and colleague, Sheriff Tottie Reynolds was always saying to her. Tottie, the first black female to achieve high office in law enforcement in the county, was fitter than any woman her age had a right to be. And, she had Paula's sedentary lifestyle pretty much pegged. Paula moved on, looking for "real garbage."

The day heated up quickly, and the roadside strip assigned to her turned into a murky bog, redolent of the natural odors of rotting vegetation as well as the stink of man-made garbage.

The sun beat down, and she stripped off her windbreaker, tying it around her waist. Sweat trickled along the side of her face and neck, making her long red hair stick to her skin. Taking off a glove, she tried to wipe her forehead and only succeeded in getting herself grubbier.

She paused, wiping her forehead again and staring down into the drainage ditch where plenty of garbage floated but where she had absolutely no intention of venturing. Nothing was worth going in there. Too messy...

But, wait. Wasn't that a pair of tennis shoes sticking up out of the weeds and dead cattails? Tennies that looked new, in fact. Paula moved down the bank, picking her way gingerly. If they were, she could be a contender for the best garbage prize. And the shoes could be washed and given to the clothes bank at the homeless shelter. She began to get excited. This could be a real treasure, if someone in need could use them. She forgot caution, and stepped too quickly...

And slipped, skimming along the muddy bank and splashing down into the filthy water of the ditch. Paula swore, loudly. She struggled to stand and fell down again, splashing mud and water all over herself.

"Paula, honey, are you okay?"

"I just slipped. Sorry for the language. But I'm in mud up to my—" She broke off her explanation and stared, unable to say another word or to move an inch.

The tennis shoes were new. *And* they were occupied.

Paula hesitated only a split second longer. If this was a dead body, she was the best one in the entire group to chance upon it. Quite possibly the only one in the group who'd ever seen one before, as well. She rose hastily, got her balance and moved forward, parting the weeds, her boots squelching in the muddy water. The body was that of a large male.

"What is it, Paula?" Susan called from up near the road. "Find something?"

Paula sniffed, warily testing the air. No smell of serious decomposition. No death smell at all. She couldn't see the face yet. "Get someone to drive to a phone and call for an ambulance," she yelled. "Rescue squad. Tottie Reynolds. The works. I think I've found a body."

Susan screamed and disappeared.

Paula inched forward, stepping carefully. If this was a dead man, it was likely he'd reached that state by unnatural means and she didn't want to disturb a crime scene any more than absolutely necessary. While she kept her gaze on the form floating in the water and weeds, she also kept alert for any items nearby. Nothing caught her attention.

But the man did.

He wasn't dead. Dead men didn't bleed, she knew, and he was bleeding from several cuts on his face. He rested on a hummock of vegetation and debris, his head almost pillowed on the mess. He'd been beaten, to judge by the bruises, purple now in the sunlight, against skin so pale it was almost pure white. A cut over one black eyebrow was gaping and bloody. A sluggish fly skittered over it and left. His eyes were shut, but he was breathing. She could see the rise and fall of his chest. The gentle movement made the stagnant water ripple.

He looked helpless and forlorn. Lost and in pain.

She felt a wash of pity like nothing that she had ever felt before. In her years as a prosecutor, Paula had seen suffering, but nothing had ever touched her in quite this way. A man, beaten and bloody, lying in a dirty ditch in the morning sunlight. She knelt beside him, heedless of the water, heedless of the mud. She touched his face... Felt his throat for a pulse... He moaned softly and turned toward her.

And Paula saw that he had also been shot. Only a superficial wound. But shot, nonetheless.

In the hell of pain, weakness and confusion that had become his whole universe, Liam Croft felt the touch of an angel, heard her soft, sweet voice and smelled her fine, expensive perfume....

And realized vaguely that he wasn't dead yet. God couldn't possibly allow the angels, no matter how lovely they might be, to wear such pricey fragrance. Not, at least, in the heaven he'd been taught about. Saints, even beautiful ones, were frugal.

So, he still lived. Grand.

He tried to open his eyes but the sun was too bright. He caught a glimpse of glowing red hair and wondered afresh if he'd not died and gone to heaven. The woman who held him was so like an angel with that long, beautiful red hair. Red as a burnished rose. Was he home? Impossible. His mission had taken him far away from home, so this was a stranger touching him.

He couldn't make out her features, but her melodic voice soothed him again. He felt her hand on his forehead, also soothing. "...all right. Help is coming...paramedics. Who...?"

He struggled, fighting the blackness lurking at the edge of his brain. She was asking something. He had answers, of course, but not for her. They came out anyway. "Silly old...b-bastard," he heard himself croak. The rasping noise startled him. Was that his own voice? "Left me to get help on my own. Don't think he knew how bad..."

"Who?" Her voice wasn't so soothing now. The question hit his eardrum like a sour note. "Who did this?" she demanded.

Liam shook his head. Or tried to. The waves of pain from the attempt at movement took him and the blackness came in a tidal wave, slamming him into a few moments of blessed oblivion. But not before it exacted a price. Before he passed out, he felt the blood start to flow down his face again. He'd been bleeding for hours. Much more blood loss would likely kill him, he knew.

Paula stifled a cry herself, one that would have echoed the man's groan of agony. The blood from his head wound flowed afresh, and just before his eyes closed, she saw them roll back. Was he dying? Right there in her arms? She held him tighter and looked over her shoulder. The bank was lined with women, watching her with a mixture of sympathy and horror, but no one seemed to want to help. "Does anyone know anything about first aid?" she called. "Don't come down, though. Just tell me what to do. This is a crime scene."

"He's not dead, is he? I just can't stand it, if he is."

"Honey, he wouldn't need first aid if he were dead."

"I took a CPR course, but..."

"Never mind, you all." Susan started dancing on her toes and waving at something off in the distance. "Here comes the ambulance. Paula, you hang on now, you hear?"

"I'm not the one with the problem doing that." Paula reached up to her shoulder and ripped at the material of her sweatshirt. The aged cloth gave, and she tore off a big strip, placing it against the man's head where the blood flowed. She didn't dare to look closely at his shoulder where the bullet wound was. It didn't seem to be bleeding much. At least not now. The entry wound was high up, giving her hope for him. She did know her bullet wounds after years of studying such mayhem for court presentations.

"Don't you die on me," she whispered, urging him to live. "You hear me?" she added. "Do you?"

"I do, lass."

Paula yelped and looked down. The man's eyes were open again and this time he was staring up at her as if he could see her clearly. His eyes were the brightest blue she'd ever seen. "You can hear me?" she asked. "Really?"

He said nothing, just stared. But there was a trace of color in his face now. Above the dark whisker bristle on his cheeks and jaw. And just a tiny turning upward of his mouth, as if he was trying to smile at her. She heard the clambering of the paramedics making their way down the bank and felt a hand on her shoulder.

"Get out of the way, ma'am," the big paramedic instructed her as he moved her aside. "We'll take care of him, now. Don't you worry none. Oh, it's you, Ms. Dixon,'' he said, recognizing her.

"Be careful," she said. "He's been shot and that makes this whole area a definite crime scene. Do what you have to, but try not to disturb the site.'' Paula stood up. The wounded man continued to watch her.

She moved away, letting the paramedics do their job. The man's gaze followed her. Only when she was halfway up the bank did he close his eyes and turn his head away. Her skin tingled in sympathy with his pain, and she felt as if her heart were rising up to choke her.

But she put feelings aside. Her emotions were in high gear, but her mind was already working on the problem of the legal mare's nest this would be for her and her office. She reached the road and the others immediately crowded around her.

"Paula, honey, are you all right?"

"You're just covered with blood and stuff!"

"Who *is* he? Do you know him?"

She shook her head, dispensing with the questions. A few minutes later, the ambulance drove off, siren howling and with the stranger safely aboard. Then, Paula went into action. "I have to call Tottie," she said, handing her garbage bag to Susan. "The blood on his shirt was from a gunshot."

"Oh, my Lord!" Susan's hands went up to her face.

"Why, that's awful." Horrified murmurs began.

"I have work to do. Excuse me." Paula spoke gently, knowing the others weren't as used to violence as she was. She went past them and hurried down the road to her car. The little sedan was clean and shiny, the seats freshly vacuumed by the auto service center she'd taken it to the other day. But the mud and blood and debris on her clothes didn't matter. Paula got in and started the engine. She had a job to do, and she had no time to waste.

HOURS LATER, she stood on the bank, watching the sheriff's deputies combing the area for any physical evidence. Tottie Reynolds, her face sweaty in the afternoon humidity and heat, clambered up the bank to stand beside her.

"Whatever happened, it didn't happen right here," the sheriff said. "Not enough blood, and not one scrap of good evidence material." She gestured to the other side of the bank. "Unless one of you made those gouge marks, it's my bet your boy came out of the swamp and fell head over hind end into the ditch."

"On his own steam?" Shivering, Paula hugged herself, then lowered her arms, self-consciously. "Have you heard from the hospital?"

"No, thought you'd take care of that angle." She paused. "What's the matter, girl? You look like a goose just stepped on your grave."

"I guess I'm pretty shook up. Maybe it was coming across him the way I did. No warning. So... unexpected."

"You see or hear anything I might need to know?" Tottie asked. "Think, Paula. Did he say anything?"

In her mind, Paula replayed the broken phrases she had heard him say. Then ... "Oh!"

"What?"

"He called me *lass*. Not lady or woman, like you'd hear from a guy around here. He had an accent, too. I can't place it right off, but..."

"Lass. English? Scots?"

"No." Paula snapped her fingers. "Irish. He's Irish, Tottie. You can bet dinner on it. That's the accent I heard." She sank down, resting on her haunches and closing her eyes. She sensed Tottie kneeling beside her knowing that Paula was preparing to reenact the scene, a procedure the two women were familiar with from long experience working cases together.

"I'm walking along the slope," she said, starting off slowly so that she could concentrate on every detail. "I see a pair of tennis shoes and figure I should take a look. So I tried to move down the bank carefully, but I slip and fall into the ditch. From there I can see the victim."

"What else?" Tottie's tone was soft, encouraging.

"He's hurt. He's lying there like he's resting, though. His clothes are plain. Jeans. A flannel shirt... No, it wasn't flannel. Wool..." She opened her eyes and looked at Tottie. "He's a foreigner, Tottie. Obviously he hasn't been around here long enough to have bought local clothes."

Tottie's eyebrows raised, but she said nothing. She continued to regard Paula calmly.

"He's a stranger and a foreigner," Paula said. "His accent makes him Irish to me. When I asked who had done those things to him, he said something about a silly old bastard who left him and didn't know how bad..." She paused. "Maybe, how badly he was hurt. Maybe whoever did it, didn't realize the extent of the injury. That's all. He didn't finish or say anything else."

Tottie stood up. "I'm sending a squad out into the swamp," she said. "If they find anybody out there, they'll bring him in for questioning." She looked down into the ditch. "Did you smell any booze on him?"

Paula thought. "No. Wood smoke, I think. The water down there smells so bad, it's hard to say for sure.'' She thought again. ''He, um, smelled funny, too. Not bad, just different. And his hands were scarred and rough. Big, with large knuckles. He's a working man, I'd say.''

Tottie smiled. ''You should have been a cop, Paula. You're wasted up there in court.''

Paula stood up, too. ''Right. And that's exactly the way I like it. If I think of anything else, I'll let you know. Now, I'm going into town and see how he's doing.''

''You boy isn't dead, or I would have heard... And take a shower first, girl. You show up at the hospital looking and smelling like that, they're liable to put you in isolation. If you weren't the assistant D.A., I might consider you a suspect, dressed and messed up like that.''

''Funny. Very funny.'' Paula grinned at her friend. ''I'll talk to you later,'' she said.

She walked the short distance to her car, got in and pulled away, waving at Tottie as she did. Tottie Reynolds watched the car until it was out of sight. The sheriff turned back to the crime scene, but she had more on her mind than the unknown man Paula had found.

Paula Dixon was her best friend. And she was in trouble, though she refused to admit it. For the past few months, Paula had been receiving threatening phone calls and hate notes through the mail. Paula wasn't worried, but Tottie was. As a prosecutor, they both knew Paula made her share of enemies. That was a given factor with the job. But these particular threats had Tottie concerned. When she had her men search the swamp, she'd also have them look for any signs of other activity in the area, she decided. With Paula's club out on cleanup duty on the highway, whoever was tormenting Paula might have considered taking advantage of the situation to keep an eye on her.

And if this Irish guy was in any way connected with anything that would harm Paula, he was going to find himself in deep, deep trouble!

PAULA DROVE INTO TOWN, past the small gas station where she had phoned Tottie's office. The building was a relic of the fifties, white stucco and tile roof. Only the pumps reflected the present decade. An RC Cola sign hung dingily in the plate-glass front window, and the whole establishment was guarded by two huge live oak trees.

Paula drove on, her glance dropping to her dirty hands gripping the steering wheel. The nails were torn and grimy. Instead of her usual reaction, she was damned proud because her hands looked useful, not pampered. Suddenly, in spite of her empathy for the wounded stranger, she felt quite euphoric. She had found a crime victim and had helped him. She had stayed with him and given him comfort and reassurance while waiting for the ambulance. A far cry from the kind of distance she usually kept from victims. In the courtroom, her function was strictly to prosecute the perpetrators of crimes, not comfort the victims. Paula smiled. Yes, she felt terrific about this day's work.

No one else in her family would understand this feeling, she thought. The only child of two only children, who had always been more concerned with their own desires than with the needs of their child she had been raised in a selfish world, replete with wealth and indulgence. All managed in a dignified way, but sterile to her. She had fled it as soon as she graduated from high school. Even though her parents still lived just a few hours' drive away, she rarely visited them or contacted them for anything other than strict filial duty. Since her first day of college, she had been on her own.

Except for her close friends, she was still alone.

Her thoughts turned to what she needed to do as she entered the city limits of Carleton Cay and drove home. The house was located in a quiet neighborhood on a back street. Just looking at its old-fashioned white frame structure made her feel safe and secure.

She unlocked the front door, knowing she was probably the only person on the block who kept her latch on when she was gone. She was probably the only person with any reason. This was a trusting neighborhood, and everyone knew it when a house was unoccupied and would watch out for the owner's property. Okay, it was a snoopy neighborhood, too. But it was her home. She closed the door. And heard the phone start to ring.

She dashed across the room and picked up the receiver. It was the hospital reporting to her. The wounded stranger was going to be all right.

Thirty minutes later, showered, but only hurriedly groomed, she was at the hospital. Her good friend and chief surgeon, Jim Cunningham, greeted her outside the surgery suite.

"He's out of danger," the surgeon said. "The bullet entered high above the clavicle. No bones broken, no vital organs injured. His biggest problem is blood loss. Otherwise, he seems to be in extremely good health. I doubt this will cause him much trouble after a few days' rest and recuperation. The head wound was superficial, too. Mild concussion, but no fractures." He paused. "Your man took a hell of a beating before he was shot, you know. And from the state of his hands, I don't think he put up a fight or defended himself."

Paula regarded Jim's long face and gray eyes. The doctor reminded her of a bloodhound. "Anything else?" she asked.

"Indeed there is." Jim opened a pocket and took out a small sealed plastic envelope. "The bullet is a lead ball, my dear. From a very old weapon like a one-shot derringer or a small pistol. I don't know that much about antique guns, so I'm not going to be able to help. Tottie's ballistics people are going to have a good time with this one." He allowed Paula to look it over and then returned the envelope to his pocket.

"Interesting," Paula said rather absently. "When can I talk to him?"

Jim considered this. "When I had the desk nurse call you, I thought he would be able to speak right away. But he's sleeping now. If you'd like to wait, that's okay. Or I could have the nurse call you when he wakes up."

"I'll wait. In the room, if I may."

"I thought you'd say that." Jim directed her down the hallway. "Just stay out of the way, in case something does go wrong and we need to get to him in a hurry."

"Have no fear." Paula smiled wryly. "Medicine is not my thing. Applying a bandage to a cut finger is about as much as I do."

Jim laughed and opened a door. "Here he is."

Paula clutched at the edges of the door. That odd feeling of empathy for this injured stranger washed over her again, leaving her feeling weak, a little dizzy and shaken. She managed to mouth a thanks to Jim and make her way into the room on her own steam, but her body felt dissociated from her mind. As if she were someone else, watching herself walk across the shiny tiled floor. She reached for the straight-back chair in the corner and sat down. Then, she looked at the man and tried to understand why she was responding so strongly to his plight.

The room was not quiet. Instruments attached to the patient monitored his pulse, blood pressure and respiration rate. Outside, hospital personnel walked, clattered and paced by the door in a never-ending pattern. She heard conversations, orders given, questions asked.

But it all seemed to have nothing to do with her. She was encased in a world that included only herself and this stranger.

He looked different now. His body, what she could see of it, was clean and bandaged across the chest and head. His skin was so white he appeared to be as bleached as the sheets. That made the bruises seem all the more offensive. Against his deathlike whiteness, his black hair and whisker stubble glistened with vitality. Since he was wearing only a skimpy hospital gown, she could see his bare arms. Each muscle seemed as if carved from marble, smooth and strong. The fine black hair on his forearms and hands fascinated her.

She got up and went over to the bed to look more closely. His hands were a mess, but the cuts and scars weren't fresh. Jim had been right. If he'd had a chance to defend himself, he hadn't taken it. She studied the wrists. No ligature marks, so he hadn't been tied up. Big wrists, as wide as her hand and then some. A long, old scar trailed up from his left hand to his elbow like a wrinkled white snake. She touched the hand and turned it over.

Callused. At the tips of his fingers, too. Like someone who...

Played a stringed instrument. She'd seen calluses like this on banjo or fiddle players. Was he a musician? She let her gaze travel up to his face.

And suddenly realized that under the bandages and whiskers and bruises, he was startlingly handsome. His features were finely etched. Not blunt or brutal as she would have expected, given the muscled body and big hands. He had a wide, high forehead, cleanly drawn, full lips and a nose that could only be described as patrician. Though his chin jutted a bit, his jawline was firm and square. Shaved and unbruised, he was liable to be gorgeous!

Who was he! Who was this man with a movie star's face and a rugged stevedore body? What was he doing in the swamp and who had worked him over before shooting him?

With a ball of lead shot, of all things. This was the kind of mystery that would bedevil her until she unraveled it. She reached down and touched the man's face, letting her fingers trail lightly over the soft skin and the one silky black eyebrow that wasn't bandaged. And he opened his eyes and looked up at her.

"Hello, darlin'," he said, a smile on his lips. "Come in to view the corpse, have you?" Then, he astounded her by turning his head and kissing the palm of her hand.

CHAPTER TWO

"No!" Paula jerked her hand away from his lips. "I'm here to get some answers."

Blue, blue eyes gazed up at her. Black lashes dropped, covering what seemed to be a sudden swirl of emotion. When his eyes opened, however, there was only the sweet, innocent blankness of a summer sky in them. "Ask away, lass," he said. "Did the Law let you in because you found me?" Before she could answer, he went on. "For which I'm thanking you, mind. I didn't fancy lying there in that cold, dirty water for the rest of me life. I..."

"Who put you there?"

He smiled, showing off his white but slightly crooked teeth. "I did, meself. Slipped down the muddy bank, I did. 'Twas dark, y'see, and I was lost."

"What's your name?"

He heaved a sigh. "Liam. Liam Croft." The sweetness fled from his expression, and his gaze became calculating. "Why, goodness me, you *are* the Law, aren't you?" Liam Croft took another breath, and expelled it again in yet another sigh. "Fancy that," he said, in regretful tones.

Paula allowed herself a small smile. "Yes, I do represent the Law. I'm Paula Dixon. The assistant county district attorney. I'm not a police person, but I am..."

"I know what you are, m' dear. I do have a little understandin' of the American justice system." His eyes appeared hooded now, like a hunting bird's, and looked just as lethal. "I should have figured it from the start." He turned his head away. "I've nothing to say to you. Please go."

"I'm not here to harm you, Mr. Croft. Please, won't you answer my questions?"

Silence as he stared at the wall.

"I'd like you to help me and I'd like to help you, but if you won't talk, I can't do either." She waited.

He turned back. "Curse it that I'm Irish," he said. "Can no more resist talking to a pretty woman than I can resist taking breath. What happened to me was no one's business but my own. Nothing to do with American law, I can assure you."

"You were shot. That's a crime here. And, I expect, in Ireland, as well."

He smiled again. "You are a hard one. I suppose it is a crime to get shot, if a body registers a complaint. That, I am not doing. So, as I see it, you've no case. Surely, you're busy enough dealing with real lawbreakers without bothering with the likes of me."

"You're no particular bother, Mr. Croft. I had no plans for the rest of the day, and I'm quite happy to sit here as long as it takes." Paula pulled the chair over and sat down again. She crossed her arms. "Was it a drug deal gone sour? Or an argument over a woman? That would make a difference in how much I pushed the sheriff to pursue this."

Liam Croft let out a whistle, soft, low and mocking, as if giving musical expression to a private opinion of her hard-nosed approach. "All right, then. No. No drugs, no passion. Sorry to disappoint you, m' dear. Nothing sensational. It was something personal *and* accidental. Plain as that.''

Paula gave him her silent, prosecutor's glare. It had worked on bigger, meaner, nastier and tougher men than he seemed to be.

It didn't work on Liam Croft. He just looked back at her. Then, he grinned. ''My, but you are a fair one, Paula Dixon,'' he said. ''Pretty as a long summer's day. Please don't be spoiling me day further by telling me you're wed.''

Paula felt herself turn red, something she hated to do and rarely did these days. ''I'm single. My work leaves little time for any relationship or romance.'' She took a deep breath, clearing her mind. *Play his game.* ''How about you? Married? Any kids?''

He laughed, wincing with pain afterward. ''Clever girl. Turn around is fair play. I see you didn't win your job by kissing the right people in the right places for it. No, I have no wife, no kiddies, though I often wish I did. 'Twould get me mother off me neck about it.''

''Your mother lives here?''

''No. In Dublin. As do most of the rest of me kin. And myself.''

''And what are you doing here? Visiting?''

'' 'Tis me business and not yours, lass.'' Liam said with a grin that made it a tease, not an insult.

Paula stood up. He was a total charmer, telling lies and truth in his own fashion, and he was obviously not about to cooperate. ''Mr. Croft, I really regret this, but I'm going to have to turn your case over to the sheriff. I'd hoped you might have understood that we consider the crime perpetrated against you to be of a very serious nature. I had also hoped that we could spare you the unnecessary aggravation of further questioning, since you've been hurt so badly, but..."

"I took a licking I deserved, lass. The shooting was an accident, just as I told you. Why, I've been hurt worse on a Saturday night coming home from the pub."

"You're a drinking man?"

"I'm Irish."

"Were you drinking with whoever beat you up? And shot you?"

He looked at the door. "Where's the nurse? I need to use the, um, whatever. To, um, relieve meself. See if you can find her for me, will you? There's a good girl."

She started to argue, certain he was just using the need for a nurse to distract her. But then, she realized she had a question or two for Jim Cunningham. If she could establish from the doctor that Croft had been drunk when he was shot, it might be of use once the case came...

To court? Would it ever come to a trial, if the victim was unwilling to testify or even make a statement?

And, should it matter this much to her? Didn't she have enough to keep her busy without sticking her nose into some private Irish brouhaha? What about those strange notes and phone calls she'd been getting lately. Perhaps her time would be better spent if she concentrated on keeping herself out of harm's way instead of getting caught up in the problems of a burly Irishman who would never thank her for it.

"I don't mean to whine about this, m' darlin', but I really do need..."

"I'll be right back," Paula promised. "Just push the call button, and a nurse will be in to help you." She pointed to the device. "See? It's pinned there to your sheet."

"Ah." Liam Croft leaned forward a bit and smiled. "So 'tis. Thank you." He picked up the gadget. "You are an angel, truly."

"I'll be back." She gathered up her purse and briefcase and started to leave the room.

"Don't be hurryin', now," he called after her as she shut the door. Cheerful as a cricket.

JIM CUNNINGHAM WAS in the doctor's lounge on the first floor. Paula cornered him just as he was getting ready to leave for home. "His blood alcohol?" she asked. "Did you get that in chemical analysis?"

"No, I don't think so," Jim said. He frowned and thought. "I'll check with Fred Turner. He passed gas on this case for me."

He went over to the phone. Paula sat down. The "gas passer," the anesthesiologist, would likely have done a test for drugs and alcohol before deciding how to anesthetize the patient for surgery. Croft's wound would not have been so serious as to force an operation before careful testing. She'd have her answer soon.

After Jim spoke briefly to the anesthesiologist he turned to Paula and said, "Whatever info you want, he's got it. He's in his lab now and he's waiting for you."

"Thanks, Jim," said Paula as she headed in the direction of the labs. "I owe you one."

Fred Turner didn't mince words. As soon as she arrived, he was ready for her.

"He was clean as a hound's tooth," Fred told her, showing her the lab report readout. "Perfect blood chemistry. If he'd been drinking, it was a long, long time before I got to him. More than overnight. Healthy a specimen as I've ever knocked out, I'll tell you that. What's going on, Paula?"

She rubbed her eyes, feeling the tension and exertion of the day finally catching up with her. "Darned if I know, Fred. I found him down in a ditch just outside town this morning. And he won't say who shot him, beat him up or even exactly how he got there."

"He's not American, you know."

"I know. Irish."

"Oh. I was going on the dental work, but I couldn't identify the country he was from. Well, you ought to be able to get something on him if he's IRA connected. The Feds'll have data on him."

Paula sat very still. She hadn't thought of that possibility. The IRA? Not Liam Croft! He seemed too gentle a sort, even though she'd glimpsed a dangerous edge to him. *Oh, for heaven's sake, Paula,* she chided herself. Since when could she identify a criminal just by looking at him? Liam Croft could be a political terrorist, just as easily as he could be a drug dealer or an unlucky lover. And it was up to her to find out which.

"Thanks, Fred," she said, gathering up her belongings again. "I appreciate all this very much and I'll get back to you soon." She headed up to the lobby and the bank of phones along the wall, dropped in change and called Washington, D.C. Time to use some old connections and call in a favor or two.

Some time later, she had no more information than she did before she made the call. Liam Croft, if that was his real name, had no "rap sheet" in the FBI's terrorist files or even in Interpol's data banks. She decided to call in a favor from an acquaintance at the CIA. He was always eager to help her out...too eager for her taste. As she predicted, he was able to "pull up" more information than her previous calls had netted. Apparently, *a* Liam Croft in his mid-thirties was listed as a licensed publican and owner of a bed-and-breakfast establishment in a suburb of Dublin. But the family name was also owned by literally hundreds of people, including, a discouraging number of *Liam* Crofts. Six farmers, a dock worker, one dentist, three priests and four teachers to list only a few. She had no way of knowing if *her* Liam Croft was the Dubliner who owned a bar, or one of the others, lying about his name and/or hometown.

Frustrating.

Well, he had to have a passport, which she could easily have traced. As the assistant D.A., she could claim the passport as evidence for the prosecution. She really didn't want to go that route, but if Mr. Liam Croft insisted on playing hardball, she would show him that two could play the game. Paula shouldered her purse, hefted the briefcase and headed back upstairs.

"He's sound asleep, Ms. Dixon," the head nurse told her, stopping her before she entered the room. "He asked me to tell you to come by in the morning, and he'll answer all your questions then."

Paula sighed. "Just as well, I guess. I'm tired, myself. Thanks for letting me know."

"Oh, that's no problem. He's such a sweet man that it's my pleasure," the nurse said, folding clean, pudgy hands together. "So courteous, a real gentleman and modest as can be. He wouldn't even let the aide stay in the room while he used the urinal.''

She was clearly caught up in the Croft charisma, Paula realized. Charmed right down to her panty-hosed toes. ''Well, that's nice,'' she said.

''And he wanted regular pajamas. Something that would cover him. Said he felt naked and cold in the hospital gown... Why, Ms. Dixon. What's the matter?''

Paula ignored the question and ran into the room. Liam Croft was gone. His bed was rumpled and empty and the window was wide open. She looked out. The drop was just a few feet, not too dangerous for a man in top physical condition. Even weak from his injuries, exposure and surgery, Croft fitted that bill easily enough.

''Call the sheriff's office,'' she snapped, turning on the horrified nurse. ''The city police, too. Tell them to put out an APB on him, but to be careful. We don't know who we're dealing with here.'' She thought a moment.

''Never mind,'' she said, revising her plan of action. ''I'll take care of it, myself.'' She hurried out, leaving behind a very startled and confused head nurse. But Paula was only aware of herself. She was furious and frightened by how badly she had misread him. She should have had Tottie assign a guard immediately. Why had she trusted him when she knew better than that? Her instincts had failed her utterly. This one was slippery as a snake.

And when she caught up with Liam Croft, or whoever he was, she was going to have his scaly hide. She might even nail it to the courthouse door!

LIAM LEANED against the low stone wall as he slowly regained his breath. He'd dropped to the ground from the hospital room and had immediately taken to his heels. Not a good thing to be doing right after all his body'd been through in the last twenty-four hours. Just that long ago, he'd been fit and spry. What a change a turn of a day's hours could bring a man.

Thank the Lord it was nightfall. The stone wall was high enough for him to crouch behind, and the shadow it cast hid him well. He slid down to sit on the cold ground, feeling the chill through the seat of the thin hospital pants that dear little nurse had brought him. She'd been sweet, and he hoped she'd come to no grief at the hands of her superiors as a result of his actions.

His fingers trembled with a combination of chill and weakness as he checked his bandages for bleeding. But the American doctors had done well by him; the bleeding had stopped. Now, the issue at hand was how to get back to the motel room without attracting attention?

If he could collect his clothes, his funds and his papers, he could be gone from this town in a twinkle. He could send the money for his care to the hospital later. For sure, if he lingered, that darlin' red-headed lawyer lady was going to have his guts for garters. Liam heaved himself to his feet, ignoring the pain that shot through his shoulder and the rubbery weakness of his legs. He'd figure a way to return and finish his task later when he was healed and strong again.

And next time, he'd succeed, by God, or know the reason why! The obligation to discharge his duty was weightier than ever, now that he knew the difficulties involved firsthand. Bloody rabbit-punched, he'd been.

Well, once was enough. He'd not be caught with his guard down, next time. Not just for his own sake but for the sake of the one who had done this to him.

But mostly, for the sake of the family. It had to be done, no matter what it cost him. For it was his duty, his sacred duty.

THE WOMEN WAITED in the motel room. "He's got to come back here." Paula crouched in the dark and lifted a millimeter of window shade to peer out. "His belongings are still here, and he's not likely to get far without clothes or money."

"You're an optimist, honey," Tottie said. "Or a fortune-teller. You were right about his staying in a motel room. But you can't say he'll come here for sure. For all we know, he's passed out again and bleeding to death in..."

"No!" Paula quickly lowered her voice. "I mean, the guys out patrolling would have found him. And I just don't think he's that badly hurt. You didn't see him in the hospital room. Tot, he's built like a Sherman tank. Arms and chest like Arnold Schwarzenegger. It'd take a lot more than a bullet and a beating to..."

"Shh." The sheriff raised her hand and cocked her head. Her voice was a mere thread, not even a whisper. "Hear that?"

Paula listened. Rustling noises emanated from the back of the motel and after a few minutes could be heard in the vicinity of the bathroom window. *Bingo*, she mouthed. Tottie nodded, unsnapped her holster, but didn't draw her gun. They waited. Liam Croft lumbered into the room. Before Paula could turn on the light and confront him with the sheriff to back her up for an arrest, he sat down on the bed, sighed and said, "You've got me again, lass. Go on. Put me in the dungeon, for I've no strength left to fight. The weakness is on me, sure."

Paula clicked on the lamp and stood up. "How'd you know it was me?"

Liam Croft smiled at her, a tired and pained smile. "Perfume. You wear the most delightful scent, Miss Prosecutor. It's in this room like a fair mist. I first got a whiff of it out in the swamp this morning and knew I'd not died yet, though the scent was pure heaven."

His gaze shifted slowly to include Tottie Reynolds. "Why, hello," he said. "Another lovely lassie with a uniform, badge and gun. Have you no men in charge around this town, then? Not that I mind, truly. I was just wondering." He closed his eyes and lay back on the bed, causing the springs to groan with his weight. "I also think I'm weary to dyin'. Mind, I've only meself to blame and that's a fact."

Tottie looked at Paula.

Paula thought quickly. He looked terrible, pale and drawn, but not anywhere near death. She could push him a little bit and not harm him. "Let's trundle him back to the hospital, Tottie," she said. "This time I want him cuffed to the bed and I want you to put a guard on him around the clock. When and *if* he's ready to give us some answers, then we..."

"I won't go. I'll stay here. You have my word I'll not move from this room. You can't make me go, I believe. I'm not accused of anything."

Tottie frowned. "You ran out on your hospital bill, Mr. Croft."

"I intended to pay." He sat up, and Paula noted that his face was even paler than before, his blue eyes like sapphires staring out of recessed settings.

"I'm an honest man, Officer. I own businesses, and I've the money to settle me debts. I just don't hold with stayin' anywhere I don't need to be." He spread out his palms. "Ladies, I know you're thinking the worst of me, but I swear before God I've done nothing wrong. Now, I ask you, could you just not leave me to rest and go about my task."

"And all *we* ask is that you let us know what that task is, Mr. Croft, so that we can see to it that no one else gets hurt." Paula moved closer. "You look like death warmed over. Are you sure you don't want to go back to the hospital?"

"I'm sure."

She considered her options. She and Tottie could spend long hours trying to get the truth out of him risking a number of things, including a civil suit for harassment if he took the notion.

Or, she could play to his obvious machismo, his apparent scant respect for women in positions of authority, and let him walk right into a trap of his own making.

"All right, Mr. Croft," she said, looking at Tottie, willing her to understand her new tactics. They'd worked accused persons often enough to have established a rapport, so she hoped it would hold this time. "No hospital, no jail and no more questions. But I can't leave you here alone. You have been hurt, shot and operated on. If you won't go back to where the doctors can take care of you, then you must stay with me. I've had some training in first aid and can at least holler for help if you get in difficulty."

Both Tottie and the Irishman regarded her in astonishment and said, "What?" at the same time. Paula smiled and explained what was on her mind.

LIAM SETTLED HIMSELF back in the big comfortable bed, thinking that his luck must indeed be changing for the better. And about time, too! He didn't trust the red-haired lassie. Not as far as he could spit into the wind. Sweet she was, but tricky to predict as a sunny day in Ireland. However, he was happy to take advantage of her kindness, whatever she had up her sleeve. This football field of a mattress was surely more to his liking that that lumpy cot they called a bed in the motel room.

And, best of all, the mattress, pillows, sheets and all the rest carried her scent. He closed his eyes and inhaled. Not just that perfume she wore, but of her body, soft, warm, sensual with sleep and...

Lord! What must he be thinking of? This was no time to be after a woman, no matter how fair and available. He had a job to do, a sacred mission for the family, and that was all he should be thinking on. Old Tobias had caught him off his mark, laying his blackthorn cane into the front of his head like that and opening that cut over his eye. Then, aiming that old pistol at him, threatening, never dreaming it'd blow off like it did, pinning him with a ball that must be twice as old as the both of them! Lord! What a mess. Soon he'd go back after the old man, and this time, he'd be ready for him.

But just now, he needed to rest. He needed his strength back. Liam sank deeper into relaxation. Just before he drifted to sleep, he gathered her sweet scent around him like a cloak of dreams.

PAULA STEPPED INTO the bedroom and watched the man sleeping in her bed. He was out like a light, finally. They had moved him bag and baggage over to her house, to the accompaniment of his nonstop chatter. She'd never encountered a man with such a gift for gab in all her life. It was strange to see him silent. She reached down and pulled the blanket up over his chest. He was such a large man, her queen-size bed was barely big enough to support him. She resisted the urge to touch his face, turned abruptly and left the room.

Tottie was sitting at the kitchen table, a mug of coffee in her hand. "You're plain out of your mind, girl," she said, sipping the steaming drink. "Taking a stranger in like this. I'm assigning an armed deputy to watch out for you, and I don't care what you say. What with those calls and notes you've been getting, you can't be too careful."

"That's your right, Tottie," Paula agreed, pouring some coffee for herself. "I admit it's a sensible idea. But still, I wish you wouldn't. I'd like this man to trust me. I think that's the only way we're going to get the truth out of him. Liam Croft is a separate issue, anyway. He's got nothing to do with my other 'little problem.'"

"Are you sure of that?"

"Come on, Tottie, how could he? I've been getting the calls and threats in the mail for weeks, now. Besides, I've been targeted before, and nothing's come of it. I wish you wouldn't worry." Paula sat down across from her friend. "Let's focus on our Irishman instead of on me. Go with me on this. You know I've got good instincts. And I think this guy needs our help."

"What I know is that this is not your usual case, and you aren't acting your usual self, Paula Dixon." Tottie regarded her friend steadily. "You fallen for him?" She tilted her head in the direction of the bedroom.

"You have got to be kidding!" Paula felt herself redden.

"Nope." Tottie continued to study her. "And judging from the color on your face, I'm not so far off the mark. He's a good-looking man, I'll give you that. But he could be dangerous, Paula. For all his charm, we don't know a thing about him, and I'm not so sure you can be objective."

"Yes. I am." Weariness came suddenly like a heavy blow. "Okay, assign someone to stay guard out on the porch, if you want. But I'd really rather have as much time with him as I can get. This is a shaky situation, legally, and the only way we can get to whoever shot him is by his testimony. He has to trust me."

"He's not going to tell you. He's going to heal up and go after him himself. Revenge, his way."

Paula drank her coffee. Thought. Shook her head. "No. That's not it. No revenge in him. He's not angry and he doesn't seem to care about his injuries. Isn't that odd? Any other man I've ever known would be howling for a chance to get even. He isn't."

"How do you know?"

"Call it my famous instinct." She set her mug down and rubbed her face. "I'm really dead," she added.

Tottie stood up. "I trust," she said, "that is not a prophecy."

The sheriff gathered up the papers they'd found in Liam Croft's room, including his Irish passport. They hadn't come across a return plane ticket, however, which was puzzling.

"I'll go ahead and get the wheels in motion to check him out from the moment he drew breath on the planet," she said. "We're going to do at least part of this by the book. I'm leaving Bull Drake outside with orders not to let your guest leave. You check in with him every so often, you hear?"

"I hear. And I obey."

Tottie was not amused and decided to issue one last warning before taking her leave. "Chuckie will be back from vacation in a week. Even Hawaii couldn't have mellowed him enough to overlook the fact that you've kept a potential client in your bed—even if you aren't sharing it with him. Are you going to have this cleaned up before your boss comes down on you like a ton of suntanned bricks?"

Paula thought about her boss, the chief D.A., Charles "Chuckie" Benson, and nodded. "I'll have it cleaned up," she said. "I have no choice." She shut her eyes and yawned.

It had been a long, long day.

LIAM WOKE to aches and pains and bright sunlight on his face. The light bothered him more than the pain, since he wasn't used to the harshness of it, whereas the results of dealing with obstreperous custom in his drinking establishment often plagued him of a Sunday morning.

And it was Sunday, sure. He could hear the church bells clanging. He groaned and rolled over. His mother would be harping at the door in a moment, telling him to get his trousers on and get to Mass or he'd lose what little he'd left of his immortal soul . . .

A scent assailed him. This was not his bed!

Liam sat up. He was in the "angel's" house.

She slept in a chair over in the corner of the bedroom, her small bare feet propped on a large ottoman and a soft, fuzzy blanket thrown over her form. She wore some kind of a loose, gray sweatshirt and pants. Red hair spilled over a little silk pillow....

The memories came crowding back. Liam looked at the sleeping angel again and then at himself. What a fix!

He moved to the edge of the bed, marveling again at the expanse of it. This was just the bed he needed with his big size. When he got back home, he'd order himself one of these beauties, sure.

He rose carefully, testing his strength. The places where Toby had bashed him were sore. The bullet wound in his shoulder hurt like the very devil. But he had no fever and even with the slight headache, felt powerfully hungry. He regarded the sleeping woman again. He'd not wake her but when she was up, he'd ask for food.

He glanced over to the low chest where she'd set his luggage last night. His clothes were inside. His kit and all. Rubbing his whiskery chin, he wandered to the window. The bells were ringing for church, all right. He hadn't dreamed that. Fascinated, he pulled back a bit of curtain and looked outside.

Lovely, it was. The neighborhood was a grand one, with fine old houses and handsome folk strolling down the sidewalks. The church must be within a block or so. Charmed by the tableau, he spent a few minutes observing the people headed for worship until he noticed they were looking at this house in a curious way. Now why would that be? he wondered.

He left the window, walked softly past his fair benefactress and made his way to the front door. Opening it, he found out why all those passersby had been so blessed curious.

"Hello, lad," he said, extending his hand to the huge, surprised, uniformed man who sat on a chair by the door. "You must be my guard. I'm Liam Croft. Delighted I am to meet you."

CHAPTER THREE

PAULA WOKE UP to the sound of music—piano and singing. Two male voices, a deep rumbling bass and a sweet full tenor. She sat up, rubbing her eyes, realizing from the light in the room that she'd slept far later than she'd planned.

The bed was empty.

Liam Croft was gone!

"Croft!" she yelled, jumping to her feet, stumbling over the mohair blanket. "I will personally see you suffer for this!" He was gone, done it to her again, and this time he had left the radio on to keep her...

Keep her asleep? That made no sense. The music had woken her.

Why would he leave the radio on? She gathered her wits, slowly, and went into the parlor where the piano she had painfully learned scales on as a child resided, a tribute to years of lessons wasted. She never touched the thing nowadays.

The music was live. Not from the radio, a record, tape or CD. Liam was seated at the piano, his fingers poised above the keys. Deputy Sheriff Dexter "Bull" Drake was standing beside him, one elbow resting on the top of the old instrument. Both men stared at her. They had been singing together.

"Uh," she said, drawing the blanket around her like a large shawl. "Hi, Bull. Morning, Liam... Mr. Croft. I woke up and didn't see you in bed and I thought..."

Bull's jaw dropped in shock.

Croft just smiled at her. "Sorry. We tried to keep it down, darlin'," he said. "Didn't wish to disturb your rest. But Mr. Drake here has the grandest knowledge of American spirituals, and he was sharin'—"

"I was just keeping an eye on him, Ms. Dixon," Drake said, his expression showing clearly that he believed she had been sleeping with a man he was instructed to consider a prisoner or at least a suspect. "He came out the front and saw me. We got to talkin', and one thing led to another and..."

"I collect folk music," Liam explained. "Wherever I go, I like to learn some of the tunes from that part of the world. The lads back home get a kick out of them when I sing them in my pub." He grinned and slapped the big deputy's arm. "We'll do this some more. Lovely stuff, and you've a grand voice."

"You, too." Drake was clearly seriously embarrassed. "I'll just take myself back on outside now," he said. He picked his cap up off the top of the piano, returned it to his head and touched the rim sheepishly.

"Ma'am," he said and left.

Paula couldn't speak.

Liam, as usual, had no problem. He stood up, his face showing concern. "Why, sure but if I don't think the man has the wrong impression of our sleeping arrangements. That'll never do. I'll just go tell him..."

"*Don't* tell him anything," Paula found her voice. "It'll just make it worse if you try to explain."

"Ah, and now you're angry with me." He shrugged expansively. "Well, never mind that. You just go make us some coffee and breakfast, and you'll be feeling better in no time a'tall. I'll..."

"You want *me* to make *you* coffee and breakfast?"

"Why, 'tis your kitchen, me girl. I wouldn't dare presume. A woman's castle, that's what a good kitchen is."

She considered arguing the point, but it was still too early for her. "Well, okay. But don't get the idea I wait on people around here. If you were hungry, you should have fixed yourself something."

"I began to visit with Mr. Drake before I could..."

"Liam, go lie down." She tossed the blanket onto the sofa. "I'll fix breakfast. And don't talk to me until I've had coffee and orange juice."

"I'm not tired." He sat down on the piano bench. "I'll serenade you while you work. How's that?"

Paula moved toward him. "You can play with that injured shoulder?"

"I can." He banged out a few chords. "Not as well as usual, of course. But you don't know the difference, do you, now?" He grinned wickedly as he hammed it up on the keyboard.

"How do you like your eggs?" she asked as she headed for the kitchen.

"From chickens, I suppose."

She stifled her natural response and entered the kitchen. One thing she'd learned a long time ago in courtroom confrontations: Never engage in an exchange of witty repartee until you're fully awake and you've got the full measure of your opponent. With Liam Croft, she was sure, it was going to take an extra effort to get his measure.

If she ever could.

THEY ATE a while later. Paula watched him shovel in mouthful after mouthful, listened to his cheery, appreciative remarks about her admittedly indifferent cooking and wondered what in the world she had got herself into. This man not only had the gift of gab, could charm the birds out of the trees, he had now added a natural talent for music to the ever-growing list of his accomplishments. Not to mention getting her to cook breakfast!

"You're pretty good with the piano.... Almost sound like a professional."

But he dismissed her praise. "I just play what I like," he said. "Learned the basics in church, but I've had no formal training a'tall. Picked up the rest here and there, awanderin' in my misspent youth."

She filed that information.

"You realize what you don't tell me, I'll find out, anyway," she said, passing him the last of the eggs and sausage. "Once Sheriff Reynolds does her computer search on you..."

His fork clattered to his plate. "My name is Liam Croft, son of Michael Croft, deceased. I'm thirty-five years old. I live in Dublin, near Phoenix Park, and I own Croft's Loft, a bed and breakfast and licensed public house just down the lane about three hundred yards. I support my mother, one as yet unmarried younger sister and am the patriarch of the Croft clan, which includes numerous individuals. The count can vary, depending on who's had a baby since I left. There were several due, as I recall. And I'm here on personal, family business that does not involve your

American justice system." He took a breath. "And I've never been arrested."

Paula stared. "Clan?"

"My family." He returned her stare steadily. "They belong to me and I to them. We are interdependent, you see." He picked up the fork and went back to polishing off his breakfast. His little finger tapped his coffee mug in silent command—fill it.

Without thinking, she poured him a refill. When she realized how casually she'd been ordered to do so, and how easily she'd responded, she felt no anger, only amazement. He must be from another planet, she decided. On a specific mission to drive her crazy!

But she could still recognize the truth when she heard it, thank goodness. "Liam. Um, Mr. Croft," she said. "I believe you. Now, if you'll just explain—"

"I won't, bless your persistence. And you've no right to make me. Look, lass, we've been over this ground already. Much as I'd like to further my acquaintance with you, I cannot. I'll mend a little while, tend to my affairs and be off before you can blink twice. How's that?" He wiped his mouth with a napkin, folded it and set it down beside his empty plate.

Not great. Paula suddenly realized she had a burning curiosity to know all there was to know about Liam Croft. "I'm still concerned," she said, forcing herself to speak in an objective and professional capacity. "Suppose whoever shot you takes it in his head to shoot someone else? It's my responsibility to make sure that doesn't happen."

He shook his head. "Not a chance, lassy. Tobias wasn't aiming to..." He frowned.

"Tobias? Tobias who?"

Liam stood up. The interrogation was over. "Thank you for breakfast. It was delicious, but I'll be bathing now, as best I can with all this bandage stuff on me, if you don't mind." He turned and left the kitchen.

Paula tapped her fingers on the table. Well, at least she had a first name to work with. She cleared the table and picked up the phone, dialing an overseas number. Her call yesterday to the CIA had answered some questions, but not enough to satisfy her. She needed to know more before she could begin to relax and trust this stranger. A trust, oddly, that she really wanted to give.

A little while later, she had as complete a confirmation of his story as it was possible to get. The call she placed had been to an old friend at New Scotland Yard, whose area of expertise was monitoring the activities of the IRA. If Liam Croft had so much as sneezed in the direction of the terrorist group, her contact would have known about it. She tried out another theory, based on what Liam had told her about his family. The Tobias he'd mentioned could be a relative who was on the wrong side of the law. But her friend had also no record of a Tobias Croft who'd been affiliated with any wrongdoing. It was most likely, her contact said, that Croft was not dangerous, but was only covering up something private.

She thanked her friend and hung up. So far, she'd turned up exactly nothing, but she didn't intend to stop trying. However, until she had some legal reason to detain him, she knew she could get into a lot of trouble, keeping him prisoner and under guard.

She went outside and told Bull he could go home. The policeman gave her a brief, futile argument before obeying. Paula was sure he'd report her dismissal of him directly to Tottie. But she would deal with the sheriff when the time came. Meantime, she went inside to speak to her strange guest.

Her bedroom door was ajar and he was standing with his back to her. He had on a clean pair of jeans, but his feet and upper torso were bare. His back gleamed like ivory in the morning light, and the play of his muscles made her breath catch.

She knocked on the door frame. "Mr. Croft, I . . ."

He whirled around, covering his chest with the towel. His clean-shaven cheeks reddened in obvious embarrassment. *Modest,* she thought. Just like the nurse at the hospital had told her. "I'm sorry," she said, turning around. "I didn't mean to walk in on you when you were dressing. But I thought you'd like to know that your story does check out."

"I know it's your house, Miss Dixon," he said. "But you really should give a person a chance to cover up before you enter a room."

She heard the rustle of cloth. Thought of the way he looked, cleaned up and shaved. Very nice.

"You may turn around now," he said.

She did. He had on a fresh shirt much the same as the one she'd seen on him yesterday. Obviously hand-made—but by whom? His hair was tousled and in disarray because of the bandage around his forehead, but he was gorgeous. The strong lines of his chin and jaw were now clearly defined. And his lips were full and sensuous—made for kissing. He was an extraordinarily handsome man. But he was frowning at her. "You still won't take my word when I tell you the truth. You feel you have to check on me."

"It's my job." She folded her arms, wishing she felt more in control of the situation. What she wanted to do was drop her professional persona and slip into something more seductive. Then, it hit her.

She *wanted* this man!

He continued to regard her thoughtfully for a moment, then turned away and went back into the bathroom where he hung up the towel neatly. She had never in all her life seen a man do that. He came out, rubbing his hands together.

"Any idea where my other clothes are?" he asked. "The ones I was wearing when you found me? That bullet hole in the blouse can be mended, and..."

"Blouse?"

"I mean shirt. Shirt. That's what you'd call it, of course. My mother made that one for me, and I'd hate to lose it."

Paula resisted probing for more information on this topic with difficulty. "I guess," she said, "that it's still at the hospital. We can go there... What's wrong?"

Liam had turned paler and seemed to sink down to sit on the bed. "I suppose I'm not altogether well, yet. It seems I haven't my normal strength at this moment." He looked weak, pained and, oddly enough, ashamed.

Paula sat beside him and put her hand on his shoulder attempting to comfort him. "Liam," she said. "You're a big, strong man. Apparently, a lot of people depend on you for leadership. That's a heavy burden, and I'm sure you carry it well. But everyone has limits, you know. Why, think what you've been through in the past twenty-four hours. Most people would still be lying in the hospital, and..."

He was staring at her. "I have a duty to my family, lass. But I must tell you, in all honesty, that I'm finding you a considerable distraction." His finger traced the curve of her cheek. "Lord forgive me, but how you have managed to touch my heart in the short time I've known you, Paula Dixon." He cupped her chin, and leaned forward and kissed her. Lightly. A friendly sort of kiss. Just a gentle, tingling touch of his lips on hers.

Paula sat very still, keeping a tight grip on herself in order to keep from responding as she wished.

If it were only up to her, she would put her arms around his neck, and pull him down onto the mattress. But his recent demonstration of modesty, together with his concern for her reputation, prevented her from making her wish a reality. He moved away from her once the kiss was done.

"You, uh, look a little better, now that you've shaved," she said, testing her voice and finding it working. Inside, she felt confused and stupid. Not so stupid, however, that she couldn't think. He was relaxed, trustful. Time to strike. "But you mustn't overdo it. Not after all the punishment you took from that Tobias person." She watched him for reaction. "He's kin to you, isn't he? And that's why you're here, isn't it?"

One tiny section of skin at the corner of his left eye jerked. Just enough to betray him. "Of course not," he lied, smiling. "Why would you be thinking a thing like that, now?"

"Because it's true." She crossed her arms. "You just told me. By your expression."

The blue eyes turned chilly. "I told you nothing, lass. And that's the truth. What you care to make of my face is your business, but I don't think it'll be carrying weight in a court of law."

She bounced up off the bed. "Damn it, I'm just trying to help you."

"I realize that." His tone was mild, unruffled by her anger. "And I appreciate it, as I have said. But I haven't asked nor do I want your help in the matter." He smiled, bringing the sun back into the room and the warmth back into his eyes. "What I would ask, however, is your company this fine Sunday morning at Mass. Will you honor me by attending with me, Paula Dixon?"

Paula felt dizzy, thrown off course by his sudden reversal. "I'm afraid I don't go to church much."

"No matter. I'm Irish, and the Lord listens well to us. We make sure of it by talking to Him all the time. I'll put in a good word for your soul." His smile and expression were beatific. "He always answers, though not always in the way we'd particularly expect. Like your finding me yesterday. Now, that was a prayer answered! Why, He could have sent anyone. But He sent you."

Liam had a point. She could think of nothing more to say on the matter.

So, they went to church together. It was an experience unique to Paula's minimal religious participation. Oh, she'd been to church with other people, and often, in her younger days. Even with men who were courting her more or less seriously and seemed to think it necessary to prove they were men of some religious conviction in order to win her heart. It hadn't won her over then, and she doubted it would now. But she had never gone to a service with a man who really believed in the whole thing.

Liam Croft went to Mass with reverence and worship, and she felt both emanating from him as she sat, stood and knelt beside him during the liturgy. His faith and feeling for the service seemed to surround him in a kind of aura that from time to time expanded to include her in its peace and odd excitement.

But she did not like the attention they attracted. Of course, in a town the size of Carleton Cay, everyone of any consequence was known. She was not only of some standing socially because of her family, but she was the first woman to reach the deputy level in the D.A.'s office. Further, Liam wasn't dressed as he "should" have been for church, in small-town America. No suit and tie. Just an odd-looking shirt and jeans. Bandages around his head and his arm in a sling—an addition she had insisted upon when she had seen how it pained him to let the arm just hang.

People stared, politely, but quite openly. Paula suppressed a sense of uneasiness. Nothing she could do about it now, anyway, she told herself. She forced herself to relax and enjoy listening when he sang. He did have a marvelous voice. Then, when the service was over, she drove Liam to the hospital to be checked out properly.

He was meek as a lamb and politely apologetic to the doctors when lectured about his abrupt departure from their care. They all had to admit, however, that he was healing at a pace beyond normal expectation. "You might ask him what kind of vitamins he takes," Jim Cunningham suggested to Paula. "If you could bottle whatever his constitution has that's putting him back together so well and so quickly, you'd make a fortune."

Paula smiled ruefully. "I think his secret is just a healthy attitude, Jim. Thanks."

"Whatever. It works. Bring him back tomorrow for a nurse to check that dressing. I don't need to see him again unless there's some problem."

"I'm sure there won't be." Paula thanked him again and went to collect her Irish lamb.

He was waiting, patiently. "I'd like to go back to the church," he said. "I need to talk to the priest."

"Have you something to confess?" she said, raising an eyebrow.

"No, darlin'." He stood and smiled at her. "I've nothing particularly sinful to confess. I was in study for the priesthood myself at one time. No, I need to ask the good Father a more secular question. Mind?"

"You?" She was stunned. "A priest?"

Another smile. Gentle and full of humor. "It didn't take. Don't you be worrying. I'm too much a worldly man, though it troubles me at times. I kissed you, didn't I, so that should prove I'm enough of a rogue to need prayers. It's grateful I am to have so many good women in my family lighting candles regularly for my soul."

"Come on." She needed time to think about this. "I'll take you over to the parish house. Father Sheridan ought to be there now."

He followed her obediently out of the hospital to the parking lot and her car. "I was persuaded to join the priesthood when I was a wee lad," he said, chatting as was obviously his wont to do. "Before I really came to know the world fully. And I loved the study. The music, particularly." He settled into the car, ignoring the seat belt. "But, alas, when my manhood discovered earthbound angels, I decided the heavenly angels could wait."

"That's interesting." Paula said, starting the car. "Seat belt," she said. "Please."

"Um. Oh." He fastened it. "But when I left the church, it was with amicable farewells to my teachers and mentors. No bad feelings on either side. I've kept close and friendly contact with them all my adult life, particularly with my special sponsors. It's one of them I wish to speak to your Father Sheridan about. I think he'll find my connections worth attention."

"Connections?" Paula steered out of the lot and down the street toward the parish house. "Is this something that ought to concern me?"

Liam didn't reply directly. But his smile gave her fair warning. "As it happens, I do have something to confess. I made a phone call while you were visiting with the good doctor about my physical condition," he allowed. "And that call will clear up a number of things for you, me darlin'. A number of things."

Paula couldn't wait to find out what sorts of things. Liam Croft was too full of surprises to be for real!

"HIS UNCLE is Monsignor Croft, Ms. Dixon," Father Sheridan said, handing her a cup of tea from the service sitting on the coffee table in front of them. "I've spoken with His Reverence long distance in Rome not twenty minutes ago, and I promise you there's no way this lad could be involved in crime and have such high-level recommendations and support from the Church."

Paula regarded the man thoughtfully. She could rely on what he said. She knew that from past experience. The priest was as Irish as Liam, but his years in the southern United States had given his brogue a softness and his manner some American ease. A squarely built, balding man with a warm smile and a blue-eyed gaze that didn't waver when he spoke to you. He was about forty, Paula figured, and well liked by his parishioners, she knew. If he said a thing was so, it was so.

Paula gave Liam a hard look. He'd put her into this embarrassing position. "I wish he'd called on you sooner, then," she said. "Liam, I'm not going to sit here and talk about you as if you weren't present. Why did you wait to pull out the big credibility guns?"

"Because I was reluctant to involve anyone else," he answered. "I was not trying to be difficult."

"Please just tell me the truth, then." She set down her cup. "We have a mediator here in Father Sheridan. Surely, you can trust him, if you won't trust me."

Liam appeared to think about it. He sat back and rubbed his big hands on his thighs.

"Come on, son. She's a fair person." Father Sheridan nodded to Paula. "Her career's been outstandingly honest and free of any hint of corruption."

Paula raised her eyebrows, but said nothing.

"If I tell the truth, and I need a lawyer," Liam said, looking at Paula, "will you recommend one?"

She blinked. "I can do that now. I recommend Tinsley Berringer. She's done quite a bit of public defense work during the past few years. She's smart, she's dedicated and..."

"And the dear lady is expecting another wee Berringer," Father Sheridan announced. "I don't know if Alex will let her take on a case these days."

Paula had to laugh at that. "I doubt if Alex has that sort of control over what Tinsley..."

"Ah, a lady who obeys her husband." Liam looked happy. "Rare to find. I approve. She's suitable, if he allows. Now, then . . ." He settled back on the couch, composing himself.

"It's my great-granduncle, Tobias Croft," he said. "He's missing, y'see, and the family wants him home."

"*Great*-granduncle?" Paula said. "How old is he?"

Liam shrugged. "We're not sure. In his late eighties for certain. That's why—"

"*He* shot you?"

"'Twas accidental as I told you."

"Please don't make fun of me, Liam. I'm not a fool."

"Ms. Dixon. Paula," the priest said, sensing trouble. "Calm down. Let him finish."

"All right." She reined in her exasperation. "Just how long has he been missing?"

"About forty or fifty years. Perhaps closer to sixty. No one's quite sure, y'understand. He left Ireland one day and just never returned. A card from here, a letter from there. But never any real attempt to communicate."

"And you all just now decided to find him?"

Liam nodded, either oblivious to her sarcasm or ignoring it. "It was time," he replied calmly. "The family decided."

Paula got up and started to pace around the parish-house parlor. "Liam, I'm trying to understand you, but it is difficult. You came here to find a man who's probably four-fifths in his grave and you get yourself beat up and shot and you claim he—"

"I don't *claim*. I say. Tobias became very angry when I suggested he might prefer to spend his last days with his loved ones rather than all alone. He whacked at me with the cane, and I didn't defend myself for fear of hurting him. When the pistol went off, it was pure accident. He was as shocked as I. When I left him to find help, he was repenting with tears, believe me."

"That's not easy."

Father Sheridan cleared his throat. "I must say I've heard fairer tales, son," he said. "Can you give us proof?"

"You mistrust me?" Liam asked.

"No, not exactly, but..."

Paula sat back down. "Liam, I think I have to believe you. If I'm ever going to make sense of this business, that is. But let me help you, please. Tell me where Tobias is, and I'll send some people to get him. They—"

"No!" Now he stood and paced, worried and upset. "I won't have him hunted and hurt by strangers. I have to do this. Me, myself. No one else."

Paula sat quietly. This was the most anger and passion he'd shown. The old man really mattered to him. Or at least, his responsibility toward him mattered. One led to the other, it seemed, where Liam Croft was concerned. Still, she was sure he wasn't telling the whole truth. Just part of it. Not lying, just...rationing it.

It made her all the more intrigued with him.

Father Sheridan spoke. "What if the three of us try to deal with your uncle?" he asked. "Would that help you?"

Liam smiled regretfully. "I think not, Father. Though it's kind of you to offer. You see, my great-granduncle has no love for the Church nor for those who serve Her. If he saw a priest coming or learned he was dealing with one, I'd lose him again. One way or another. No, he'll have to be brought in gently and with love. But carefully and with consideration of his years and attitudes." He bent his head for a moment.

"Mind if I take some time to myself?" he asked. "I promise not to go any farther than the church next door."

"Well, I don't know...."

"I'll walk over with you, son," Father Sheridan said. "Ms. Dixon can have both our heads on a platter if I let you escape."

"If he goes," Paula said, "I have to. He's still in my custody, and I'm responsible for..."

"I'm going to pray, Paula Dixon." Liam sat down beside her and took her hand in his. "And you, darlin', are not conducive company, whereas the good Father is. Now, if I trusted you enough to tell you about my dear relative, you can be trusting me with a little quiet praying time, can't you?"

"I—"

"Good." Liam stood up. "Come on, Father. Let's go see what God would like for me to do about this mess."

And once more, Paula found she had nothing else to say on the matter. After that, what *could* she say?

CHAPTER FOUR

THE REMAINDER OF Sunday passed quietly, with Liam sleeping or just resting most of the time.

While Paula thought.

But on Monday morning in Paula's office, Tottie Reynolds was hardly impressed when she found out just what Paula had been thinking so hard about.

"You're completely out of your mind," Tottie declared, slamming her palm down on Paula's desk. "I thought so before, but now, I'm sure of it!"

Paula shifted papers. "I'm not crazy," she said calmly. "I know exactly what I'm doing."

"Right. And keeping a stranger on in your house with no deputy or anybody to protect you if he gets to acting funny is *exactly* what you're doing!" Tottie paused for effect. "*That* is crazy."

"It's stupid, maybe," Paula admitted. "But not crazy. As sure as I know I'm sitting here discussing this with you, I'm sure Liam is incapable of—"

"Liam? *Liam,* is it? Not Mr. Croft anymore?" Tottie stepped back, planted her hands on her hips and glared. "Girl, you have lost it. And don't you for one minute think that man is incapable of anything. They're all capable, every last one of them, and you know it as well as I do."

"He's a very religious man, Tottie. He spent almost two hours in church yesterday afternoon, praying with Father Sheridan."

"I don't care how much he prays. Have you asked what he's *praying* for?"

Paula glared back, defying the sheriff's grim expression. Then, she started to laugh. "I don't believe I'm sitting here listening to you fuss at me about a man being in my house, Tottie. You have no right to do that. I am not a child, and you are not my mother, aunt or guardian."

"No, I'm not." Tottie folded her arms across her chest. "I'm your friend."

Paula stopped laughing. "I know," she said.

"I'm your friend, and right now I'm the only one who can talk sense to you. Paula, this whole town is talking about you and your... houseguest. You can't just keep him there."

"I can. And I will. I'm getting damn tired of doing things or not doing them to protect my career and standing in the community. This goes way beyond what happens to me! He needs my help."

Tottie sighed, exasperation showing on her smooth face. She ran her hand over her hair and sank into a chair. "What kind of help?" she asked.

Paula leaned forward, twirling a pencil in her fingers. "It's kind of complicated," she said. "I don't know all the details, but it seems he really was shot by accident. By his great-granduncle."

"Say what?" Tottie settled back in the chair, resting her elbow on the arm and her head on her hand. She looked extremely skeptical.

"His great-granduncle," Paula repeated. "The old man has been gone from home and hearth for nearly half a century, and the Crofts all decided it was time for Tobias to come home.''

"I am not following this. Help me out, please," Tottie said.

"Well . . ." Paula hesitated. "Like I said, it's complicated."

"Like *I* said, it's horse manure!" Tottie sat up straight again. "I don't know what this guy's looking up, or why. He should be happy as a clam landing in your bed, but—"

"He's alone in it!" Paula stood up, her temper finally goaded. "I'm sleeping out on the porch on the daybed, now that I'm sure he's in no danger."

"Oh, well. I'm sure glad to hear *he's* safe. And hearing you're out on the porch all night just makes me all warm and cozy, too. Paula Dixon. I repeat, you have lost your mind!" Tottie shouted.

The door to Paula's office opened. Her secretary, Diane Pfaff, a woman of questionable skills and even more questionable loyalty to her boss, stuck her head in. "They can hear you two yelling all the way down to the county clerk's office. What's going on?"

"Nothing," Paula said, sitting back down.

"Not a thing," Tottie said, settling back into her chair.

"Hmm." Diane regarded the two women. "I thought I heard something about someone losing their mind. Guess I was wrong." She stared at them a moment longer, then shut the door.

Tottie pulled a face. "She'll blab about this to boss man Chuckie, and then the fat will be in the fire for sure."

"I'm already in the frying pan. What difference will it make?"

"Diane's a snitch, Paula. Everyone knows she's lusted after Chuckie for years. She'll tell him anything, just to get his attention. She gossips about you all the time, too. I don't understand why you keep her in your department."

Paula shrugged, relieved to have the subject changed from Liam to her secretary. "She's a civil servant. Impossible to fire. If I requested her transfer, who knows who they'd assign to replace her. At least the devil you know is better than the one you don't."

The door opened again. "Phone, Ms. Dixon," Diane announced. "It's Mr. Benson. Long distance. From *Hawaii*." The door shut.

Paula groaned and reached for the phone.

Tottie got up. "I'll be leaving you now," she said. "You got enough troubles without me fussing at you, too."

"Thanks." Paula watched the sheriff leave. "Hello, Charles?" she said into the receiver. "How's Hawaii? Nice weather?"

For the next ten minutes, she listened to her boss. And District Attorney Charles Benson did not talk to her about the weather in paradise.

THE STALKER SCUTTERED around the edge of the house. Bushes and hedges surrounding the backyard shielded him from nosy neighbors, and he was sure his target was not at home. It was all right if he made some noise.

But you couldn't be too careful. That's what Momma always said.

He knelt by the back-porch door for a few minutes, listening, straining every nerve.

Silence. Golden silence. He smiled to himself and reached up for the screen-door handle.

It opened easily, like warm butter sliding off a plate.

He slipped inside.

The porch had been transformed into a bedroom. The narrow daybed was carefully made up with sheets and a light blanket. He frowned. Who was sleeping out here? He knelt down again and sniffed at the pillow. Perfume.

Well, well, well!

Then he stood up and unslung the backpack he wore. Maybe she moved out here for the summer, even though it was still cold at night. Funny, but what the heck did he know about women like her? She must be pretty sure of herself. The porch area was protected only by screens and the overhanging roof.

Easy to get into, even if the door had been locked. He smiled, but it was not a happy expression.

He took out a jar from the backpack, pulled back the blanket and dumped the contents of the jar on the clean, white sheets. He watched, pleased, as the material spread slowly and stained deeply. Not so white, now.

He started to laugh. Giggle, really. The kind of delicate, sniffling sound Momma always made when something struck her funny. Thinking of Momma made him laugh harder. Giggling higher and more shrilly. But not with happiness. With relish that soon she'd—

What was that?

Door opening. Heavy footfalls from the back of the house . . .

"Are you back so soon then, darlin'? I didn't expect to see you until after five."

A deep, sleepy male voice startled and frightened him. But also sent a shiver of excitement through him. Pleasurable excitement. Quickly, he gathered up his backpack and the empty jar and flew out of the screen door, not bothering to practice any stealth. The screen banged shut, and the intruder heard the angry roar of another man as he vaulted the hedge, dodged the obstacles and raced down the sidewalk toward safety.

And from behind, he heard more sounds that made him want to stop and laugh again with glee. The man had not known about those obstacles! Too bad. Tooooo baaaaad!

ALTHOUGH SHE'D been off the phone for almost an hour, Paula was still quivering with suppressed rage at her boss when Diane, using the intercom this time, informed her she had another phone call.

"Who is it, Diane?" she asked, keying her intercom button. "I really don't want to be interrupted again unless it's important."

"*He* says it is, Ms. Dixon," Diane replied. "He says there's an emergency at your house."

Liam! He was in trouble again! Paula picked up the phone. "What's wrong?" she asked.

The torrent of commentary that flooded her ear was completely unintelligible. She made out a word or two here and there, but for the most part, she had no clue what he was shouting at her over the phone.

"Liam," she said, trying to break in. "Liam, I can't understand..."

The torrent continued without a pause. Now she was sure he wasn't even speaking English. Was this Gaelic? she wondered. Diane burst into the office. "Someone's been killed at your house," she cried. "I just got a call from the police on your other line. They want..."

Killed. At your house!

Paula slammed down the receiver and ran. By the time she screeched to a halt halfway up her street, police cars lined the curb in front of her home. Heart beating wildly and fear churning in her stomach, Paula pulled up and double-parked by the squad car she recognized as belonging to Tottie Reynolds. For a moment, the fear of what she might find threatened to overcome her and keep her glued to the seat of her car. She told herself to get a grip. She'd be no use to anybody if she didn't. Then, she opened the door and got out.

People were screaming.

She ran up the steps to the front porch. The screaming voices were male. And they weren't yelling in fright, but in anger, and apparently at one another. She had no trouble picking out Liam's deep tones and use of unrecognizable words. The other voices were undoubtedly from cops. She didn't hear Tottie.

As she stood there, listening, Tottie came out the front door. Her expression was stony and grim.

"Who's dead?" Paula almost couldn't speak. This was her house! Someone was dead in it!

"Nobody," Tottie replied. She glanced behind her in the direction of the arguing voices. "But that might not be the case in a few minutes. You'd better go in and see if you can get someone's Irish down."

"Liam?"

"That's right." Tottie stepped aside as Paula went through the front door. "I don't think I've ever seen a man as mad."

Paula hesitated. "Tottie, what happened?"

"Someone snuck onto your back porch and dumped about a gallon of blood on your daybed."

"What?"

"You heard me. I guess your houseguest was taking a nap or something and heard some woman laughing and thought it was you. When he went out to see, he saw the mess and someone else's tail end disappearing over the hedge."

"A woman? Who?"

Tottie shrugged. "Don't know. Not even sure it was a female. Moved real fast. Your guest tried to give chase but the quarry disappeared. And Mr. Croft, who had a slight accident in the rush to capture the villain, then returned to the house and dialed every emergency number he could find on your phone. Seems he likes to cover all the bases."

"And?"

"And we can't tell anything right now," Tottie replied. "I'm going to have the lab run tests on the blood, but aside from telling us what it came from..."

"Not *who?*"

"I don't think it's human."

"It's pig blood!" Liam roared into the room. "I've smelled enough in butchers' shops to know." He was limping, favoring his left leg. His arm was out of the sling, and deep scratches ran along the left side of his neck and face. His shirt was torn. "Bloody hell," he muttered.

"Liam, are you all right?" Paula stood still, not knowing exactly how to react. He was red in the face with rage, and the veins at his temples were throbbing. "Did you get hurt?" she asked.

Liam ignored her. Or seemed to. He turned on Tottie. "Those idiots you call policemen are refusing to search house-to-house in the neighborhood," he said, looming over the sheriff. "If this were Ireland, the gardai'd be out, pounding doors and..."

"It's not Ireland!" Paula shouted, demanding and getting his attention. "Liam, what happened?"

"Ah, darlin' Paula." He gazed at her, blue eyes simmering with sadness, with regret. "Taking a little rest, I was, and then I heard your voice singing. At least, it sounded female. Anyway, when I went to see, I found your bed all defiled and the scoundrel in the very act of leapin' the hedgerow. So I gave pursuit, and—"

"And you landed in Mrs. Pritchard's rose garden, didn't you?" Paula went over to him and examined the scratches. "Come into the kitchen," she said. "Let me put some ointment on those."

"I'm all right," he said. "Go and look at your bed."

"I really don't want to," she confessed, ashamed to admit to her feelings of having been violated in front of Liam and Tottie. "I..."

"Paula," Tottie said, her tone gentle. "I hate to alarm you, but I have a nasty feeling that whoever's been sending you all the notes and making all the phone calls just left his calling card."

"But—" Paula started to say.

Liam interrupted. "What notes? What phone calls? What calling card?"

Paula was about to tell him not to worry about it, that it was none of his concern. Then, she realized something: she'd made his problem *her* concern. And it wasn't just because she was a prosecutor, either.

It was because she liked Liam and found herself caring about him and his strange situation. Could he possibly be feeling something similar for her?

"About six months ago," she said, "I started to receive odd notes and threats by mail and telephone. This sort of thing happens to prosecutors, so none of us, especially me, thought too much of it."

"You were threatened? And no one thought a thing of it?" Liam's expression showed how he felt about that. The veins in his temples started pulsing again. "What sort of society cares nothing for protectin' their womenfolk?"

Paula was about to reply that it was her problem, not society's, that she'd chosen her profession with its risks as well as its rewards, but just then, one of the city police officials came into the living room. Paula almost groaned aloud when she saw who it was. *Mr. Sexism* of Carleton Cay's police force, in person. Forrest Gradon.

Detective Forrest Gradon hadn't modified the intensity of his dislike for her in all the years they'd been forced to work together, no matter how much she'd tried to accommodate the man. Thin, acid of personality and Deep South to his toes, he was a cop from the old school who disapproved of women meddling in the "masculine" business of crime and punishment. "Ms. Dixon, ma'am," he said, greeting her. "Y'all oughta come on out back, please."

"Detective Gradon," she said, acknowledging him with a nod. "I will. In a minute. First, I have a few things to clear up with Mr. Croft."

Gradon cleared his throat. "No, ma'am. I suggest you come with me right now. We have—"

"You heard the lady," Liam interrupted. "Mister Gradon, you will wait until she..."

"I suggest *you* keep your damned face out of this, you—" Gradon began, turning on Liam.

Paula edged between them, hoping to avert any trouble. But the men moved away just enough to face each other and...

Liam's fists were balled and his neck seemed to swell as his shoulder muscles bunched. He moved toward Gradon and the detective took a step backward right onto Paula's foot. Startled and in pain, she yelped and pushed him away.

Instinctively, Detective Gradon elbowed her. At first, it was accidental, but then his intention to hurt her was unmistakable. His lips were thin with rage and his small eyes gleamed with cold fury. This time, he deliberately aimed his elbow so it would hit her square on the jaw, and Paula went down like a knocked-out prize-fighter. As she drifted to the floor, she heard from a thousand miles away the bull-like bellowing of an enraged male. Then something struck her forehead, stars appeared in front of her eyes, pain knifed through her head and darkness came.

"PAULA?"

Gentle slaps on her face.

"Paula!"

Not so gentle slaps. A sharp and nasty odor—ammonia. Paula groaned and opened her eyes.

A doctor was looking intently at her. She knew him but she just couldn't remember his name. There was a nurse with him. A black woman she didn't recognize at all....

"Paula!"

Another black woman, very familiar... Face tense with emotion ... Concern ... Oh, yes ... She was...

"Tottie?"

Tottie's facial muscles relaxed. "Thank goodness, girl!" she exclaimed. "I thought for a while there you were planning to sleep through Christmas. When we brought you here to the hospital, you were out cold."

"You did sustain a blow to the head when you fell," Jim Cunningham said. "Definitely a concussion there," he added. The nurse nodded.

Now she knew who he was. Now she remembered....

"Liam," she said, trying to sit up. The pain in her head made her dizzy and nauseated. She lay back down. "Where's Liam?"

"Liam Croft is cooling his temper and his heels in jail right now," Tottie declared, her tone flinty. "And don't you go worrying about him. After Gradon hit you, Liam went for Gradon. He nearly put the man in traction for life!"

"But he was defending me." Paula closed her eyes, remembering what she could of the incident. "Gradon hurt me, and—"

"And so he hurt Gradon," Tottie said. "An eye for an eye? Is that the way the justice system works now? I know Gradon probably hit you deliberately, but I can't swear to it, and I was even there. Are we supposed to let Liam Croft play judge and jury and administer justice?"

"No, of course not, but—"

"You *have* gone soft in the head. And it's not from getting knocked out, either."

"Sheriff Reynolds, don't you think you're being a bit rough on Paula?" Jim asked, smiling at Paula as he spoke. "She's been through a lot."

Tottie shrugged. "Maybe, but sometimes, being ornery is the only way to get her attention." Her brown eyes looked surprisingly as though they were filling with tears. "You take care of her, hear me?" she added harshly.

When Paula opened her eyes again, Tottie was gone.

"That's a pretty good friend you have there," Jim said, recording notes in a chart. "Worries about you."

"I know. We go back a long way." Paula reached up and touched a lumpy bandage at the side of her forehead. "What happened, Jim? I honestly don't remember hitting my head."

The doctor smiled. "Well, your boyfriend—"

"He's not my boyfriend. No matter what everyone in this town would like to believe."

"Well, then, Mr. Croft, your houseguest, started to make Irish stew out of the detective who, uh, accidently, bumped you with his elbow, sending you to the floor via the edge of your coffee table. Said houseguest is now in jail for striking, no, attacking a police officer. The detective is on the third floor, here."

Paula held her forehead. "How bad is he?"

"Not bad, considering what might have happened. Before your Irishman could do permanent damage, he seemed to get control of himself, I'm told. So Gradon's bruised, but unbroken. Angry as a soaked hen, but he'll survive. Long enough to see your friend spending some serious jail time, if—"

"Get me a phone."

"Paula, I'm your doctor. You've taken quite a blow. You shouldn't—"

She sat up. Nausea and dizziness hit her, but she ignored them. *No time.* "A phone, please. Now," she said, quietly.

"All right," Jim said, sighing. "I might as well approve, because you'll do what you want until the day they set up your memorial stone."

Paula managed to grin at him.

"Get her a phone, please," he said to the nurse.

The nurse pursed her lips in disapproval. But she obeyed. Paula held the cellular phone and punched in a special, unlisted number. After twenty rings, the party answered.

"Berringer and Berringer," the woman said, her voice hollow, indicating a long-distance transmission. "Attorneys-at-Law."

"Hey, Tinsley," Paula said. "It's Paula. I think I have a client for you and Alex."

"Hi, Paula!" Tinsley Berringer replied, her tone full of delight. "How're you doing?"

Paula touched her bandaged forehead. "Well, I guess that's a matter of opinion. What about the client? Interested?"

Tinsley hesitated. "We're swamped right now, Paula. Alex isn't doing anything but writing at the moment. His next book is due in two weeks, and I—"

"I know," Paula interrupted. "Your next kid is due in two months. I wouldn't have called you, but I think this case is tailor-made for your special talents. And even if Alex isn't taking other cases, I'll bet this one will intrigue him enough to get him back in court. Say you'll come into town and at least meet the guy. Please."

"You're pleading?" Tinsley's tone held a teasing edge. "Is he someone significant to you?"

"Maybe. I don't know yet, but maybe."

"Well, that is enough for me! I don't know about Alex, but my curiosity demands to be satisfied. We'll see you as soon as I can tear him away from his last chapter, find a baby-sitter and get the boat across the channel."

"Great. Tinsley, I can't thank you enough! And Tinsley..."

"What?"

"I'm not at the office. I'm in the hospital. You'll have to meet me here." She glanced at Jim Cunningham. "I don't think they'll let me go unless someone offers to take me home and watch me for a while."

The doctor nodded solemnly. "That'll be all right with me," he said.

"What happened?" Tinsley asked, her voice full of concern and alarm.

"I just hit my head a little too hard. Come on in. I'll tell you all about it when I see you."

"We're on our way!"

Several hours later, Jim Cunningham agreed to release Paula from the hospital into the care of her friends, the Berringers. Both Alex and Tinsley had come over from their island, and were grilling her as if she were a star witness in a legal proceeding. Their questioning included several topics. Their first interest seemed to be in the threats and the blood dumped on her daybed.

"How long have you been getting the threatening notes and calls?" Tinsley wanted to know. "And why the hell hasn't someone taken your situation more seriously?''

She walked awkwardly, a big woman, made larger by advanced pregnancy. But her personal charisma and healthy blond beauty gave her a natural, earthy grace that dominated her condition. She pushed Paula in her wheelchair along the hallway while Alex moved ahead to open doors.

"It all started a couple of months ago, I guess," Paula replied, fidgeting. She had promised to stay put in the wheelchair until she was safely esconced in the Berringers' Jeep, but she felt hampered by not being able to move freely. "I kept it to myself for the first few weeks, figuring it was just some crackpot who would drop it, if there was no reaction from me."

"That didn't work," Alex commented darkly. The tall, lean writer had been through a similar kind of stalking-hell a few years before. And a few years even before that, before Tinsley had come into his life, he'd had a brief romantic relationship with Paula Dixon. They were still friends, and he cared what happened to her. "Rejection rarely does, if the perpetrator is serious."

"We don't know if it's a man," Paula said.

"Women don't stalk," Alex replied.

"Not exactly true," Tinsley countered. "They will stalk, if they're motivated enough."

"Well," Alex said, "a woman might watch someone for a while. Particularly if it's her erring husband and his paramour, but to actually hunt someone for the purpose of harming them, I just don't know of a precedent."

"But I haven't been harmed," Paula said, looking from one Berringer to the other. "My daybed was ruined, apparently. I haven't seen it, myself, but—"

"Telephone calls and notes," Tinsley said, musing. "That's a common stalking technique. Maintains the distance, but closes in on the target."

"But the blood's pure vandalism," Alex said.

"Two perps?" they both said at the same time.

"Please, folks," Paula said from her low vantage point in the chair. "Can we table the detective work until later? My head's killing me, and I want to take you to meet Liam before I pass out again."

"Sorry," Tinsley said. "We were going off on a tangent again, weren't we?"

Paula didn't agree, but she smiled at the couple. They tended toward tangents when working together. But it was one of the attributes that made them good, innovative, creative legal minds.

Alex held open the last door and Tinsley pushed Paula's chair outside into the late-spring sunshine. Birds carried on in courtship melodies. The air smelled of sweet flowers, and small insects buzzed in the blooming bushes and trees. "I'll go get the Jeep," he said to his wife. To Paula, he said, "While I'm gone, you fill Tinsley in on the case you want us to take."

"All right."

By the time Alex pulled up the rusty old Jeep to the hospital entrance and Paula was finally allowed to get out of the chair, she had explained all she knew about Liam Croft to Tinsley Berringer. Since her friend had been standing behind her, Paula had not been able to gage Tinsley's reactions, so she was astonished when her friend suggested to her husband that they might actually *know* Liam's uncle. For some time, the old man had been a bit of a legend among the folks who lived in and near the swamp along the coast.

"Could be," Alex agreed. "It's unlikely there're two such mean and ancient hermits out there."

"We'll have to ask your Irishman for details," Tinsley declared. "Maybe we can help him with his great-uncle, too."

"Great-granduncle, I think," Paula said. "Apparently, he's really old. And really stubborn."

"Sounds like the same guy," Alex said. He put his foot on the gas and pulled away from the curb. "Shooting his own relative." He shook his head. "Some kind of wild man, I'd say."

"It was an accident," Paula said from her perch in the back seat. "Liam insists he didn't mean to do it."

"Right," Tinsley said dryly. "And what is your Liam in jail for at this moment?"

"Assaulting a police officer," Paula admitted reluctantly.

"Sounds to me like violence tends to run in the family," Alex commented.

"Wait until you meet him," Paula said. "Unless he's provoked, Liam Croft is the nicest man you can imagine. Gentle, modest and kind. He once studied for the priesthood."

"And that makes him a saint," Tinsley said, even more dryly.

"No. But it makes him… Well, you'll see when you meet him," Paula replied.

"I can hardly wait," Tinsley murmured. Alex shushed her.

And Paula wondered what they would really think of him and if they would accept his case of their own accord, and not because of their long-standing friendship with her.

It would all depend on the impression Liam made, she thought, so there was nothing to worry about. He was so charming, they were sure to like him and believe in him.

Weren't they?

CHAPTER FIVE

"WHAT DO YOU MEAN, we can't see him?" Paula asked the desk sergeant, Gloria Wilson, a veteran policewoman she'd known for years.

"Gloria, it's *me*. Paula Dixon. Come on! I'm a prosecuting attorney in this county! And Mr. and Mrs. Berringer are legal counsel for the accused." The woman's face betrayed absolutely no expression.

"Doesn't change a thing," she said. "Still can't see him."

"Why?" Paula's head felt as if it were going to burst. "I demand to know why!" Nausea and dizziness rocked her and she grabbed the counter to keep from falling.

Tinsley reached out to help support her. Alex stepped up to the desk, his "Southern gentleman" smile and manner solidly in place.

"Tell me, Sergeant," he said, his tone mild and pleasant. "Do you mean we may not see him, or we *can't* see him?" He smiled, as if he knew a special secret.

The woman's expression changed instantly. First, she looked puzzled, then suspicious. "How'd you find out?" she asked. "Nobody's supposed to know."

"Know what?" Paula regained her balance and strength. "Know what? What's going on?" Tinsley's hands tightened warningly on her friend's arms, and

Alex reached over and touched Paula's hand reassuringly.

"Sergeant Wilson knows, and she's going to tell us," he said, still smiling benignly. "'Course if she prefers not to, we can just take ourselves down to the courthouse and get ourselves a writ."

"He's escaped," Gloria said, leaning forward toward them, her voice a whisper. "It's never happened before, but somehow, he managed it."

"Escaped!" Paula's vision grew blurred. "Oh, my God. Now he's *really* a fugitive!"

"Easy," Tinsley said. "Let's hear the whole story before we think the worst."

"*I'll* tell you the whole story," said Officer Bull Drake as he came into the room, sporting a bruise on his jaw. "He took me completely by surprise," he said. "Knocked me right into next week, I swear! That Irishman's got a mean left, let me tell you. Never even saw it coming."

Something about the expression in his eyes and the unusual tone of his voice made Paula suspicious. "All right, Bull," she said. "Tell us the whole story. Don't leave out one single detail."

"Yes, ma'am." At which point Bull launched into an improbable tale of Irish derring-do and American stupidity. When he was finished, Paula just glared at him.

"You're lying," she said.

"Oh no he's not," Gloria declared, defending her colleague. "It all happened just like Officer Drake says."

"The hell it did," Tinsley said, folding her arms over her middle. "I may not be from around here, originally, but a cover-up is a cover-up, no matter where I hear it. You two are up to something, aren't you?"

Alex moved closer to the policeman. "That's not much of a bruise on your face, Bull." He rubbed the other man's jaw even as Bull tried to pull away. "Just as I suspected—makeup!" he said, holding his purple-smudged finger up for the women to inspect.

"Okay, you two," Paula said. "Out with it. The truth!"

Gloria looked at Bull, who looked at Gloria.

"Now!" Paula slammed her hand down on the desk.

"We let him go," Bull admitted. Gloria nodded.

"You what?"

"Liam just did what any red-blooded man would do," Bull said. "The lieutenant was hurting you, and—"

"Gradon deserved to get thumped," Gloria said. "If there ever was a man who deserved it, he's the one!"

"That's hardly the point," Alex said, playing devil's advocate. "He's a police officer, and Mr. Croft put him in the hospital. Surely, even you know, he can't be allowed to go free."

Neither officer replied. "Bull," Paula pleaded, "where is Liam?"

Silence.

"Does Tottie know about this?"

"No, ma'am." For the first time, the two conspirators looked worried. "And we sure would appreciate it if you wouldn't tell her all you know," begged Bull.

"Because she'd bust us both down to rookie," Gloria said.

"Below rookie," Bull added dolefully. "Way, way down below."

Paula shook her head. "I won't betray you, since you told me the truth. But what made you take such a stupid chance?"

Bull drew himself up to his considerable height. "Simple, Ms. Dixon. I like the man. He's got old-fashioned honor in him real deep. Something you don't see much of nowadays. He takes care of people. He was defending you. He needs to go get his old uncle out of the swamp. And he intends to guard..." He trailed off, his face turning dark with a deep blush.

"Guard who?" Paula glared.

"Um, you know."

"Who!"

"Oh, Ms. Dixon, he likes you a lot, and with that crazy person sending you threats, getting in your house and dumping blood. And us not able to do a thing about it, yet... Well, Liam might be able to where we can't, since he's willing to risk..."

Paula swore as she pushed herself away from the desk and collapsed into a chair by the wall. "I don't need a guard. I don't need defending. I didn't ask him to do any of this," she said, putting her face in her hands. "Now he's a fugitive because of me."

Gloria cleared her throat. "Well, he's not exactly a fugitive, actually."

Paula looked up. "What do you mean?" she said.

"I don't get it," Tinsley said, sitting down next to Paula. "He broke jail, but no one's looking for him?"

"He didn't break jail, honey," Alex said. "He was released on his own recognizance. But not through all the proper channels, I'm willing to bet. Right?" He looked at Gloria and Bull.

"Um," Bull said.

"Right!" Gloria chimed.

"Right," Bull echoed.

"They can't do that," Paula said. "It takes a judge to—"

"It's okay, Paula. Settle down." Tinsley said, standing back up. "For now, it'll have to do." She gave Gloria and Bull a stern look. "Don't go volunteering this information to anyone else, you two. We won't say anything, if you won't."

"No, ma'am," Bull said, obviously relieved. "Our lips are sealed."

"There's a little something more, however," Tinsley went on, turning to Gloria, after Bull nodded and smiled agreement, as if he was willing now to go along with anything she asked. "We need help."

Gloria was less eager to cooperate. "What more do you want from us?" she asked.

"Just to know where Mr. Croft is," Alex said.

"Can't do that," Bull replied, sobering. "We promised."

"*Un*promise," Paula said. "He's going to be in big, big trouble if either Sheriff Reynolds or Detective Gradon finds out he's flown the coop. Now, if I can get to him first and talk some sense into him, I can help him to avoid a great deal of that trouble."

"He needs legal counsel," Tinsley added. "He did deck a cop, after all."

"One who deserved it."

"And he did leave official custody without going through proper channels."

"He escaped, like we said." Bull and Gloria swapped conspiratorial smiles again.

"Well, that's one version of what happened." A new voice entered the conversation as Tottie Reynolds entered the room. Gloria and Bull looked as if they were each about to faint.

"Here's another," the sheriff said, glaring at her subordinate officers. "The Irishman bribed his way out," she went on, closing in on the pair. "He gave you money to let him go, and you took it!"

"We never did!" Bull declared.

"All he gave us was his thanks," Gloria stated, standing and returning her superior officer's glare. "And his gratitude. That is all we took, and if you don't believe us, then you can just go looking for some new officers right this minute!"

Tottie stepped back a bit. "I can't replace you," she said, her manner gentling. "You know that. But I can't believe you two would do something like this." She looked at Paula. "Can you explain it to me?"

Paula swallowed hard and nodded. "It's Liam. He's so easy to like," she said softly, the pain in her head almost too much to bear. "He charms his way into everybody's heart so that everybody wants to help him."

"A dangerous, dangerous man," Tinsley said gloomily. "I met one like that once." She patted her middle. "And look what happened to me."

Tottie shook her head. "However it happened, I've got to get him back," she said to Gloria and Bull. "Now tell us where he went."

The two officers were silent.

"My Lord!" Paula cried. "All we want to do is make sure he doesn't get hurt!"

"He won't," Bull said, smiling. "Believe me, that's one man who can take on the world by himself and win."

Paula sat down again, groaning with frustration and pain. "No one," she said, "is that invincible. No one."

"Probably not," Alex agreed. "But my dear old friend, he seems to have done what no one else could have with regards to you."

"And just what is that?" She looked up at her one-time lover.

"Made you love him more than you love yourself or your work."

Paula could only stare in amazement at Alex. He couldn't be right!

To her relief, the discussion turned to more practical matters.

"We'll have to set this right through the system," Tottie said. "Bull, Gloria, I can understand your being taken in by this guy. If he could get to Paula, I guess he could get to almost anyone." She paused. "Except me, of course." She glanced at Paula, who was now only able to sit quietly and nurse her combined emotional and physical miseries. "But I'll do what I can for him," the sheriff added. "You're my friend, Paula, and if you care about him this much, I'll do what I can."

"Thanks," Paula murmured. "I guess I do."

"We'll stay with her," Tinsley said. "She's going to need watching and caring for until that concussion is healed, and Liam might just come to her house to see if she's all right if what you're suggesting about the feelings between them is true."

"It's conjecture," Paula said, mostly to herself. "I was just being nice to him."

"Paula, honey, forgive me, but niceness is not one of your leading qualities," Alex said, his tone kind, in spite of his words. "Fair, yes. Honorable, yes. Honest, yes. As the day is long. You're a wonderful woman, but you are as tough as nails, and you know it. You'd never have taken any other man into your home, nor would you be defending him like you are now. Going against the letter of the law. Paula, you don't do that. Ever. This one's got to mean something to you."

Paula looked up at the others. All four of them were nodding in agreement. "Okay," she said. "I'm soft on the guy. I admit it. Now what?"

"NOW WHAT, then?" Tobias Croft glared at his great-grandnephew, Liam Croft. Liam was about three steps away, well within striking distance. Tobias rested his gnarled hands on the knob of his blackthorn cane and considered how much of a chance he had to deck the youngster once again.

And if he, by honor's standards, should.

After all, he'd shot the lad barely a week ago, though by accident, and sorely hurt him. 'Twasn't right, that. The boy was only here, trying his level best to help, though he'd not taken into account that his help was unsolicited.

A boy. Still a child. That's all young Liam was.

But a boy who was a blood relative, and, it seemed, a good soul with an earnest, true conscience, who didn't give up a quest or mission easily because of pain or trial. That was to be taken into consideration when it came to thinking of whether to thrash him again.

No. 'Twouldn't do. Now was the time for sittin' and reasonin' together.

"I suppose ye could sit," Tobias said grudgingly, indicating the one other chair in his cabin. "And perhaps ye'll open the jug for us to have a drink together."

Liam controlled the urge to smile with relief. By sharing his liquor, Tobias was saying he wouldn't start a fight again. It would offend his Gaelic sense of hospitality.

Liam went over to the old wooden sideboard and located the brown jug and two relatively clean mugs, poured a generous amount in each and returned to sit near the old man. He handed over one mug. The two men drank.

"It's not just for the family or myself, now that I want you to come with me," Liam said, speaking only after the fiery effects of the moonshine had begun to leave his throat. "It's also for the lass I met after our last meeting and the little accident that occurred."

"Lass?" Tobias took another deep swig. "Pretty, is she, then?"

"As an angel," Liam replied, smiling openly. "With shining blue eyes and red hair and freckles, though she does try hiding them under some makeup."

Tobias chuckled. "But ye've already seen her without that makeup stuff nor anything else. There's the lad!"

Liam stood, knocking his chair over. "She's not an easy woman, Uncle. And I'll not be havin' you speak so of her!"

Tobias stood. "I'm sorry, Nephew. I meant no harm."

"She's an honorable young woman," Liam said. "A virtuous one." He told Tobias about Paula's position in the community and about the high esteem the priest, Father Sheridan, held her in. He also explained how the priest had helped convince her that he, Liam, was to be trusted, himself. "So, she's not only virtuous, Uncle. She's smart, too."

"Good, then." Tobias raised his mug. "Here's to her smart virtue." He drained the drink.

Liam did the same.

He picked up his chair, poured some more poteen and sat down again. "Someone's trying to harm her, Uncle," he said. "And I mean to keep that from happening."

Tobias frowned. "What's she to ye, then? A friend? Or more?"

Liam was silent.

"Ah," Tobias said. "Ye've found love, have you?"

Liam thought for a moment. "How could I? I don't think she's the one for me. She's not the marrying kind of woman, or she'd already be in a home with a husband and a houseful of children and..." He hesitated. "No, she's not for home and hearth. Not her."

"None of the best ones are, lad," Tobias said. "The ones you've got to court to the altar make the best wives. Take it from one who knows. I had meself one like that."

"Uncle, I didn't know you'd married. No one back home said..."

Tobias stared at his drink. "No one back home knew. For she's dead and gone now. We had only two years together before a fever took her from me. I told none of the family about her. Hurt too damn much to remember, even does in the telling, now. But I loved that lass more than life itself." He looked up. "If ye think ye might have found one like her for yourself, perhaps I'll help ye. Perhaps, I will."

Liam still did not speak.

"Ye do not know, yet, do ye?" Tobias got up, filled the mugs a third time and sat down. He watched as Liam drained his dry. "Ye've feelings, but ye do not know what sort," the old man said.

Now, Liam nodded. Now, he was the one staring at the emptiness of his mug. "Well," said Tobias, "that is a start." He grinned, exposing surprisingly strong, white teeth for a man his age. "At least ye don't know ye *don't* love her." He chuckled.

Liam chuckled, too. Then laughed. Moments later, both Croft men were roaring with laughter. And the sound made human music in the humid air of the swampland.

Then, the laughter quieted, and Liam told Tobias what had happened and what might be happening to Paula Dixon, even as they spoke.

WHAT WAS HAPPENING to her right at that moment was a trip in Alex's motorboat across the channel from the mainland to the Berringers' island. After some more discussion, Tottie, Alex and Tinsley agreed that for Paula to go back to her own home, even with escort and guard, would only invite further trouble. If nothing else, it would preclude the kind of total rest she needed, because she would be constantly on the alert for Liam, if not for her persecutor. Until some more leads developed regarding the person or persons harassing her, she would be better off out of reach. All agreed the island was as good a place as any.

Paula, still struggling with the remnants of her headache as the small craft danced across the waves, wasn't so sure. She really had wanted to stay home in case Liam did show up. The place was certainly under constant surveillance by Tottie's team, but Paula wanted to be directly involved if and when the law caught up with her Irishman.

Her Irishman.

"Feeling okay?" Alex asked as he regarded her with concern. Tinsley was driving the boat. "Channel's not rough, but you're looking a little green."

"It's her head," Tinsley yelled over the roar of the motor. "Concussions do that. I know."

"I'll be all right," Paula replied. "Just as soon as I get some rest."

"That's what you need, all right," Tinsley called out cheerfully, as she skillfully steered the motorboat into docking position. "That, and knowing your friend is safe."

Friend. Paula considered the word as they pulled up at the Berringers' dock.

Yes, Liam was a friend.

She would like for him to be more than that, she believed. He excited her, and she liked that. The kiss he'd given her Sunday morning had stirred her blood, no doubt about it. But nothing further physical had happened between them. And friendship had developed instead of romance.

She liked him. He'd been an ideal houseguest—polite, kind, considerate and fun at the same time.

Well, he was a little on the demanding side when it came to being waited on, but she figured that was just the way he'd been raised. The Irish customs were different than American ones. He was used to women doing the cooking and cleaning for him, while he ran the business of the family's bed and breakfast as well as the pub down the street.

Family. She couldn't imagine living with hers. One and all from her parents to her grandparents on both sides, disapproved of her life as unbefitting a Dixon.

Tinsley got out of the launch with an agility that belied her pregnancy and set the lines on the moorings. Paula stood and swayed with the gentle swell of the water.

"Watch your step here." Alex helped Paula up and onto the dock. The wood still had a fresh look to it. It had been rebuilt by the island people several years ago after an enemy of Alex's had blown the old place sky-high.

Out of love and respect for Alex, they had also rebuilt his home, and he and Tinsley and their children lived there almost year-round, except when they took the whole crew back to Tinsley's home in Wyoming for a visit, or when Tinsley went on a poetry-reading tour.

She was still one of the most popular of America's cowboy poets and had continued that creative career along with her work in law, as well as being a full-time mother and wife. She never ceased to amaze Paula with her strength and energy.

Okay, so she had plenty of help from the local women and men with child care, cleaning and cooking for her family. Still, Tinsley Berringer, Paula reflected, really was a superwoman! Something she knew she could never be. She had chosen to remain single in order to dedicate herself to her career. While she did admire women like Tinsley, Paula knew her own limits and didn't try to exceed them. Marriage was not altogether out of the question, but it would take a unique sort of man to share the future she had mapped out for herself.

As they walked together up the dock toward the beach fronting the house, the Berringer children came running from all directions to greet their parents. The oldest boy, Ted, led the considerable pack. Not all of the kids were Alex and Tinsley's natural children. Many were island orphans or other children who had been in need of a loving home like the Berringers'. They seemed willing to take in an unlimited number of youngsters. Those they couldn't actually house were bunking with other islanders, but were still part of the extended Berringer family.

Paula flinched as the small, screaming horde reached them and demanded their parents' attention. She liked children, but preferred one at a time, and only when they were old enough to have learned to behave themselves.

Fortunately, Tinsley had a firm hand on her brood and gave strict orders that Paula was to be left alone to rest and recover and that any serious noise-making was to be done on the other side of the island, if at all. The kids grinned impishly, but agreed. Not one of them felt it necessary to challenge Tinsley. Obviously, what she said went.

And so, she rested in one of the many bedrooms in the Berringer home. The dwelling was large but plain, utilitarian and built with care to withstand the weather that could strike the island during the stormy months. But it was a home. Comfortable, solid, safe...

Like Liam...

Then, Paula Dixon fell asleep, dreaming of *her* Irishman.

THE WATCHER OBSERVED her house through the lace curtains of the third-floor bedroom window across the street. Police were swarming everywhere, running around like ants below.

But *she* was nowhere to be found. Not here, not at the hospital, not at her office. Nowhere.

The watcher pulled the curtains shut with a vicious jerk and turned away. If she wasn't home, it would do no good to deface the house further. She could be anywhere. Even somewhere where she'd never know what damage had been done.

And if she didn't know, didn't get scared or hurt or angry about it, there was no point. Ideas and plans swam in his head as he walked slowly down the long staircase. This had become more than just a game of hatred and revenge. He'd actually begun to enjoy taking risks and tempting fate. He'd discovered this new thrill-seeker in himself when the strange man in "her" house had caught him in the act. He'd felt . . .

Good.

Scared, sure, but good, too. And it had been fun watching the big man yell and trip and fall into the rosebushes, hurting himself in the process. Great fun!

The question now was, how could he get the most fun out of destroying Paula Dixon.

And keep Momma happy at the same time.

Yes, that was the question.

"IF YOU'RE TRICKIN' ME with your story just to get me out of me house and into town, ye'll live only long enough to seriously regret it, lad," Tobias Croft muttered, his walk steadied by the cane and his words only slightly slurred by the enormous amount of raw whiskey he had consumed over the past few hours. He waved the ever-present blackthorn walking stick in the humid swamp air. "For I'll beat the living tar out of ye, I swear it."

"I believe you, Uncle," Liam replied. His words were more slurred and his gait not nearly as steady as that of the octogenarian. He'd tried pacing his drinking, but it had still affected him. That was one powerful punch Uncle had brewed up, it was! If he were to serve it at home in his pub, he'd have a row on his hands within a matter of minutes. Went right to a man's noodle, it did. Fine stuff!

"And I'm not deceiving you with my story about the girl, I promise," he said. "When you meet her, you'll understand." He tripped on a large tree root that crossed the path they were using and almost fell.

"Perhaps." Tobias put out a gnarled hand and helped his great-grandnephew regain his balance. "And that priest fella sounds like one you can trust. As far as ye can trust any of 'em, a course."

"He's a good man," Liam said. "When Officer Drake let me out of jail, I went to consult him. The father advised me to return to custody, but he also sympathized with my dilemma. A man with heart, he is."

"They all should be," Tobias muttered. "But they ain't."

The pair walked on in silence for a while. Around them, the swampland began to give way to firmer, drier ground. Liam felt his head clear a bit, and he set a more determined pace.

Tobias had no problem keeping up.

"We'll hitch a ride back into town," Liam said. "'Twas the way I got out here. Folk are charitable enough here in the country."

"I know. That's why I've chosen to live out the rest of me days here."

"It's not the same as family, regardless of how neighborly people are," Liam said, his lips loose because of the drink. He had not intended to bring up the subject of Tobias's return to Ireland until all was well once again with Paula Dixon. "And your family—"

"Are a bunch of vultures, waiting for an old man to croak so they can pick me bones clean." Tobias shook his fist in the air. "Don't try me, lad. I won't be budging from me home."

"Aye." Liam shoved his hands into his pockets. "Whatever you want, Uncle. But I do thank you for coming out with me, now."

"'Tis only for the lass."

Liam smiled. It didn't matter how he'd gotten Tobias out of the swamp. Once out, he might see reason more clearly and eventually be open to his relatives' pleas for his return to his home soil. Surely, after all these years, the old man would want to see Ireland once more. How could any true son of Erin not?

"Yonder's the road," he said, pointing across the field. "That's where I fell into the ditch and was ministered to by Ms. Dixon."

"Then 'tis a hallowed place." Tobias walked ahead of Liam, taking the grade down into the ditch and up the other slope to the roadway without hesitation or difficulty. Liam followed more carefully.

As he reached the road, he saw his great-granduncle raise his stick to signal a passing car. But the vehicle, a red sports model, roared on by, ignoring the pair. Ah, well, Liam thought. Wasn't enough room for three in such a car, anyway.

And then, the face of the driver registered on his brain.

"It's her!" he yelled, running a few yards, then stopping and waving his fist in the air. "Or him!" He hailed curses after the vanishing car.

"What's come over ye, Liam?" Tobias said, grabbing his great-grandnephew's arm. "Have the rest of your senses gone begging, then?"

"No!" Liam's expression hardened. "I think not. I do think, however, that whoever was in that red car was the one who I nearly caught at Paula's house. Man or woman, I don't know. But that matters not. Uncle, we have a lead to our villain!" He took another step down the road, then stopped.

"I also think that if the blackguard saw us, that we might be in grave danger, Uncle," he said.

CHAPTER SIX

PAULA WOKE UP to a strange "whomping" sound. Right outside her window something was stirring the air and sand into a small hurricane. A helicopter! She threw off the covers and sat up, assimilating her surroundings. She was still at Tinsley and Alex's place.

Her head felt back to normal, except for a mild ache where she had struck the coffee table. She looked at her watch, and realized she had slept through the night well into the next morning. There was a knock at the door.

"I'm up," Paula called out. "Come on in."

Tinsley stuck her head around the opened door. "I can't imagine anyone's sleeping through all that racket," she said. "But they want you, so you'd have to have gotten up, regardless."

"They?" Paula stood, rubbing sleep from her eyes. She wore one of Tinsley's nightdresses, and the large garment draped like a tent on her comparably small frame. "They, who?"

"Tottie. And your department back on the mainland." Tinsley came into the room. "Paula, Liam turned himself in late last night."

"What?"

"He and that great-granduncle he told you about. A very unusual old man, according to Gloria."

"Are they all right?" Paula clutched at the folds of the nightdress.

"They're fine." Tinsley smiled. "Except your Liam is a bit worse for wear after a night of drinking the old man's moonshine. But they're both all right, considering how far they hiked to get into town."

"Hiked?" Paula looked around for her clothes. "They didn't catch a ride? Where's my stuff?"

Tinsley directed her to the closet. Paula's clothing, fresh and clean, hung there.

"Thanks," Paula said. "Go on. They didn't try to hitch a ride? I can understand Liam's walking, maybe. But the old man? How come?"

"According to Liam, just as they reached the road, intending to hitch a ride, a driver sped by them in a red sports car. Liam swears it was the same person he saw running from your yard after dumping the blood on your daybed. He also said he couldn't tell if it was a man or a woman."

"That's really odd."

"Yes, but that's what he claims. But never mind. It's not important, yet. After that, Liam refused to try hitchhiking. They just walked the whole way into Carleton Cay. Hoofed it right across country, keeping away from the roads just in case whoever had been driving the red sports car had spotted them and had returned to look for them."

Paula grabbed the clothes. "I want to get over to the mainland as quickly as I can."

"That's why Tottie sent the helicopter," Tinsley said. "She knew you'd be in a fit to get the story straight from the horse's mouth."

"I am. I sure am!" Paula started hauling on clothing. "And when I see him, I'm liable to take his head off!"

"Sure you will." Tinsley leaned against the door frame and smiled.

"He broke the law!" Paula ran fingers through her hair, avoiding the bandaged area. Her hair was stiff and wiry, but she had no time to wash or even comb it. "And by turning himself in," she added more thoughtfully, "he's blown the cover we gave him."

Tinsley nodded, understanding. "'Fraid so. Alex and I talked about it while we were waiting for the helicopter to arrive, and we concluded that Liam has done himself serious harm by returning with his uncle like he did.

"Our defense strategy would have been to play on the sympathies of the jurors emphasizing how Liam was so desperate to get to and help his aging relative that he actually 'left' official custody to see to the old man's well-being. But..."

"But since they both walked the distance, you aren't liable to get much mileage out of that. The old man must be in darn good shape. Not much of a sympathy factor there."

"Right. And the prosecution would have a field day with us."

"The prosecution." Paula sighed. "And that's me."

"Indeed it is. So, any ideas?"

"None. I guess I'll have to see what he has to say for himself." She felt a surge of energy. "*And* to see if he can give me any details that might help me get a tracer on that red car."

Alex came into the bedroom. "They're waiting for you, Paula. Want us to come along?"

"No. I've taken up so much of your time and hospitality already." She hugged her friends. "Just get over by boat when you can, and I'll set you up as his lawyers. If you're still willing to take the case."

"Wouldn't miss it for the world," Tinsley declared.

"No, indeed," Alex added. "The more monkey wrenches this Liam Croft tosses, the more interesting it all gets."

Paula smiled. "That is one way to look at it," she said. "*One* way."

THE RIDE OVER was uneventful. Paula's arrival at the courthouse was not. The lawn was swarming with curious people as the helicopter hovered over the landing pad, and she could see the local news van parked at the curb.

Somehow the station had gotten wind that something unusual was going on. The moment she stepped from the chopper, a TV microphone was thrust in her face, by none other than Jefferson Ebert, TV personality and the local reporter for Carleton Cay county. A man who, at one time or another, had been a source of aggravation to anyone who had held public office in the county.

Now, it was her turn.

"Is it true you have an IRA terrorist in jail, Ms. Dixon?" he asked, his free hand holding down his longish, styled hair against the blasts of wind from the helicopter blades. "Is it true that he escaped, then gave himself up again because of you? Is there a romance in this?" Ebert smirked at the camcorder, held by his assistant.

"There's no romance, no IRA person, terrorist or otherwise, in Carleton Cay," Paula declared, flushed with anger and embarrassment. She avoided the camera, knowing what she must look like. "Now, Jeff, please move. I have work to do."

"Is it true you were attacked and injured by a police officer? A man who has held a grudge for years against women in law enforcement. That the officer is in critical condition because your live-in lover—"

"Jeff, get out of my way!"

"Is it true ... Oh!"

Paula dodged the microphone and let her elbow slide into the reporter's arm, jolting him gently, but effectively out of the way. Then she dashed into the courthouse, slamming the door behind her. Ebert was right on her heels, however, embarrassing questions coming from him like bullets.

"Slow him down," she ordered the cop at the desk. The policeman on duty halted Ebert long enough for Paula to get beyond the public area and to head up the back stairs toward her office on the second floor.

In the second-floor reception area, Diane Pfaff sat at her desk and did not speak or look up when Paula raced by. Paula opened the door and went into her office.

What awaited her there was even more of a dismaying sight than the television crew on the courthouse lawn. Tottie was there, somber, stone-faced, in her official capacity. Gloria and Bull stood at attention against the back wall, like dishonored soldiers. Liam, handcuffed securely, sat in one of the client chairs. He looked pale and tired. He glanced at her and smiled wanly. She wanted to go to him immediately, but didn't. An extremely old man, his walking stick clasped in trembling hands, sat in another client chair.

And at her desk, seated in *her* chair, was her boss, Charlie Benson. He looked rested, tanned and mad as hell.

Tinsley must not have known he was back. Paula wished she could have had at least a few minutes' warning before facing her boss. But... It was show-time now.

"Why, here's our Ms. Dixon," he said, smiling coldly, the way he did when covering great anger. "Welcome to the party, my dear assistant. I think you know everyone here."

"Hello, Charlie," she said, gathering up her courage, knowing she was as deep in trouble as she'd ever been in her entire career.

Her entire life! Forget the career. "Welcome back," she added. It couldn't hurt to try politeness, she decided quickly.

But it did.

Charles Benson, district attorney of Carleton Cay County, erupted like a Hawaiian volcano. He stood up, turned redder than his tie and began to list her errors and her lack of judgment in this case and her minimal chances for reconciling herself with the D.A.'s office.

"You will never hold public trust again," he thundered. "And furthermore, you look like you've just been dragged through—"

"She looks grand," Liam interrupted loudly, struggling against his handcuffs. "And if you insult her again, I'll..."

"Ease, laddie," the old man said, reaching over and touching Liam on the arm with the tip of his cane.

"I'm keepin' track of each and every evil word he's uttered, fear not."

Charlie started to speak again, but Liam preempted him, talking loudly. "Ms. Paula Dixon, this is my great-granduncle, Mr. Tobias Croft. Uncle, this is Miss Dixon."

The old man stood up and extended a hand. His grip was almost as strong as Liam's, she noticed. "Ye're as beautiful as me nephew spoke ye, lass," he said, smiling out of an incredibly leathery and wrinkled face. "It's me great and grand pleasure to meet ye, seein' as ye rescued the boy when he..."

"This is not a social occasion!" Charlie bellowed.

Paula released the old man's hand and watched him as he sat back down.

He did not, she noted, assume the same position. He was now on the edge of his chair, gripping his cane.

He was ready to strike.

Paula took a step forward, thinking that moving between an angry Irishman and an upset public servant was exactly what had set this present situation up. When she had moved between Liam and Gradon, she had set the stage. But she had to avert any further violence or trouble. "Charles, I'm sorry if I've created a problem for the department here, but I—"

"All right. All right." Calming slightly, Charlie sat. He folded his hands on Paula's desk, and shut his eyes as if to gather his thoughts along with his temper. "Let me rephrase what I've been trying to say—Ms. Dixon, you have pushed this office right up the creek with this Irish mess of yours. Now, I am going to give you one day. *One.* This one. To get it all straightened out." He pointed at Liam. "Either have this man arrested for assaulting an officer or prove to me that you have reason to release him. Legally, not emotionally."

"Sir, I—"

"And not into *your* custody! We've had enough scandal."

"No, sir. I mean, yes, sir."

"Good." Charlie stood and straightened his tie. "That's done."

"Sir," Tottie began. "I need—"

"You need to meet me in my office in five minutes," the district attorney said. "Sheriff Reynolds, we have some serious talking to do about the way you manage your deputies."

"Sir," Tottie repeated, clearly trying to break through to Benson. "I don't—"

Charlie didn't let her finish. "And before you come to my office, you put that troublesome Irishman in a holding cell. Until his lawyer can arrange bail, he's staying here, behind bars."

"His lawyers are the Berringers," Paula said. "I'm sure they'll have him out in no time," she added for Liam's sake. "Meanwhile, sir, if it's all right, I'd like to keep Mr. Tobias Croft with me for—"

"It is not all right with me. I want you here, at your place, working, Ms. Dixon. Working! Not nursemaiding some old Irish drunk who—"

That was as far as he got before Tobias Croft's cane caught him smartly across both shins. The old man threw with perfect accuracy. The crack of wood on bone was like a gunshot.

Charlie howled with pain and fell to the floor.

"When you get a chance," Paula whispered to Tottie, "call in Father Sheridan. He might be able to help with all this."

"I already did," Tottie whispered back. "He'll be over as soon as he can."

From the floor, Charlie screamed for Bull and Gloria to act.

They hesitated, then gently, but firmly, they removed Liam's extra handcuffs from the chair, keeping the cuffs at his wrist on. One on each side of him, they guided him toward the door. He looked back once at Paula. Scowling, a dark expression on his face.

He was blaming her for this, she thought. She yearned to explain, but now was not the time.

Tottie helped Charlie up and took Tobias along as she led the limping D.A. toward the door. At the door, Charlie stopped and said, "Get on it, Ms. Dixon. You were a witness to the attack, so you know what charges to add. Throw the book at the old man." It was not a suggestion, but an order.

"Yes, sir," she said, her heart sinking.

Tobias looked back at her and grinned. His blue eyes, buried deep in wrinkles and years, looked exactly like his great-grandnephew's eyes.

And Paula's heart ached.

HOURS LATER, Paula felt as if she'd been run over by a truck. She needed to take a break or her brain would turn to jelly. Even Alex and Tinsley's arrival hadn't made her feel much better. Her headache was back, a dim demon of the one that had plagued her before, but a definite presence. Time to pause for a few minutes. She needed to think about herself for a change. Otherwise she was going to be of no help at all to Liam and his uncle.

She was a mess. And it wasn't just because of Liam and his great-granduncle. She was beginning to reassess her life. She liked doing her job—and she did it well—but she did not like the way she had to play politics in order to keep it. The longer she played, the less she liked it.

The less she liked herself, as well.

She got up and wandered over to the window. Dusk was settling in, and evening would soon bring warm spring darkness to the streets of the town. The TV crew was gone; the crowd had disappeared. Two little boys rode bikes down the street. Cars drove slowly by. Office workers heading home. Diane had left the office at least thirty minutes ago.

No matter how high up she got in public office, Paula would always have to play politics. Was this what she really wanted to do with her life?

What else was there for her?

Paula leaned forward, watching. A few pedestrians strolled along. It all looked so peaceful.

Carleton Cay had been her home for years. She had worked so hard and turned her back on so much to get where she was. She had been born into an easy life, and she had rejected that. She had struggled for this office. So why wasn't she more upset with the prospect of losing it? Was it all what she really wanted? Had she so compromised herself with Liam Croft and his actions that she would have to think about leaving? Or would people forgive, if not forget, her folly when he was gone? And how did she really feel? Right now, she wasn't sure.

In all fairness, she had to admit she had been wrong. Charlie, for all his pompous righteousness, was correct. For an assistant D.A. to take a shooting victim into her home, knowing little to nothing about him was the height of personal and professional foolishness.

Suddenly, she realized she was finished here. Even if she managed to get Liam exonerated, she was finished. Her career and her social life in Carelton Cay were over.

Strangely, she didn't feel any regret. Maybe she was too tired. Maybe too emotionally overwhelmed to realize the implications. She continued to watch the scene two stories below. The sky darkened. Father Sheridan hurried down the front steps of the courthouse, a lone figure in black.

Paula leaned out the window. "Father?" she called. He didn't stop.

Paula turned away from the window. She thought for a moment, then made a decision. She left her office and dashed down the back stairway in pursuit of the priest. If Liam had shared anything important with him, she wanted to know about it.

She had reached the ground floor of the courthouse and was opening the wide door to the outside when the world exploded.

Paula was tossed like a feather by a hot blast of air. She felt herself falling again, and anticipated pain, but this time she was lucky. She landed on the lawn, the thick carpet of spring grass cushioning her body. She rolled, then lay still.

What had happened?

From behind her, she heard people shouting, screaming. She looked up.

And almost screamed herself.

The entire area of the courthouse where her office was located was gone. Destroyed. The window she had been staring out of minutes before was blown away, along with several feet of brick wall along either side and above and below.

If she hadn't started to follow Father Sheridan, she would have been blown to bits!

Paula sat up on the grass and began to shiver. Then, to shake. Her body trembled in reaction to her narrow escape.

A siren sounded. More screams. This time from inside the building.

Liam.

Tobias, Tottie, Bull, Gloria, Alex and Tinsley! Even Charlie?

Smoke billowed from the devastated area. Against the evening sky, she could see the bright flare of flame. Paula forced herself to get to her feet. She ran back to the building, stumbling on one step, but making it to the front door. The door was intact, though the glass section was fractured. She went inside.

Smoke and shouting filled the air. Tears filled her eyes. She grabbed at the first figure she saw. "The prisoners?" she asked. "Has anyone seen to them?"

It was Tinsley. "Paula! You're all right?"

"Yes! Is Liam . . . ?"

"He's upstairs," Tinsley said, her voice carrying over the turmoil. "Trying to find you. Bull let him loose. Alex went with him. And the old man. I tried to stop him, but—"

"Move, ladies!" Several men in fire-fighter gear pushed past them, heading for the stairs. "Get outside," one yelled at them. "Smoke's getting worse."

"You go out," Paula told Tinsley. "You have the baby to think of. I'll try to find the men."

Tinsley coughed and nodded agreement. She disappeared in the direction of the front door, where the air was clearer. Paula moved forward, seeking the stairway.

She immediately encountered another person. This one obviously didn't expect to see her. Whoever it was pushed her aside without a word of apology and ran past. She didn't even get a good glimpse of the person's form. The smoke was thickening fast; and the smell of burning material was strong and acrid. She coughed again, pressed her loose shirtsleeve over her nose and moved forward again.

This time, she found the stairs. She shut her stinging eyes and went upward. Up into hell.

The second floor was full of people, mostly fire fighters trying to deal with the flames. Paula ignored all orders that she get out. She shoved her way toward the part of the building where her office used to be.

"Liam?" She called out and coughed violently. "Alex? Where are you?" Her choking voice was too thin to carry.

"Lady, get out of here!" A fireman pushed by, snarling the order at her this time. "The floor's likely to collapse at any moment!"

"There are people up here," she said to him, grabbing at his sleeve. "Got to get them."

"They know," he shouted. "But they want to find the assistant D.A.'s body, and we can't get them to budge until they do."

Paula drew in a deep breath, ignoring the caustic smoke searing her lungs. "Liam Croft, you Irish idiot!" she yelled. "It's Paula! I'm over here!"

"Paula?" Liam's voice was fainter than hers had been. "Paula, darlin'! Is that your spirit callin' me, then?"

"No, ye young idiot!" Tobias's voice was stronger. "It's herself! She's not dead."

"She's over by the stairs," Alex said, his tone joyful. "She's alive!"

"But then, who is that?" Liam sounded confused. "Who died?"

"Sir, you have to get out of here," the fireman called. "You and your friends go! We'll dig out whoever's in there." Paula started forward. Someone was in her office?

Who?

Liam broke through the smoke. He stared at her. Then he grabbed her.

And kissed her as hard as she'd ever been kissed. No lust, just passion. Passion that went beyond the physical. He kissed as if he would blend her with himself and never let her go again!

"Leave off," Tobias said, gently tapping his nephew on the back with his cane. "Get the lass below to safety, *then* kiss her."

Liam stopped kissing, but did not release her. Paula relaxed in his grasp. It was good to be held right now. She wasn't sure how much longer her legs would support her.

Alex appeared, his eyes wide with concern. "Tinsley?" he asked. "Did you see her?"

"She's outside," Paula answered. "I came up after you all."

"We came for you," Liam said. "We were told you'd died in the blast." His hands were shaking, but his grip was firm.

"We still have a chance o' doin' that oursel's," Tobias announced. "Unless we all get the bloody hell out of here."

"Right!" Alex started steering the four of them down the stairs. "Come on. This way."

"We're with you," Liam said, half carrying Paula as well helping his uncle to find his footing on the steps. Then Liam picked Paula up easily as if she weighed nothing. She clung to the strong arms supporting her and shut her eyes against the smoke and her ears against the shouts of the firemen.

They finally reached the outside and the fresh air. Though it was now full night, the lights from the fire trucks made it look like midday.

Paula choked and gasped for breath. She had drawn smoke deep into her lungs calling Liam, and she knew she'd pay for it now. He bent over her, muttering words she could not understand. Tinsley, Alex and even Tobias came near and watched anxiously while she struggled for air.

Then she asked, "Who was in my office? I left just moments before..." She paused for another fit of coughing. Liam's big hand was warm and soothing on her back. "Who could have been there?"

No one answered right away.

"They thought 'twas you, lass," Tobias said. "Me lad here went near mad when he heard. But seein' you're here and well, well, I..."

Tinsley knelt down. "Paula, I heard the paramedics talking. They think they know who it is."

Paula stopped breathing.

"They think it's Tottie," Tinsley said, tears filling her eyes.

Paula's cry of denial ripped out from a place deep in her heart.

CHAPTER SEVEN

AFTER PAULA RECEIVED medical attention for smoke inhalation, she and the others had boarded Alex's boat and traveled to Berringer's Island. With Tottie possibly dead, Sergeant Gloria Wilson was now ranking law enforcement officer. Paula trusted her to handle matters for the time being. She, herself, was certainly in no shape to do so. Until she recovered some more, Gloria and Bull and the few junior officers would have to do most of the work.

No one had been able to locate Charlie. Diane Pfaff was also missing. Puzzle on puzzle. They supposedly had left work around five, but never made it home, according to family or neighbors. Had they been trapped in the building and simply not found?

On Berringer's Island, where Paula was now recuperating, Alex set up a command post, ready to receive information by phone, fax or smoke signal, and Paula was forced to settle back and let the Berringers run the show.

She was still too weak to do much else but grieve quietly for Tottie.

And consider her situation regarding Liam.

Like a large, devoted dog, he had not left her side since the moment he'd embraced her so fervently in the smoke-filled hallway of the courthouse. When Jim Cunningham had examined her in the emergency room, he'd attempted to make Liam go out into the hallway, but the Irishman had refused with just one hard look at the physician. No words were exchanged.

And Liam had stayed, unchallenged. Jim had given her oxygen and warned her to rest for a few days before trying any stressful physical activities. Paula had nodded weary consent, but Liam had *listened*. Now, as she sat in a big easy chair in the main room of the Berringer home, Liam had found a place on the floor beside her and held on to her hand as if it were a piece of gold.

Tobias had taken over one of the large couches, covered himself with a throw blanket and was snoring peacefully. His heavy cane lay on the couch right by his side.

"Here's some tea," Tinsley said, bringing a tray in from the kitchen. "Clara and Janna made it for us." Two island women and one girl had come to fix food for the group. No one had called for help. The islanders had just been there, waiting, when the Berringers had returned. The children were all taken care of, staying with families willing to baby-sit until the crisis was over.

Liam got up to help Tinsley with the tea. He performed the task with such ease and grace that Paula had a hard time linking this image of him with that of the man who had casually tapped his coffee cup for service back at her place. He was, however, she had to remember, in the bed-and-breakfast business back in Ireland, so he must have watched women serve tea thousands of times.

That would explain his gracious behavior now. He handed her a cup, and she smiled thanks. As they sipped the hot liquid silently, Liam made an announcement that was almost more startling than the explosion had been.

"I'm taking Paula back to Ireland with me," he said, addressing the Berringers. "If she stays, even out here on your island, she's going to be killed. And others might suffer more, as well. So, I'm taking her away."

"What?" Paula said, shaken out of her cocoon. "What did you say? I can't go to Ireland!"

"Why not? I think it's the right idea," Tinsley said.

Alex nodded. "Makes perfect sense to me. I think, given the situation, we can get the authorities to clear you and Tobias of any charges, pending or set, as well, Liam. I'll get on it right now." He went over to one of his computers and began to type.

Paula started to protest. Liam knelt by her chair. "Look, darlin'. Since I've met you, you've been under siege and outright attack. Whoever's responsible is probably geared up for the final strike. You know how this kind of lunatic operates. He or she always accelerates outrages until they reach the point of murder."

Paula quieted. "Until now, I didn't expect that." She thought of Tottie, and tears stung her eyes again. "I survived, but I was lucky."

"God was guarding you," Liam said. "And now it's my turn."

That statement made Paula remember the priest. "Did anyone see Father Sheridan before the explosion?" she asked.

"Don't be changing the subject," Liam said. "It's Ireland for you, Paula Dixon. No argument."

"I'm not trying to change the subject." Paula stood up. throwing off the light blanket that Liam had wrapped around her earlier. "That's why I wasn't in my office when it blew."

"Explain." Tinsley set her cup down. Behind her, Tobias snored, snorted and woke up. He regarded Paula steadily, as if he'd been listening all the while. Alex left his computer and sat down on the floor beside his wife. Even Liam settled to listen.

Paula told them what had happened, leaving out no detail that she could remember. When she was finished, there was silence.

"Cannot have been the father set the bomb," Liam stated, breaking the silence. "He's a good man."

"He's a priest," Tobias muttered.

"Okay," Paula said. "I know Tottie . . ." Her voice broke for a moment. "Tottie said she'd called him in to help mediate with the legal situation."

"What situation?" Tobias asked. "Me?"

"Partly." Paula smiled at him. "You were part of the reason Liam was in trouble, Mr. Croft."

Tobias scowled. "Aye," he admitted. "That I was. No doubt about it."

"So if Father Sheridan was supposed to show up and help out early on, why did he wait until evening?" Tinsley asked. "And we were both with Liam." She looked at her husband. "Did you see the priest?"

Alex shook his head.

"Why would the father wish Paula harmed?" Liam asked. "Makes no sense. You must look for a motivation."

"Just speculating," Tinsley said. "But could he be acting for someone else?" She paused. "Liam, how did you know it was a bomb?"

"Smell," Liam replied. "I've lived near where enough of them went off from time to time to know." He shifted position. "It's not a smell you forget."

"No, it's not," Alex agreed. He and Tinsley looked at each other. The old house he had lived in before they married had been destroyed by such an explosion. "I thought the odor was familiar."

"I think we'd better try to find Father Sheridan," Paula said. "If he had nothing to do with the explosion, we need to know that so we can eliminate him as a suspect. We need to know why he was at the courthouse, if he didn't talk to you or—"

"Wait, there," Liam said. "You're sounding like an investigator, Paula, darlin'. And you're not. You're the victim, and you're going away to safety with me."

Paula was about to argue but just then the telephone rang. Alex jumped up and grabbed the receiver. He said hello, then listened.

As he listened, a relieved expression came over his face. He covered the phone for a moment. "Tottie's alive," he said to Paula. He didn't elaborate, but listened a few moments longer and then spoke into the receiver. "That's good news," he said. "And, Gloria, please tell the Fed guy to get in touch with me as soon as he gets into town. I have some information..." He paused. "No, I'd rather tell it to the outside investigator, if you don't mind." Another pause. "Yes, ma'am. But—"

"Give me the phone," Paula said, reaching for it. When she was on the line, she said, "Sergeant Wilson, whatever Mr. Berringer says comes directly from me. So you do as he asks, understand?"

"If you say so," Gloria replied, her tone reluctant. Then her voice changed. "Did you hear me tell Mr. Berringer? Tottie's not dead! She was still alive when they finally dug her out of the rubble of your office. She's at the hospital in intensive care."

Paula sat back down, her leg muscles giving way in relief and cautious joy. "How is she?"

"Not good. But she's still alive. And fighting."

"She would be. Keep us posted, please."

"I will."

"Anything else?"

"No," Gloria answered. "Bull's been looking all over creation for Mr. Benson and Miss Pfaff. But no sign of them. No bodies in the courthouse ruins or downstairs in the police headquarters."

"Any bodies at all?"

"No. Everybody got out. The sheriff was the only one seriously injured."

More relief! "Gloria, was the whole place destroyed?"

"'Fraid so. Not much left but debris. Just as they got Tottie out on the lawn, the upper floors collapsed. It was real close."

"Thank goodness they made it. But all those records..." Paula covered her face with her hand. "My God, it's going to take decades to reconstruct what was lost."

"Yes. I guess the memories of some of us are going to be pretty valuable, now."

That lit a thought. "Gloria, do you have any way of reconstructing the record of who was in the building this afternoon?"

"I wasn't at the desk. Officer Booth was."

"Ask him. See if... Hey!"

Alex took the receiver away from her. Liam took her hand and held it. Firmly.

"Sergeant Wilson, this is Alex Berringer again. Ms. Dixon really does need to rest after her ordeal. Let's not get her involved actively in any investigation, all right?"

"It's my job!" Paula protested. "My duty!"

"Your duty, m'dear, is to stay alive," Liam said, his blue eyes gazing into hers. "And if I must, I shall see you unwillingly to my home just to keep you safe." The intensity of his gaze increased. "But I'd rather you come willingly."

"I—" Paula began.

"Oh, just do it," Tinsley said, interrupting. "Go with him. There are other people who can do the dirty work here, Paula, and you know it. Investigating acts of terrorism is out of local hands, anyway. If they've sent a federal investigator, you'd just be standing around watching."

Paula considered this. "You're right," she said. She rubbed her free hand over her eyes. "I'm so tired and beat-up that I can't think straight. I need to rest and get my head together. But, you're right. If I stay here, more things will happen, and maybe the next time, someone will die." She looked at Liam. "I'll come home with you, Liam. Just to get out of the way for a while."

"Good," he said. "I'll be making the arrangements while you sleep."

"Fine." She shut her eyes. "Whatever you do is fine with me."

"In living memory," Alex said softly, "Paula Dixon has never been known to be so agreeable and submissive to anyone, much less a man. What have you done to her, Liam Croft?"

Liam smiled. "I've talked sense at her."

"That never made any difference before," Alex replied.

"Very funny," Paula said, opening her eyes. "I'm just tired, that's all. I can't think, much less plan."

"You were trying there for a few minutes," Tinsley said, her tone serious. "And doing a good job of it, too. I like the idea of finding out who was inside the courthouse today. With all the excitement, anyone could have planted that bomb, even Father Sheridan. He could have done it innocently, you know. Just accepted a package from someone and left it in the right place. Security has never been much of an issue around here."

"Before this," Paula said glumly. "I wish I knew what it was that started it all. I wish I knew what I'd done to make someone mad enough to do things like..." She yawned widely.

"We'll all talk to the investigator tomorrow," Tinsley said firmly. "Now, you really should get to bed, Paula. You look like you're about to pass out right there in the chair."

Paula stifled another yawn. "Seems all I do here is sleep," she said. "I hate being so weak!"

"Girl, listen to me." Tobias spoke for the first time in a while. "Ye've a long life left to ye. If ye care for yourself, first and foremost, get sleep. Time for fightin's later on. It's comin', though, and ye'll be in it, don't fear."

Liam regarded his uncle. "Do you see something of the future?" he asked softly. "And what of yourself, Uncle?"

"I don't see a thing," Tobias snapped. "I'm just talkin' sense, like you were. Now, meself, I'm staying here on this island with these good people, if they'll have me. I am not returnin' home with you, Liam. Ye've done your job. Now, go with the woman. Find your future."

Liam frowned. "The family'll be sorely disappointed."

"Not with you bringing her home with ye." Tobias pointed at Paula.

Paula narrowed her eyes. "Why should that take their minds off you, Mr. Croft. You're a relative. I'm not. They sent Liam after you, not me. You're the reason he came here in the first place."

"Aye. But they'll be much happier seein' your pretty face than me old, ugly one."

"Uncle, I—"

"Liam," Paula said softly, putting her hand on his shoulder. "Let's not fuss about it now. After this is all cleared up and I come back home, you and Tobias can work out what you want to do."

"That sounds fair," Alex said. "Shouldn't take too long to find the bad guy now that there's government help, in any event. And Mr. Croft, you're welcome to stay here on the island with us. You'll be safe, since you're certainly not a target. I know we can find someone to take you in for the time."

Tobias nodded. It was settled.

But for Liam, nothing was really settled. He sat very still, feeling the warmth of Paula's hand on him.

Realizing in a slow, sinking, pleasurable/painful kind of a way that he wanted to feel far more than mere warmth.

Realizing that if he did get her home, he'd not be likely to let her go easily. Nor control his longing for her, either.

And realizing how dangerous all this could actually be for him. Dangerous and wondrous, as Tobias had said.

Love?

He remembered how he'd felt when he thought she was dead. How his heart had leapt when he'd heard her call him and he knew she was alive.

He would not give her up! It was indeed possible that he had fallen in love with her, as Tobias had suggested.

And instinctively, he realized if he let her know any of that, he'd lose her, sure.

Helping her was not as important to his people as getting Tobias back, but it was what he had to do. They would have to be told. If they didn't understand, he would resign. Give up his position as head of the clan. She was *that* important to him. Perhaps, that was a sign it was indeed love he was feeling.

"So, then," he said, casually rising to his feet and away from her touch. "Paula's to come, and you're to stay. And I'll accept the situation for the family, Uncle. You're right. With Paula there, not much else will get any attention. So it's better we wait to welcome you back into the fold." He still lied well, he thought. Good Irish blarney at work once more.

Tobias nodded, crossing his arms over his chest. A posture, Liam knew, that meant taking him home would take more work than anyone suspected.

"I think that sounds best," Paula said.

Liam brushed his hair back from his forehead. "I'm for sleep, then," he said. "It's been a hard few days, and I admit I'm weary. Dead tired, as you say."

"Good." Paula stood up. "I was beginning to think you really were indestructible. It's nice to hear you admit a little human frailty."

Liam raised his eyebrows. He looked at her and smiled. "You thought I wasn't a normal man?" he asked, his smile turning to a teasing grin.

Paula blushed, color rising in her face. She glanced away from his gaze. "Well, of course not. But, after all, in the space of a few days, you've been beaten, shot, chased an intruder from my home, fallen head-first into a rose garden, hit a cop, been arrested, escaped from jail, got liquored up, walked nearly fifty miles in the dark with an elderly companion, and—"

"I'm fitter'n him," Tobias said, pointing his cane at Liam. "He couldn't handle the booze, so I was doing most of the leading. Don't forget that, girlie."

"Hush, now, Uncle," Liam said, still smiling. "She'll think I'm not up to normal Irish drinking standards, if you go on that way."

"Not likely," Paula said, still showing a touch of blush on her pale cheeks.

"I suggest we abandon this discussion until tomorrow. We all need sleep," Tinsley said, getting slowly to her feet. "Come on. I'll show you which kid's room you each get."

"I'm thinking of a shower, too," Liam said. "I fear the combination of swamp, sweat and smoke is getting right thick on me."

IT WASN'T LONG BEFORE water was running and the mellow sounds of Liam's singing began. Listening, Paula had to smile. The man did sing like an angel when he bathed.

And the idea of a shower seemed an excellent one. She went into the smaller bathroom off her assigned bedroom and did the same. After cleaning up, she dragged on Tinsley's old nightgown and crawled into the same bed she had vacated less than twenty-four hours before.

It seemed like a lifetime instead of a day.

She thought of Tottie and prayed for her friend's recovery. Nothing she could do now but wait for news, she told herself.

A soft knock at her door. "Come in," she said, sitting up, turning on the bedside light and wiping her eyes.

Liam entered. He wore sweatpants and a T-shirt, clearly borrowed from the shorter, leaner Alex. "Can we visit just a bit?" he asked.

She nodded.

He shut the door. Taking a child's chair from the desk, he positioned himself next to her bed. But he didn't touch her.

"I thought you might like to talk about your friend, the sheriff," he said softly. "I know you are close." He clasped his hands, as if in prayer, and rested his elbows on his knees. His expression was tender, consoling. His tone was so gentle and kind, it reached right to her heart.

Fresh tears started. "We are close. We grew up together," Paula said.

"Tell me about it."

She looked away. "Not much to tell. My life's been pretty ordinary up to now. You'd be bored."

"I find that hard to believe, and I have nothing else to do but listen."

She hesitated. Talking about herself was always difficult. "Okay. I come from a little town about thirty miles from here."

He raised an eyebrow. "A village? You seem more a city person."

Paula smiled. "Thanks, I think. No, my hometown is Dixon Acres."

"Your family name?"

"Uh-huh. It's really just an old antebellum plantation expanded into a town. My family owned—"

"Ante? That's previous to your Civil War?"

"My family has been on the land for over two hundred years, Liam."

"Ah." He smiled, pleased for some reason.

"But I left."

"Why?"

Paula plunged on. "I hate my family's past. I'm not happy with its present. I don't belong to it."

Now, he was not pleased. "I'm not understandin'. It *is* your family."

"But we were slave owners," she said. "Exploiters. I have to admit I'm hardly proud of my heritage. And to be with my parents, you'd think those times were still around. The style, the rules of behavior. They... don't exactly approve of the ways I've chosen to live."

"Being a lawyer? Being friends with Tottie?"

She nodded. "My insistence on working for a living is a family disgrace. Dixon ladies marry—they don't work. And Tottie? That's been a battleground ever since I can remember. Not that my parents ever forbade me to be friends with Tottie—they wouldn't dare—but their disapproval was obvious. As I told you earlier, I've known Tottie all my life. Our hometown is so tiny we were the only girls the same age in our school. We both chose law as the basis for our professions. Our career paths have paralleled." She paused. Took a deep breath. "Tottie is the only person I know who *really* tells me the truth about myself when I need to hear it. Even if she knows I won't listen."

"You're fortunate to have such a friend," Liam said. "In spite of the pain you feel now for her, you have a treasure when you have a true comrade."

"I guess so." She reached for a tissue and wiped her eyes, then blew her nose. "I just wish I could get my hands on whoever did it to her. For five minutes. That's all I'd need!" She sniffed and looked up at the ceiling. "Right now, I don't care about the legal part. I'd just tear him limb from limb."

Liam smiled. "Spoken like the warrior you are."

Paula looked at him. "Me?"

He nodded. "I'm Catholic. I don't believe in reincarnation. But it's like you have the soul of an ancient High King dwelling in you at times. I see the fire and fight in your eyes. It blazes, darlin'. Fairly blazes."

"But I'm running away. I agreed to go. That's not standing your ground and fighting, is it?"

"No." Now he reached for her hand and held it tightly as he had earlier. "You're staging a strategic retreat. That's not running. That's good battle planning."

His words did more for her spirit than any soft consolation. She felt stronger, steadier. Paula stared at him. "Liam, who *are* you?"

His smile was wry. "Just as you see."

"I see..." She shook her head. "I don't know what I see, anymore."

"Even a strategic retreat brings some confusion. Don't you worry. It'll pass. You'll see your way clear."

"In Ireland?"

"Likely."

They looked at each other.

Paula felt her skin warm and something deep inside her open and flower. She sat very, very still, her hands in her sheet-covered lap, her lips parted, scarcely breathing. Her heart started a slow thudding that gradually increased in tempo until her pulse was racing.

He reached out and touched her face, and a shudder went through her body. She smelled the clean, male scent of him in the small room. Paula shut her eyes for a moment, unable to continue gazing at him, so intense and powerful was the feeling.

His fingers moved down to caress her throat. So gently, it was almost not a touch. So surely, he made every nerve quiver.

She heard him whisper her name.

No. Not here.

She opened her eyes. He withdrew his hand and clasped them once more in front of him, back bowed, eyes gazing at the floor. Moonlight filtered in through the slatted shades on the window, and she saw him clearly.

Lord, he was a beautiful man! That jet-black hair, the strong, carved features, the fair skin and the eyes that... Eyes that saw right to her heart. She hadn't said a word, but he knew it was not time for lovemaking for them.

Yet.

"I'm thinking," he said. "About you and your other friend."

Paula cleared her throat. "Tottie?"

"No. This man, Alex. He and you were lovers?"

Paula smiled. Was Liam jealous? "A long time ago. Over ten years, in fact. It didn't last very long. We were not a good pair."

"But you still are good friends?"

Paula frowned. What was he getting at? "Sure. It took some time, but we have learned to like each other. And Alex was never meant for any other woman than Tinsley."

"Yes." Liam looked up. "I can see that. 'Tis a lovely thing."

"It is. They're fortunate. And very happy."

"Could you ever be thinking the same for yourself?"

"What?" She looked at him. His eyes were full on her, wide with something dark and cautious, like an animal testing new ground. "You mean me? Married and Mother Earth to a hundred kids like Tinsley is?"

"No. You're not her. You'd always do things your way. I just wondered if you'd ever considered partnering for life."

Paula blinked, unsure. Was this some odd kind of proposal? No, it couldn't be! If Liam was going to ask a thing like that, he'd come straight out and do it.

At least, that's what she thought he'd do.

Not that she really knew the man. They'd shared crises, yes. But that was no way to get to know a person fully.

She answered his question. "Honestly, no. I haven't, because I've always thought of myself as an individual, standing alone. I guess because of alienation from my family. Tinsley and Alex are two parts of a whole. Apart, they were broken. Together, they're . . . well, complete."

"And you're content . . . complete by yourself?"

She shrugged. "I don't know if I'd put it that way, but, yes, I like being alone."

Now, he smiled. "You won't be alone in Ireland, Paula Dixon."

"Your family?"

"A person is never alone in Ireland," he said. Then he stood. "There are just far too many folk wanting to talk, night and day. I'll be leavin' you to sleep now." He put his hand on her head, a blessinglike gesture. "Have some peace for a while. I'll go pray for your friend."

"Th-thank you." The tears came again at his kindness.

"She's a strong one," he added softly. "She's like you."

"But even the strong can die."

"No such talk from you, now. In the morning, things'll look better and clearer to you. So, sleep." He bent and kissed her lips, lightly.

And then he was gone.

CHAPTER EIGHT

THE NEXT MORNING, Paula felt worse, not better. Her sleep had been fitful and crowded with strange images and dreams. Instead of peace, she felt anxiety. Instead of hope, despair. Instead of being rested, she felt exhausted, and had just dozed off again when Tinsley knocked on the door and said that the federal agent assigned to the courthouse case was in the front room waiting to speak to her.

"Oh," Paula groaned, pulling the light blanket up over her head. "Now?"

"Stop whining." Tinsley came in and pulled off the blanket. "There's a robe in the closet, and coffee waiting for you out there. Come on. The man's a busy guy."

"I ache over every inch, Tinsley," Paula complained, getting out of bed and trying to stretch. "I forgot about the somersault I did down the courthouse steps."

"Oh." Tinsley lost her bantering tone. "So did I! Sorry. I'll tell him you're just too beat to talk today, and that he can come back—"

"No." Paula held up a hand. "Just give me a few minutes, okay?"

"You have them." Tinsley left.

Paula managed to get into the clothes Tinsley had put out for her. One of these days, she thought, I'm actually going to go home like a real person and sleep in my own bed and wear my own clothes. Meanwhile, Tinsley's generosity was welcome, even if the shorts and sweatshirt were several sizes too large for Paula's figure, just as Alex's clothing had been too small for Liam.

Liam. Last night he had been . . .

Wonderful. He'd given her just what she'd needed, and then left without taking a thing for himself. She'd never been near a man like that before.

She opened the bedroom door, just in time to hear him singing once more from somewhere outside. She heard children, too. Singing with him, and laughing. Tobias appeared in the doorway of his room.

"Lad's got the throat of an angel, don't he?" the old man said. "Fair makes you weep with joy to hear him when he's really going to it."

"He's got a great voice," Paula agreed. "How are you this morning, sir?"

"Better'n ye look, lass," Tobias said, regarding her closely. "Ye don't seem quite right."

"I'm not. I feel pretty rocky. I guess yesterday's catching up with me."

"'Tis more than that," Tobias said. "Old'ns like me, we sometimes know things about a person just by looking at them. Future things as well as past things. I'll think on it," he added mysteriously. "Let's go now to meet this government gent." He extended his elbow, inviting her to take his arm.

"All right. I'd be pleased." Paula accepted the offer, and they walked arm in arm into the front room. Tobias Croft, she thought, had the same charm as his great-grandnephew.

It just came in a slightly older package.

The federal agent was seated in the living room, but he wasn't merely waiting patiently for her to appear. He and Alex had obviously hit it off. A man of about thirty, he wore a finely made suit, and his grooming was impeccable. In contrast, Alex Berringer was unshaven and dressed in ancient jeans and an old T-shirt.

But they had already had a meeting of minds, it seemed. The agent and Alex were hunched over a computer, speaking in low tones and punching keys. Since they both ignored her, Paula led Tobias past them and into the kitchen.

Tinsley had coffee, juice, tea and rolls set up at the big wooden table. Tobias sat down and tucked into the food immediately. Paula sipped coffee slowly, hoping her brain would engage gears before she had to speak to the newcomer. From somewhere outside, she heard Liam again. This time, he was talking, not singing.

But he sounded like he was talking to a lover. She frowned. Who in the world . . . ?

"Your Irishman seems to have taken a real liking to our latest baby," Tinsley said, pointing out the window. "It was love at first sight, if you ask me."

Paula got up and went over to look out. Down by the shore, Liam, wearing only the tight sweatpants, walked with a willowly young female. Paula smiled at the sight. "When was she born?" she asked, watching Liam walk a small horse down the beach.

"This January," Tinsley said. "For a filly, she's got quite a strong build. Alex says we ought to try reining her to race. Just watch."

Liam led the filly by a halter rope. A moment later, he and the young horse started to run. Sand flew and surf splashed beneath bare feet and hooves. Sunlight flashed off the animal's black coat and Liam's black hair. Muscles bunched and rippled. Both man and horse were splendid! And following them came a horde of laughing, squealing children. A game of chase was in progress. Liam and the filly sped up, leaving the kids far behind. Then, they slowed, allowing the gang to catch up. Nearly. Just as the leader of the children was almost able to reach out and grab the horse's tail, off the two were again. By the time the parade disappeared around the headland, Paula was entranced and laughing.

"How does he do it?" she asked no one in particular. "How does he charm every creature that comes his way?"

"He's Irish," Tobias said from his post at the table and the food. "'Tis only natural."

"He's also a troublemaker," a strange voice said. "That seems natural to him, too."

"That's not at all true!" Paula turned and regarded the federal agent. "He's only dealt with the situations that have come his way," she said angrily. "You can't blame him for anything."

"No, Ms. Dixon," the man said. "Don't misunderstand me. I'm not blaming anyone." He extended his hand to her. "I'm Agent Casey Sears."

"Mr. Sears." Paula shook his hand, briefly. "Why did you call Liam a troublemaker, then?"

Sears smiled. "Because, ma'am, he is. I have a dossier on him, and from one place to the next, whenever he's been away from his home ground, he's carried a chip on his shoulder that's led to trouble. Granted, he hasn't always started it, but he's certainly more than willing to finish a fight, once it's off and running, according to my information."

"He's a spirited lad," Tobias said, taking a long drink of tea. "And you have no business looking into his business."

"That's true," Paula said. "I checked him out myself when I first found him. Nothing in his past indicates—"

"Excuse me, but you don't have the resources of the U.S. government at your fingertips," Sears said. "Did you learn that when he was in the military, he was trained in all kinds of explosive techniques?"

"Well, no, I didn't. But he couldn't have set that bomb in my office, Mr. Sears. He was in jail downstairs."

"The bomb was not in your office, Ms. Dixon. It was just outside. And Mr. Croft could have used an accomplice."

"Father Sheridan?" The name slipped out before she could stop herself. If she'd been more awake, it wouldn't have happened, but it was too late. Sears grabbed at the priest's name like a panther jumping on a rabbit. "The priest does have connections that are questionable," he said. "We have nothing specific, of course, but—"

"Connections?" Paula sat back down, this time taking a seat right beside Tobias. "You mean IRA?"

"Well, we don't know for sure, of course, but—"

"Then you should be making no such insinuations," Tobias said. His fingers twitched as if he wished he had his cane in hand. "I have no use for churchmen, myself, involving themselves in a man's private business as they do, but if Liam says the man is good, then he is good."

"Sir." Sears sat down in a chair opposite them. "I mean no disrespect, but you did just meet your great-grandnephew, Liam Croft, a few days ago for the first time. He wasn't even born, nor, for that matter, was his mother, when you left your home in Ireland. And then, when he tried to use force to get you to go with him, you resisted to the point of actually shooting your own relative. Did you not?"

"'Twas an accident."

"Were you frightened of him?"

"Hell, no," Tobias roared.

But Sears smiled winningly. "Sir, I'm sorry. I don't mean to call your courage into question. I can see you have enough for many men."

"Don't ye forget it, lad," Tobias said.

Paula shifted position, uneasily. Sears's manner was calm and polite. Professional. She found she couldn't dislike him, in spite of not liking what he was inferring. The man was only doing his job. And doing it in the same way she would, if she weren't emotionally involved.

"Mr. Sears," she said, putting her hands on the table. "If Liam and the father are involved in what happened at the courthouse yesterday, how do you explain that they have entered the scene only recently, while the harassment and threats I've been getting have been going on for months."

The government agent shook his head. "I'm sorry, Ms. Dixon. But only you say that."

"What?"

Alex lounged in the kitchen doorway. "Apparently, your boss and secretary claim you've had no calls, no letters, no threats, Paula," he said. "And they suggest that Liam himself poured the blood on your daybed."

"What!" She stood up. "You're kidding?"

"No." Alex came into the room and accepted a cup of coffee from his wife. "That is the story. And the only one who can confirm your version is Tottie."

"Where is Charlie? And Diane?" Paula's fists clenched and unclenched. "I thought they were missing."

"They turned up," Sears said. "We've spoken to them. We have no reason to doubt their testimony." He looked at Paula.

Maybe you don't, Paula thought, *but I know they are lying!* For some reason, Charlie and Diane were conspiring against her.

She rubbed her temples where the headache was starting again. She was too weary to put anything together.

"Good morning to you, people!" Liam bounded into the kitchen through the back door. His bare, muscular chest glistened with sweat, and a glow of health enveloped him and moved with him. The scar from the bullet he'd received less than two weeks ago was merely a pinkish pucker on his shoulder. He slowed, then stopped when he saw the somber tableau. "What's this?" he asked. "Not bad news about Sheriff Reynolds?"

"Tottie's still in critical condition," Alex told him. "But she's stable. This is Federal Agent Casey Sears. He's assigned to investigate the explosion at the courthouse."

"Ah." Liam moved to the table. "Mr. Sears," he said, extending his hand. "Liam Croft. Hope you catch the bastard."

Sears shook hands, clearly a bit startled by Liam's hearty friendliness. "We're trying."

"Good, then." He turned to Tinsley. "That is some fine little filly you have there, Mrs. Berringer, I have to tell you. She's a racer already. Fair loves to run, she does."

"I know." Tinsley handed him a mug of tea. "I should have her exercised like that every day."

"Let the youngsters do it," Liam said, taking the remaining chair and setting it over next to Paula. "They love to run with her. It's good for them. Gets rid of some of the extra energy the little imps store up."

A shriek from outside punctuated his words. A playful shout. Someone yelled for Mom, indignantly.

"I'll keep that in mind." Smiling, Tinsley excused herself and went outside to referee. Sounds of children's laughter billowed in before she shut the door.

"So," Liam said, giving Paula a look out of the corner of his eye and drinking his tea. "Mr. Sears, what may we do to help you in this investigation." He turned slightly to regard the agent.

Paula said nothing, but under the table, she wove her hands together. *Here it comes,* she thought.

"You can start by telling me of your relationship with Father Sheridan," Sears said.

Liam shrugged. "'Tis nothing special. He's a priest. I'm a Catholic. We're both Irish. Why?"

"I'd like to ask the questions, if you don't mind, sir," Sears said formally. "Did you know him when you were in seminary?"

"'Course not. He's years older than me. Why?"

This went on for a while, Liam answering every question innocently, then turning it right back to Casey Sears. The agent began to show frustration.

"Mr. Croft, did you or did you not learn about explosive materials when you joined the military in—"

"Yes," Liam interrupted. "And I hated the bloody stuff. I left the service for a variety of reasons. That was one. Ask my old sergeant, if you must dig into my life. Sean Creedon. He's now the superintendent of the Garda Siochana in Dublin City. But a waste of time it is, I tell you. Because I was locked up when this bomb was set, and I feel . . . a strong attachment for Ms. Dixon, which would preclude any violence intended or otherwise on my part. Even if I had motive. Which I do not." He stood up. "Now. Mr. Sears, if you'll excuse me, I need to shower and make arrangements for travel."

"Don't be in too much of a hurry to leave," Sears said, also standing. "Until I sift through all the ashes of this situation, no one involved is to leave this county, much less this country."

"Is that so?" Liam raised an eyebrow.

"Yes, it is."

"Oh, I don't think so," Alex said. He sat down. "Listen to me, Casey. And please think seriously about this suggestion. Wouldn't Paula be better off somewhere else? Somewhere she'll have more safety than what we can provide her with here?"

Sears was silent.

"It's not as if we'd be disappearing on you, Mr. Sears." Liam sat back down beside Paula. Without thinking much about it, she reached for his hand. "If you've studied me, you know I'm not going anywhere but home. You can find me, if you want me."

The agent seemed to consider things for a moment. "Hmm. A number of factors combine to make this idea palatable to me. I'll see if I can clear it through my office." He smiled now; a decision made. "A special situation like this requires a special set of documents. That way, I'll have you under some obligation to me. And be able to bring you back right away, if things don't work out."

"Indeed you will." Liam smiled and held out his hand. "If necessary, we will come back of our own choice."

They shook.

After that, the tension level lowered. Casey Sears behaved like a good sport over the situation, though Paula was sure the agent would not give up on the "Liam track" until he was firmly convinced of the guilt of someone else.

She spoke, finally, interrupting the conversation. "If I'm traveling tomorrow, I've got to get back to my own house for a little while to pack," she said.

"No way," Sears said. "It's too dangerous. I can't have you taking that kind of risk."

"Mr. Sears, before the explosion, I was taking that kind of risk every day, only I didn't know it." She stood up once more. "I need my passport and money, and I will return to my own home and get my own clothes, thanks very much."

"No," said Liam quietly. "You won't."

"Excuse me!"

"Mr. Sears is correct, Paula," he said. "The enemy may be watching and waiting for just such an opportunity to put a bullet into you."

"Liam's right," Alex said. "Listen to him, Paula."

"Don't worry about the passport," Sears said. "As I said, I'll arrange for special documents for both you and Liam. His were at the courthouse and were destroyed in the fire after the blast."

"And don't worry about money, either. I'll loan you whatever you need," Alex added.

"She needs nothing," Liam said. "Thank you, but she's my responsibility now. Money is not a problem. And as for clothing, why I've more sisters, cousins and aunts than there are grown women on this island. The family can outfit her properly."

"Good luck, lass," Tobias breathed. "If they're like they were when I lived among 'em, ye'll need all the luck ye can get. Regular pack of banshees, them."

"I still don't see why I can't at least send someone to get my things," Paula said. "Surely, that would be all right with everyone? Gloria or one of the policemen could..."

Sears cleared his throat, interrupting and asking for attention. "Ms. Dixon," he said, "would you mind stepping outside and speaking to me privately? I think I can explain something that will convince you to do things our way."

Paula hesitated.

"Please," Sears said. His expression was earnest.

"All right, if it's important. I'll listen."

They went out through the back door.

Liam sat still for a moment. Then, he turned to Alex. "Perhaps I'm wrong to do this," he said, "but I'm going to ask you a question, Alex."

"Fire away." Alex got up and poured himself another cup of coffee. "What do you need to know?"

"Paula's family." Liam leaned forward, resting his elbows on the table and clasping his hands together. "Last night, she spoke to me of them. Briefly, as is her way. I sensed great alienation. I wondered why."

Alex sat down and smiled. "And you knew you wouldn't get it out of Paula, didn't you?"

"I did."

"You know her well for a man who's known her only a few days." Alex drank coffee. "It took me over a year to begin to figure her out."

"I have nothing figured. I merely sense things."

"That's good enough. Paula's a hard person to know. Almost impossible, if she chooses to stay closed to you. As for her family, she's . . . Would you understand the term 'changeling'?"

"Surely. 'Tis a fairy child put in a human cradle to replace the real child."

"Well, in a way, that's Paula. While she does love her parents, she cannot stand to be with them for long. They simply don't accept her as she is. She never did fit into her *place* in the Dixon ladies' world of petticoats and pink lemonade and politeness. She rebelled from birth, as I understand it. Climbed trees instead of practicing piano. Played with Tottie instead of the other white girls of her class and station. Went into law instead of majoring in literature and marrying right after graduation. Generally, she refused to fit in, to compromise or conform."

"A warrior," Liam said softly.

"Pardon?"

"Just a thought I had last night."

Tobias cleared his throat. "She's meant for a Croft," he said, staring off into nowhere.

Liam regarded his relative. "You're seein' now, aren't you, Uncle?"

Tobias blinked. "What's that ye said?"

Liam smiled. "Nothing, Uncle. Nothing a'tall."

PAULA LISTENED carefully to what Casey Sears was saying. The two stood on the edge of a seagrass patch just before the beach sand took over. The sound of the surf would cover their voices, Paula realized.

"I didn't want to reveal this to the others for security reasons," he said, "but since you're being stubborn, I suppose I must tell you. As I said, there are a number of factors that made me decide to let you go to Dublin with your friend."

"Such as?"

"We have a plan, involving your house."

"A plan?"

"Yes. It makes sense to believe that the person after you has been watching you for months. In spite of what your boss and secretary say, I tend to believe your version about the duration of the harassment. I don't understand the discrepancy, yet, but perhaps they have chosen to ignore facts you see more clearly. In any case, the courthouse bombing was no spur-of-the-moment deal. A long-range strategy, suggesting a complex mind at work, seems to be what we're dealing with here."

"I see."

"Yes. I didn't know about the proposed Ireland trip, of course, but I did plan to ask you to go into hiding. And what we intend to do while you're out of sight is wait a little while ourselves and then use a decoy. Someone to draw the enemy out into the open. But we want to wait so as to increase the tension."

"So that when 'I' do appear, the temptation to take a shot at me will be downright irresistible?"

"Exactly." Sears beamed. "I see you understand my thinking."

"I object strongly to putting another person in danger because of my problem!"

"Ms. Dixon, you are not the only one in danger anymore. Not since the courthouse blew up. Be reasonable. Can't you see that human life must mean nothing to this person? I'm willing to bet that if an attack could be launched against you on this island right now, it wouldn't matter one bit to the bastard if little children and other innocents died, just so long as you suffered."

"It sounds to me like you really believe this is a terrorist at work. Not just a stalker."

"I have experience in this sort of thing."

"I don't like any of this."

"No one asked you to like it. Just cooperate, please. I do know what I'm doing."

She turned and gazed toward the mainland. "He's over there, somewhere, plotting right now."

"Yes, he is. Or she is."

Paula turned. "You think it might be a woman?"

"Women have been known to do such work with great skill. If they're motivated, anyone can be deadly."

"True." She felt an emptiness inside. "All right. I'll do as you say. No going back home."

"Good." He smiled. "I appreciate your attitude, Ms. Dixon."

She didn't reply. They went back to the house.

CHAPTER NINE

IRELAND WAS very green and very lovely, Paula thought as their plane flew over impossibly vivid emerald countryside on the way into the airport at Dublin. They were about to land in the nation's capital, but the land below was still rural, segmented into fields, dotted with the brown and cream-colored oblong shapes of cattle and sheep. The only buildings she could see were small stone cottages. Then, a larger, taller shape came into view below.

"Is that a castle?" she asked Liam, pointing down.

Liam roused and glanced out of the window, "Could be," he said in the uncharacteristic laconic manner he had taken on since they left Berringer's Island a full day ago. "We've lots of 'em here." He settled back in his seat and stared into nothing. His big hands held on to the armrests.

Paula sat back, too, and regarded him.

He looked strange. Something was wrong.

She'd fallen asleep almost as soon as the jet taxied down the runway in Atlanta. Although she had noticed he'd been silent on the short hop from Savannah, she hadn't thought much of it, being too weary herself. Now, rested, she realized her companion was not his normal self. "Liam, what's the matter?" she asked.

"I'm thinking."

"About?"

"Things."

"What things?"

He cleared his throat. "Is your seat belt fastened? We're about to land."

"Liam!"

He gripped the armrests. "I'm thinking how best to present you to my family," he said.

"*That's* kept you so quiet all this time? I don't believe it!"

"All right, then." He cleared his throat again. "I do not like to fly, if you must know." His knuckles were dead white. "I'd sooner take a hard beating."

Paula did her best, but she could not stop a laugh. "You? Afraid of flying?"

"Yes." The veins stood out on the backs of his hands, and she saw a drop of sweat trickle down the side of his face. "To be honest, I'm terrified of being up high in the air. Have been all my life. Heights and flying do me in."

She stopped laughing and covered his hand with hers. "How did you get to America to hunt for Tobias?" she asked. "Surely you flew."

"I took passage on a freighter."

"You are kidding me."

The plane shuddered as landing gear went down.

Liam closed his eyes tightly. He turned his hand over and clung to hers in a grip so fierce, she thought her bones would be crushed. "I don't joke about this fear," he said. "Ever."

"I'm sorry," she said softly. "Forgive me for laughing."

He held on to her.

And then, they landed. Smoothly.

Liam breathed again.

"Why didn't you say something when all the plans were being made?" Paula asked him as the jet taxied to the gate. "I'm sure Alex could have somehow made other arrangements if he'd known you were a real white-knuckled flyer."

"No. We had to fly. There was no other way to get you to safety quickly." Liam's smile was wry. "You're too important for my problem to interfere. And I'm too bloody pigheaded to let your friends know my weakness, I suppose," he said. "Let off about it now, love. It matters no longer. We're here, safe and sound." The jet came to a stop. "Come on," he said, reaching for her hand. "Let me show you my home."

Entry into the country was no problem for either of them. The special papers provided by Casey Sears held up under customs scrutiny with no difficulty, though they both received curious looks from the officials. In contrast to his show of nerves on the plane, Liam remained calm and pleasant through the entire procedure and when it was over, he retrieved their baggage and guided her outside.

The air smelled like rain, though the sun shone. The grassy areas were radiant, and flowers bloomed in colorful abundance everywhere. Paula sniffed appreciatively. "I smell the ocean," she said. "Even with all the odors from the airport, I can still smell the sea."

"I smell home," Liam said. "And it delights my heart. I welcome you to my country." He gazed at her for a moment. He did not touch her, but his eyes explained that he would have liked to.

Very much.

He didn't take her home to meet his family right away, however. Getting a taxi at the airport, he instructed the driver to head for Islandbridge. "I have a place there," he said. "You can have some privacy for a little while."

She didn't feel like asking what would happen to her privacy after that.

Once they were seated inside, Liam and the driver began to chat amiably about local sports events, politics and the weather in such heavily accented English that Paula lost track of the conversation almost immediately. Relieved at Liam's return to his normal loquaciousness, she sat back and watched the scenery go by.

The vehicle roared out of the airport and down the highway. Paula flinched at the driver's tactics until she remembered that driving here was on the opposite side of the road. After a short while, they left the modern thoroughfare and entered a nineteenth century world of brick buildings and Georgian doorways. She gazed out, entranced. The city reminded her a little of Charleston. Or maybe Boston.

But it was different. Subtle differences in the buildings. Obvious differences in street signs, which were written in both English and Gaelic. Then, there were the people.

Along the narrow sidewalks walked young women with small children, elderly folk making their way to shops for food or the pub for drink, a group of teens, tradesmen, all somehow stamped with a distinction of appearance and dress that reminded her she was not in America anymore. This was different. Another country. Other customs. Other ways.

The cabbie, following Liam's directions, drove down a hill, past what looked like a park, turned onto another main road and then, before Paula could squeak protest, wheeled right in front of oncoming traffic and off onto a ramp that led down into a large courtyard surrounded by attractive two-storied apartment buildings.

"We'll set you up here for now," Liam explained, moving easily back into unaccented English. "I have several flats in this complex that I rent out for long-term guests or when the bed and breakfast fills. At least one's empty, I know. So you'll live there for the time being."

"Where will you be?" Suddenly, she was nervous about being separated from him.

He sensed that and smiled. "Just up the street from here. Shoutin' distance. Don't you worry."

"I wasn't. I just wanted to know."

The cabdriver said something about pretty lasses and men and being nearby, and Liam laughed. Then he replied in Gaelic. Both laughed. Paula did not inquire the details of the exchange.

Liam joked with the driver for a moment longer, then paid him and turned to her. "The flat down by the river is the one for you," he said.

"Okay." She followed him along the brick sidewalk. "How'll you get in?"

"Wait and see."

The apartments on the ground floor had little fenced-in yards with tiny lawns and miniature planted areas with bushes and flowers. All neat and tidy. He led her to the last place on the right and opened the small gate. Beyond the buildings, the ground fell off in a gentle slope to a river. Another brick walkway meandered along the bank, and several children were fishing in the water. On the other side ducks and geese nested and foraged in the wild shrubbery and grasses. Trees grew tall, obscuring the view beyond.

Liam set down the bags and did some foraging under a clump of bushes. He dug up a set of keys. "In case of emergency," he said, grinning.

"I'm impressed," she admitted. "You've thought of everything."

"Perhaps," he said. He went to the door and started opening locks. "Don't follow me right away. There's an alarm system I have to disengage, and that involves a bit of a scramble." The last of three locks opened, and she heard the beep-beeping of a triggered intruder alarm begin.

Liam dashed through the entryway, into the main room and over to a small closet set against the opposite wall. He flung open the door and revealed a small but complex alarm system. A few number punches, and the beeping stopped. He turned.

"Come in," he said.

She did.

The apartment was cozy, compact and smelled slightly musty. There was a trace of some sweet aroma, but Paula assumed she was bringing in the scent of some of the flowers with her. "This is nice," she said.

"'Tis," Liam replied. "I bought into this complex when they first put out the plans." His smile was that of a businessman who had scored a good deal. "I've never regretted it, though all the promises have yet to be kept." He gestured riverwards. "They hoped to build a boat dock out here, but it hasn't been realized."

"Developers will do that." She went over to the kitchen area and studied the appliances. "You're going to have to show me how all this works," she said.

"It's very different from what I'm used to." She hunkered down and studied the tiny washing machine set under the counter to the left of the kitchen sink.

Liam's hand rested on her shoulder. "I'll show you," he said. "But later." His fingers tightened. "I've things to do and people to see before you're completely settled and safe."

Paula stood up. "What do you mean? I thought the whole idea of my coming here was that I'd be safe. Otherwise, it was a waste of time and money to—"

"Hush," he said softly. His hand was still on her shoulder, and standing so near him, she realized once more how big he was. How solid and strong.

How compelling.

"I have plans merely to tighten the safety net," he said. "This is my home, and I have connections your friends would not think of using."

Paula felt a tendril of concern enter her mind. "What sort of connections?"

He just smiled. "Let me show you how the hot water heater works," he said. "'Twould be a terrible thing to ask you to take a chilly shower your first morning in Dublin."

A few minutes later, Paula understood how to work the various appliances and gadgets in the flat, had been shown the mysteries of the alarm system and given the keys to the place with instructions how to use them all to secure herself. And Liam was gone without answering a single question.

He was talented that way, she thought as she unpacked the clothes and the toiletries Tinsley had given her. Able to sidestep a direct question with skill and such charm that the interrogator didn't realize what had happened, until later.

Like now. What "connections" could he be talking about? Surely not criminal or terrorist! He'd been checked out by the best the United States government had.

So he had to be clean!

Didn't he?

She waited a half hour until the hot water heater had warmed a sufficient amount for a shower. After bathing and changing into a shirt and jeans, she felt wide-awake and not at all ready for the nap Liam had suggested. The plane flight was the longest she'd ever taken, but she had slept so much of the journey that she felt awake and relatively fit.

The aches and pains of the trauma of the past few days were still lingering, of course, but she was pleased that her body had the resilience to rebound as it had.

She must not be in as bad shape as she had thought.

As Tottie had teasingly accused her of being...

The almost-forgotten painful emotions of the past days returned with a rush. Her best friend lay in the hospital. Maybe dying. And there was nothing she could do! The itch of frustrated fury started deep inside her, but she managed to control it. There would be a time for anger and action, just as there was a time for hiding and grieving.

And when that time came, whoever had hurt Tottie and nearly killed a number of people, including herself, would seriously regret his actions!

Or her actions.

If only she had a single lead, she knew she could find the culprit.

But, she was here. Out of the way. Out of the game for the time being. For the sake of others as well as

herself. Frustrating as it was, she had to admit it was
still the best thing to have done.

But she needed to do *something*. Move around. If
she sat here, waiting on Liam's return, she'd just
worry herself into a real state.

So Paula decided to go for a walk. Explore a little.
Clear her mind. She'd never been out of the U.S. before, and she might as well take advantage of the opportunity to get the flavor of another land. She
carefully set the alarm and locked up as Liam had instructed her.

Then, she set out to see what she could see.

LIAM WALKED the distance from the flat to the block
just beyond the main entrance to Phoenix Park.
There, he turned up the street and climbed the hill
until he reached the compound where his family, home
and businesses were located. Along the way, he passed
many people he knew, but he spoke only simple
greetings and ignored the curious looks and questions
that his presence caused among his neighbors and ac-
quaintances.

Questions enough would be flying once he encountered the family. He did not need to seek more.
Reaching the front door of the Croft compound, he
paused. The high Georgian doorway with its gleaming brass fixtures and bright red paint had always been
a welcome sight to his eyes when he returned from a
long journey.

Today, all he wanted to do was turn and run back to
the tiny flat and Paula.

And there? What would he do there? Surely everyone could tell what he wanted to do, he thought. He

wanted to be with her. In every way it was possible for a man to be with a woman, he—

"Liam?" The female voice came from a second-floor window. "Is that you, Liam Croft?"

He looked upward. It was his favorite sister, Annie. "Good morning, darlin' sister," he said, full smile on his face. "It is meself, in the living flesh. And how are you this fine day?"

Annie Purchase leaned out the window and grinned back at him. "Where's the old man, then?" she asked, her rosy-cheeked face aglow with curiosity. "Ye found him already?"

Liam didn't answer directly. "Where's Mum?" he asked. "I need to speak to her."

"Out back, talking to the garden, I suppose," Annie replied. "But what about the old man? Where is he?"

"He didn't come with me," Liam said. He stepped forward and opened the door to his home. As the big wooden door swung shut, he heard Annie's cry of disappointment echoing from the upstairs.

Inside, everything looked tidy and proper. Liam paused, absorbing the ambience that was unique to the place. Old wood, brass, antique prints on the walls, the smell of beeswax candles, lemon furniture polish, the metallic odor of silver and brass, the stale aroma of his male relatives' pipes and cigarettes . . .

Home.

Annie came rushing down the front stairs into the foyer. "Mum will have a fit," she said, her tightly curled red hair coming loose in straggly strands from the kerchief that bound it up while she worked. "Ye know how much she counted on Great-Granduncle to return home." She threw her arms around her broth-

NO RISK, NO OBLIGATION TO BUY...NOW OR EVER!

GUARANTEED

PLAY "ROLL A DOUBLE" AND GET FIVE FREE GIFTS!

HERE'S HOW TO PLAY:

1. Peel off label from front cover. Place it in space provided at right. With a coin, carefully scratch off the silver dice. Then check the claim chart to see what we have for you – FREE BOOKS and a gift – ALL YOURS! ALL FREE!

2. Send back this card and you'll receive brand-new Harlequin Superromance® novels. These books have a cover price of $3.50 each, but they are yours to keep absolutely free.

3. There's no catch. You're under no obligation to buy anything. We charge nothing – ZERO – for your first shipment. And you don't have to make any minimum number of purchases – not even one!

4. The fact is thousands of readers enjoy receiving books by mail from the Harlequin Reader Service® before they're available in stores. They like the convenience of home delivery and they love our discount prices!

5. We hope that after receiving your free books you'll want to remain a subscriber. But the choice is yours – to continue or cancel, anytime at all! So why not take us up on our invitation, with no risk of any kind. You'll be glad you did!

You'll look like a million dollars when you wear this lovely necklace! Its cobra-link chain is a generous 18" long, and the multi-faceted Austrian crystal sparkles like a diamond!

THE HARLEQUIN READER SERVICE®: HERE'S HOW IT WORKS

Accepting free books puts you under no obligation to buy anything. You may keep the books and gift and return the shipping statement marked "cancel". If you do not cancel, about a month later we will send you 4 additional novels, and bill you just $2.96 each plus 25¢ delivery and GST*. That's the complete price, and – compared to cover prices of $3.50 each – quite a bargain! You may cancel at any time, but if you choose to continue, every month we'll send you 4 more books, which you may either purchase at the discount price...or return at our expense and cancel your subscription.

*Terms and prices subject to change without notice.
Canadian residents will be charged applicable provincial taxes and GST.

019561919-L2A5X3-BR01

HARLEQUIN READER SERVICE
PO BOX 609
FORT ERIE ON L2A 9Z9

If offer card is missing, write to : The Harlequin Reader Service, P.O. Box 609, Fort Erie, Ontario L2A 5X3

MAIL≫POSTE

Canada Post Corporation / Société canadienne des postes

Postage paid
if mailed in Canada

Port payé
si posté au Canada

Business
Reply

Réponse
d'affaires

0195619199   01

er's neck. "But anyway, welcome home," she said, hugging him. "Even if ye're as alone as when ye left."

"I'm not alone," Liam said, returning her embrace, then stepping back. "I brought a friend with me."

Annie regarded him. "Friend? Ye sound funny when ye said that."

"I should."

"And why's that, might I ask?"

Liam couldn't answer. The truth seemed to stick in his throat. And this was the sister to whom he was very close. What would happen when he tried to explain Paula to the others? To his mother? He felt his face reddening.

"Oh, my." Annie studied his expression. "Tell me it's not so, dear brother! Ye've not taken an American woman next to your heart! Is she one of those liberated kind?"

"I—"

"Liam?" His mother's voice sounded from the back of the house. "Did I hear Liam out there just now?"

"I'm home, Mum," he said, moving past Annie and signaling her to silence with his finger to his lips. "And I have much to report."

"I'd say ye must," Annie muttered. But she made no further comment. Liam's mother came out to greet him.

"Darlin' boy," she said, gathering him in for a motherly embrace and kiss. "I've been praying day and night for ye."

"I've needed it." Liam held his mother out at arm's length.

Morgan Croft was a sturdy woman, still possessed of much of the great beauty that had graced her youth. Though her body had thickened through fourteen pregnancies and births, the finely drawn features of her face were still evident. Her skin was only slightly wrinkled, and her jawline showed just a little sag. But her hair, once raven black as his was, had long since turned as silver as the family tea service on the old oak sideboard.

"And where's Uncle Tobias, then?" she asked, her eyes like blue steel and her lips pulled into a tight line. "Did ye stash him down at one of the flats?"

"We need to talk, Mum," Liam said. "Tobias isn't here. He couldn't come—"

"*Wouldn't* come." Morgan Croft turned away from her oldest child. "Did ye explain to him why he was needed?"

"No. That I did not. I thought he should come back of his own free will, rather than with us beggin' for a favor. It would then seem we didn't care for the man, himself."

Morgan's squared shoulders sagged. "You men and your pride! Why cannot ye think of the family first and your own damned pride second?"

"Mum, I did, but I had no chance to tell him of the signing. A...a situation arose that took my entire—"

"No situation is worth losing this." Morgan Croft gestured, indicating the whole Croft complex. Ye know what will happen if Tobias dies and does not sign his name to the papers."

"I do. But—"

"Then you must return. Bring him here."

Liam sighed. "Mum, I cannot. I said we must talk. So far, all I've done is listen."

"Ye don't seem to be able to do that so well!"

"Nor, do you!"

And then, the bomb dropped.

"I did not bring Tobias to you," he yelled at his mother. "I brought a woman who—"

"A woman?" Morgan Croft's voice echoed through the halls of the Croft domicile.

"Aye. And she and I—"

"Ye'll not live with her under this roof!"

"I will! This is my home," he shouted back, his face the color of a summer thunderstorm. "Further, I am elected leader, not yourself, in case you're forgettin'. So I have a right to live here as long as I choose. I choose to stay. And more than that, Mum, she will live here with me!"

"You intend to marry her, then?" she asked, her voice suddenly soft, motherly. Astonished.

"If she'll have me," Liam replied, also returning to a softer tone and manner. "Mum, I do love her, though I've known her but a short time."

"And does she return your love, Liam?" Morgan asked. "Does she love ye and wish marriage to ye?"

"That I do not know," he said. "And I fear with all my heart that she may not."

"Oh." Tears ran down his mother's face. "Well, then," Morgan said, moving toward her son once more and embracing him, "we shall have to help the lass see her way clearly. This American. She will come to your way of thinking, believe me."

THAT WOMAN was walking and thinking, letting her legs take her where they would while she contemplated the mystery surrounding her present life. Who was after her? Why? What was the next step she should take? Should she let Agent Sears do all the work? Or initiate some sort of investigation from here, as Alex had suggested.

Paula walked on, but she soon found herself at a large intersection. The river and the apartment complex was behind her. Should she turn and go back?

Or keep on and see what turned up?

She kept on. She crossed the main road, aware of her surroundings for the first time. She had reached the top of a hill, and over to her right stood a grim stone fortress of a building. It looked like a prison. Curious, she approached it.

Kilmainham Jail. She was right. It was a prison. Or had been. Now, according to the sign outside the gate, it was a museum of sorts and open to the public. She checked her pockets. Liam had given her some Irish money, though she had no idea how much each denomination was in dollars. Admission was one-fifty. Not too much, regardless.

She went inside, leaving the sunshine for the damp grayness of prison walls.

And discovered far more than she had imagined.

LIAM AND SOME of his family sat in the huge kitchen that served the bed and breakfast, the tavern, the main dining hall and the various households within the compound that comprised the Croft estate. He had changed out of Alex's clothes, had showered and put on his own things. A comfortable pair of trousers and a favorite hand-knit sweater. Wool socks. Good heavy brogues on his feet.

A fire crackled in the big cooking fireplace in spite of the season. His mother had set out tea and scones. The works, as the Americans would say.

Americans. No one was very pleased that one of them now occupied the riverside flat down the road a bit.

Too bad. She was there until she was safe! There, or, God willing, here. Meanwhile, the Crofts were here for a conference. Thirty or so adults and eleven teenagers old enough to have a voice in the proceedings.

"So, ye failed in your mission, did ye now?"

Liam regarded the speaker. His uncle, Johnny Croft, a lean and hungry type who had always resented losing out on the clan leadership first to his sister, Morgan, then to his younger nephew. By his side sat his daughter, Noreen, a young woman who seemed content enough with her lot.

The Croft clan leader was elected by family. No regard to age, sex or status was given. A person was chosen because the family trusted him, or her, to lead. For many years, Morgan had been head of the clan. She had been elected before her marriage and had kept her maiden name even after being wed. In fact, her husband had taken *her* name. Leadership responsibility took precedence over nearly everything else in the life of the clan.

Now, it was Liam's job.

"I did," he answered the question calmly. "If you regard a delay a failure. I don't."

"But it will be, if the old one dies," said Aunt Tess. "He must sign the document, or we might lose the land."

Liam tried a smile. "He's nowhere near death, Aunt," he said. "He's tough as old leather and twice as strong. Beat me silly, he did. And put a ball shot into me shoulder on top of that. A few days later, he hiked with me—"

"What's this about a woman?" The interruption and question came from a youngster, Peter Purchase, Annie's oldest. He was a thin lad, unusually intense. He had declared himself for the Church and was preparing to go the same route Liam himself had tried in his early years.

"I brought her with me," Liam said, addressing the boy directly. "She's—"

"She's turned your head, Liam Croft," Johnny declared, disgust in his tone. "Made you lose sight of your mission. She's why ye failed to bring the old man home."

"Not so." Morgan Croft stood. "I've heard Liam speak in detail of what has happened. At an appropriate time, he'll tell it to everyone. But I know, and I stand by his actions and decision. He has behaved as a good and true Irishman should. This woman is in danger. He brought her here so she'll be safe."

"And what of all of us?" Gerald Daily asked. He put his hand over his wife's. "What of the family? What of our safety. And future?"

Patsy Daily was Liam's youngest sister, and she held her ties to the Croft fortune and land with a tight fist. Her husband, Gerald, had learned to do the same, Liam reflected.

"I made a decision to wait," Liam said. "We don't know for certain that the lack of Tobias's signature would land us out on the street." He stood. "I do know that if Miss Dixon remained where she was, she would likely be hurt or killed."

"So you brought her here?" Tess made a face. "And what if the villain follows? What then?"

Liam smiled. "Then, we have the advantage, don't we? We are the Crofts. We've lived and fought on this scrap of land for over a thousand years. And if someone tries to harm her here, why, we know what to do, don't we?"

His family, his clan looked back at him, steadily.

And then, most of them smiled in response.

PAULA LEFT the cold stone corridors of Kilmainham with her head and heart full. Young men and women had been imprisoned and executed there not so many years ago for wanting to be free. If Liam had been alive then, she was willing to bet he would have been in the front lines of the rebellion.

And probably been stood against a stone wall and shot for his crime.

She shivered in spite of the warm sunshine.

The emotional experience of the prison tired her, so she made her way back to the flat, intending to take that nap. She stopped along the way to buy some groceries from a little shop, and it was the extra load she carried that saved her.

CHAPTER TEN

IF SHE HADN'T SET the bag down on the front stoop in order to make the run into the flat to deactivate the alarm, she might not have noticed that the little light was off.

Someone was inside. Or had been inside and deactivated the system already.

Paula straightened, key in hand. If she opened the door, what might await her? Liam? A stranger?

Another bomb?

She backed away from the door, tripping over the small step, but regaining her balance immediately. Adrenaline began to flow. She was on full alert. Even her skin tingled in alarm.

Somehow she knew it wasn't Liam in there. Turning on her toes, she sped out of the yard, leaving the metal gate open and her sack of groceries still on the stoop. She ran up the ramp and onto the sidewalk that led along the road. Heavy traffic roared by. She kept glancing over her shoulder to see if she was being followed.

But no one seemed to be paying her any special attention. She was just one of many red-haired, blue-jeaned women. She kept moving, not running, but walking rapidly.

About a block away from the flat, she slowed. She couldn't deal with this alone. Where was Liam? She had no idea which way he'd gone after leaving her. She was tired and disoriented and not sure what her next step should be. She needed to find him. But he hadn't even hinted where he would be.

She looked around. She was on the shady side of the road. The neighborhood looked seedy, but not particularly dangerous. Weeds and trash collected in small vacant lots and a number of storefronts were boarded up. Hard times. Across the street, however, things changed.

Across the street was a park. Beyond the stone and iron fence, she saw trees, flowers, grass and people strolling. Beyond that, farther down the street were open stores and businesses. At home, a public park in a big city would not offer a sense of security, but this one did. It looked clean and fresh, and she could see several policemen. She hurried to the corner, and watching the traffic carefully, crossed to the other side.

The entrance to the park was farther down, so she walked along, still glancing back to check for anything or anyone suspicious.

Nothing.

Was she overreacting? The idea of running from nothing made her blush.

Hell! The idea of running from *something* made her furious! If she wasn't so shook up and still so weary, she'd have done something! And possibly taken a stick of dynamite in the face for her foolish courage. *Come on, Paula, think!* Quit reacting!

She reached the gates to the park. It was a huge place. She could see that, just from looking in the entrance. Lots of people . . .

"Help you find something, Miss?"

Paula turned toward the voice. A policeman stood there, regarding her with a friendly, but curious expression. For a moment, she considered asking him to go back and check out the flat with her.

But that's what Paula Dixon, assistant district attorney, would do. Right now, she was Paula Dixon, refugee. She knew enough about Ireland to figure the word *bomb* would trigger a powerful reaction from the authorities. Besides, involving the police at all would only bring more trouble, especially if nothing was wrong. So, she smiled. "No, I'm just out for some air," she said. "Thanks, though."

"Ah, an American?" The policeman was tall and good-looking with eyes almost as blue as Liam's and sandy hair. "Here on holiday?"

"Yes, I..." Paula glanced beyond him and a sign caught her eye. "Why, what in the world...?" She moved past him, still staring up at the sign. It graced the entrance to a lovely section of town.

"Croft Lane," the cop said, following her. "It's part of one of the oldest and largest Irish-held landholdings left in the Dublin area."

"Excuse me?" She turned and regarded the officer. "Oldest and largest? As in years and size?"

He grinned, obviously pleased to have her attention once more. "Aye. It's legendary, Miss. Many a tale of bravery and sacrifice surrounds the Croft estate." He moved closer. "My beat takes me along the lane. Care to come with me?"

"I certainly would." Paula stifled the emotions she was feeling. Liam, if this *was* his family place, had deliberately misled her. Anyone who owned this turf must be rich and powerful as all get-out! "Lead on, Officer," she said, forgetting for a moment to be a starry-eyed tourist and snapping the phrase like an order. She even stepped ahead of the man before she remembered her role.

Falling back to walk beside him, she asked, "So, how long have you been on this beat? Do you know the Crofts?"

They were strolling up a hill. But unlike the one she had walked earlier that led her to the jail, this one was lined with trees. Bright flowers spilled from window boxes. Everything along the way looked clean and prosperous.

"I've been here a few months," he said. "I've met some of the family, of course. But the clan leader's been away on business, so I—"

"Clan leader? What's his name?" Paula stopped.

"Why, everyone knows Mr. Croft, Miss." The cop signaled a greeting to one of the passersby. "Everyone."

"What...is...his...first...name?"

"Liam, Miss. Liam Croft. Are you all right, Miss?"

"I am fine," she said, enunciating the words carefully. "Just...fine." She looked around. "He owns all this?"

"His family—"

"Show me where he lives."

"Are you certain you're all right? You've turned right pale, and—"

"I'm fine." All the strong emotion that the jail tour had caused, all the fear and tension that had been building since she fled the flat, all that threatened to boil up and over into anger. Unreasonable anger, perhaps, but anger, nevertheless. Liam had deceived her. Who exactly was he? One thing was for sure, he was no simple bed-and-breakfast owner. Knowing she was very close to the edge, Paula sat hard on her temper. "Just...take...me...to...Liam Croft."

"I don't know if that's such a good idea, Miss. Why don't you tell me why you wish to see him."

"That's my business, not yours." The authority she'd held as a prosecutor for almost ten years came flooding to the fore. "Now, do as I asked, or I will be speaking to your superior."

The policeman's pleasant attitude vanished. "I suspect that might be a good idea, Miss." He took her by the elbow. "Come along with me, now."

A moment later, she was under arrest.

THE FIRST THING that set off the alarms in Liam's brain was the sight of the gate ajar and the bag of groceries on the front stoop of the flat. He got out of his car. "Stay inside," he said to his mother and Annie, who were in the back seat. They had come along to meet the American woman who had turned his life and plans upside down. "Something's not right," he added.

"Liam, call the police," his mother said. "Don't go up there."

He ignored the advice. "Paula," he called out. "Paula, are you there?"

No answer.

He moved closer. The front door was closed and locked, but the alarm light was off. Behind him, he heard his mother and sister telling him to stop, but he moved faster, circling around to the back of the building and approaching the flat from the rear. The back door was still locked, and he had not shown

Paula how to get from the smaller bedroom into the storage room where the back door exited.

If she had left those groceries at the front, and the back wasn't disturbed, had she gone out shopping and then returned to find the alarm turned off? Had she been quick enough to think perhaps someone had set a trap for her in the time she was gone?

Maybe set another bomb? Nausea suddenly hit him.

Liam's hand was on the back doorknob and the key was in his hand. He pulled away, his heart starting to pound. She could not have been followed and found! Not by her enemy! Not here!

But if he took the chance and opened the door and a device exploded . . .

He left the area and returned to his car. "I don't know what's going on," he said, addressing his mother and sister. "But I think I'd better notify the gardai."

"Go there now," his mother said.

Liam obeyed. Headquarters was right around the corner.

And that was where he found Paula.

When he walked into the headquarters of the Garda Siochana in Phoenix Park, the desk officer, an old friend, looked up and grinned at him. "Hello, Liam Croft," he said. "Cannot imagine why you're here, lad."

"Hello, Pat. Why do you say that?" Liam put both hands on the desk and leaned forward to whisper. "This is no social call. I need to talk to someone in the bomb squad," he said.

"Why?" Patrick laughed. "We've got your little bombshell all packaged up and ready."

"What?"

"The girl, laddie." Wide grin. "You certainly upset her, you know. Fair set her pretty heart—"

Liam reached over and grabbed the officer's uniform shirt, pulling him out of his chair and halfway across the desk. "Is Paula Dixon here?" he yelled. "Is she hurt? Where is she? What have you done with her?"

"Ease off, Liam." Superintendent Sean Creedon appeared in the doorway of his office and signaled to the other officers. "She's fine. But I think you'd best be explaining a few things to us about her."

"Indeed I will." Relieved beyond measure to hear she was all right, Liam smiled at his old friend. Going into the office, he shut the door and quickly expressed his fears and described Paula's situation.

A few minutes later, Paula, looking beautiful, bedraggled and furious, was brought in by a policewoman. The policeman who had arrested Paula also entered. Paula took the chair she was led to and sat, her arms and legs crossed, her expression angry and her mouth silent.

Her attitude puzzled him, but he was so glad to see her safe and well enough to be mad, that he felt nothing but relief and gratitude to her watchful guardian angel. That angel should be given a raise in pay, he thought. He had done overtime for certain sure.

"Hello, darlin'," he said. "'Tis a fair sight you are."

"The hell I am," she said, snapping the words out in that manner he was getting to know well. She was afraid and so she acted angry.

Liam decided to keep quiet as well until he understood the situation. She should have been overjoyed to see him, given the fright she must have had back at the flat. How had she gotten herself arrested? What was wrong, now?

"She now claims to be a prosecutor back in the States," the policewoman said, addressing the senior gardai officer who had been in the office when Liam entered. The man, also an old friend of Liam's, had already dispatched a bomb team to the flat. Now, he was sorting out matters. And that included Paula Dixon.

"She is, Sean," Liam said. "Don't let her present appearance fool you. Those are not her clothes."

For that, he got another killing glare from Paula.

But no words. What the devil was eating at her?

"Sean," he said, speaking to the superintendent, "could you kindly be putting me in the know? Paula Dixon is an elected officer of the court back in her home county. A solicitor of some renown and good reputation. She's a victim, not a—"

"You lied to me," Paula said softly.

"I did no such thing, darlin'! I've been truthful with you from the start."

"Ha!"

"Settle down then, you two," Sean said sternly. Just then, another officer came in and handed the superintendent a piece of paper. Sean read it, then looked up. "What's the noise with the bomb scare, Liam? Our team reports nothing at all amiss at your flat. Just the alarm turned off. No one there, and only signs of a woman occupying the place. I assume that must be Miss Dixon."

"It is." Liam sat back, relief pouring through him and sobering him. "Nothing?" he said. "Ah."

"I didn't know what was in there," Paula said, speaking to no one in particular. "I just saw that the alarm light was off. I'm tired, not thinking any too clearly. I suppose I panicked."

Without thinking about it, Liam reached out and took her hand. "Given the past, no wonder. I'm sorry I wasn't with you. Forgive me, Paula."

"Safe? Bombs? The past?" Sean rose from his chair. "I'm thinking someone had better put me in the full picture."

"Sean, this is a delicate matter. Do you think we can speak freely?"

"Aye." Sean returned to his seat. "These're all to be trusted here."

"Everyone but Liam Croft," Paula muttered.

"What now has you in such a terrible spin, Paula?" Liam asked, beginning to reach the end of his patience. "I'm not understandin'!"

"You told me you ran a bed and breakfast," she snapped. "And now I find out you're some kind of... I don't know. A lord, or something."

"A lord?" Laughter returned. "Oh, have you misread me once more, darlin'! No titles for me. I'm no bloody aristocrat, believe me."

"I wish I could!"

"I think," Sean said, interrupting, "that explanations between the two of you had best wait. For I will hear what's going on, or I'll see the both of you in court."

"Very well." Liam settled back, intending to begin with the tale of his search for Tobias.

But Paula took the spotlight. In dispassionate, curt American legalese, she explained the processes and events that led up to the present moment. Every detail, except those private moments she and Liam had shared, was set out and thoroughly explained for the

Irish authorities. When she was done, Sean regarded her respectfully. "It seems, Miss Dixon, that you have been telling us the truth. At least about who you are and what you do. I doubt you could make all that up on the spot, no matter how much of a clever liar you might be. I tend to believe you. You won't mind if we do some checking, of course."

"Certainly not. In your place, I'd do exactly... I've done the same." Once more, she gave Liam an angry look. "Just remember that you might not turn up all you want when you look. If you have any questions, I'll be glad to supply what answers I can."

The man who had arrested her cleared his throat. "Might I ask one question of her, sir?" he asked, speaking to Creedon.

"Do so."

"Miss Dixon, why are you so upset with Mr. Croft? I believe that anger with him led you to strike out at me. It was that anger that made me bring you in for questioning. I'm willing to let the incident go by, if you'll just explain."

Liam watched her. She turned red as sunset. "He misrepresented himself to me. I believed him. That made me mad. And I was upset about the flat, thinking whoever was after me at home had managed by an evil miracle to follow me here. And... I just lost my temper. I'm sorry. It won't happen again."

"I still don't understand," Liam said. "I do run a bed and breakfast, and pub, as I told you. And I was in South Carolina to find Tobias for the family."

"He's telling the truth, Miss," the officer said.

"He may be telling the truth," Paula said, "but far from all of it. He's got a *street* with his last name on it, for crying out loud!"

"So?"

Liam honestly looked innocent and bewildered. Paula began to wonder if she had made a mistake. Though she couldn't think how. A man who headed a family with a street named after them and who held property in a prosperous section of any city was no mere bartender and innkeeper.

And anyway, why had it made her so angry to think he'd lied to her? Perhaps, he hadn't. In his eyes, perhaps he had told the truth.

She needed to try to understand. "Let me put it as simply as I can," she said. She indicated the policeman. "I was told by this man that you owned one of the largest and oldest estates in the city. Is that right?"

"My family—"

"The hell with your family! I want to know about you!"

"Ease down, Miss," the senior man said. "Or we'll be rethinking charges."

"Sorry." Paula turned back to Liam. "You explain," she said. "I'll try to keep quiet and listen."

"Fair enough. But if it's all right, I'd rather go do this someplace else."

Sean considered. "As long as that someplace is someplace I can reach you at a moment's notice. We don't take lightly to bomb scares here, as you well know. If you fear someone's after Miss Dixon, we can provide proper protection."

"Protective custody?" Liam grimaced. "I think not. But we will stay in contact, Sean. Count on it." He stood and held out his hand to her. "Paula," he said, "come with me. I'll try to answer your questions with all the honesty I can muster."

In spite of her anger and emotional turmoil, all she wanted to do at that moment was to fall against his chest and have his arms around her. What a day it had been! And in her heart, she wanted to trust him again.

She took his hand with as much dignity as she could muster. "All right," she said. "Let's go. And Liam?"

"Yes? Whatever you want, love!"

"I am hungry. Starved, in fact. I bought those groceries so I could eat. If you really do have a restaurant, or something, could we . . . ?"

"Go there? Aye. I believe we can." He offered her his arm, and Paula took it.

Then, he led her outside.

More surprises. Paula took in the old, battered compact car with two women in the back seat. They were staring at her, and she saw their close resemblance to Liam. They were undoubtedly part of his famous family. But the car was interesting. No truly wealthy man would be driving such a heap. Not in her experience.

And it was his car. He took her around to the left side and opened the door. "Paula Dixon, this is my mum, Mrs. Morgan Croft, and my sister, Mrs. Annie Purchase."

From feminine faces, Liam's blue eyes regarded her. "Welcome to Ireland," the silver-haired one said.

"Such a welcome," said the younger one. "To be arrested not hours after settin' foot on the soil! Goodness! Liam, what were you thinkin', leaving her alone like that?"

Paula got in the car. "He was thinking I had sense enough to stay put until he came back for me," she said. "I suspect if I hadn't left the flat, no one would have come in and..." She didn't finish. She had no idea how much he'd told his family.

Liam settled behind the wheel. He smiled at her, looking for all the world like a large, satisfied cat. "So you admit you would have been better to do as I said?" he asked.

"Maybe."

He turned back to address the other women. "Miss Dixon is a bit hungry, Mum. D'ye suppose we can find her a decent place to eat?"

AN HOUR LATER, Paula groaned. "I can't eat another bite, I swear." She pushed her dessert plate away. "It was all wonderful, and I've eaten enough for ten."

Liam, who had been standing by the fireplace, silently watching her, spoke. "You've eaten fair enough for an army, Paula Dixon. Perhaps your bad temper was simply from starvation and not because I caused you grief."

She blushed. "My temper was from a number of causes."

He came over to the table. At a hand signal, Annie and Mrs. Croft disappeared without a word into the back part of the house.

Paula blinked. What kind of power did this man have in his own home? For women to scuttle away like that at a wave of his hand, was downright medieval! Up to now, she'd enjoyed the chatting and bantering from both women. But did it cover a more sinister side of the household?

And were there more? No one else had put in an appearance, but she felt many presences around her.

Like ghosts.

Liam put his hands palm down on the old wooden table. "Talk to me, Paula," he said. "Tell me everything you did from the moment I left you."

"Don't command me. I'm not one of your womenfolk."

He looked at her sternly, and she wanted to cower. The power of command was on him, no doubt about it! But she held her ground.

"I only wish to help," he said, speaking slowly. "If I seem harsh, forgive me. I fear for your life."

She took a deep breath. If he was no lord or aristocrat, he certainly behaved like one. The physical trappings may not be there. In addition to the old car, he wore plain clothes. Plainer than the ones he'd taken to America. He looked like a college professor in heavy shoes, an old baggy sweater and corduroy pants. But his manner was of one who expected and received obedience when he spoke.

However, he did have a point. She was still in danger.

"Okay. Here's what I did." She explained about showering, then feeling like taking a walk. She described her ramblings that led her to Kilmainham. She intended to gloss over that part, but he touched her hand with his.

"And what did you think of Kilmainham?" he asked.

Tears filled her eyes. "I . . ." She couldn't speak.

"Aye," he said softly, understanding.

And then he surprised her again by leaning forward and kissing her lightly on the lips. "Your first experience of the real Ireland, I take it," he said.

"Y-yes." She tapped her fingertips on the table.

"You've a lot to learn, Paula Dixon. It's not just shamrocks and leprechauns here."

"I guess not." She looked down at the table. She could not meet his eyes.

"It's blood and hatred and tears and pain and loss and a history more frightening than any tale you'd tell your children," he said, getting back up and moving over to the fireplace. "And this land, this house, this heritage right here is ours by right of all that suffering."

"Ours?"

"The family's." He smiled at her. "You still think it's mine, don't you." He waved his hand. "All this."

"I thought so. Now, I'm not so sure."

"It's not mine. It's *ours*. You must understand, Paula. I'm the clan leader. Elected. Not born. It's a sacred honor to hold this office in the Croft clan. Before me, it was my mum who was leader."

"Your mother?"

"Yes."

"But she acts like your servant, Liam." Paula stood up. "I guess I really don't understand you people. But," she added softly, "I'd like to try."

Liam felt his heart jump a beat. "What did you say?"

"I said that I'd like to try. I…I'm not sure why, but I do want to try."

He stood very still. "I see you don't know. Perhaps, just perhaps, I do."

"Then tell me. Please."

"I don't know that I can. Not now." He held out his hand. "But I know I can show you." He moved closer.

"Liam, I don't—"

"Hush!" He captured her hand and pulled her to him.

And then, he kissed her as he had after the explosion.

CHAPTER ELEVEN

HE KISSED HER, embracing her as if he would draw her inside himself. She yielded to it, sensing that his was a demanding passion.

And that was what she wanted. A passion that wouldn't take less than everything she had to give.

A lover who wouldn't take less than everything.

Was this what she'd been searching for all her life? Was Liam the man she'd waited for? This foreigner. This stranger. This man who belonged to another land, another world.

He broke the kiss and held her tightly. "Back in America, I nearly died when I thought you were dead," he whispered in her ear. "And I nearly died today when I thought you were gone. Or taken."

"I'm right here," she replied. "And it's not likely I'm going anywhere else for a while."

Liam held her off at arm's length. "I love you, you know," he said plainly, simply. So honestly, she felt tears in her eyes. "I think I've loved you from the moment I opened my eyes in that bloody awful ditch and saw you looking down at me, caring for me," he added. "I thought you were an angel, remember? Until I smelled your sweet perfume."

"Liam, I—"

"Don't say a word," he commanded, his tone harsh. "I'll not take another blow to my heart right now. And you're not sure of anything, yet. We've time, thanks to the bastard who's out to harm you. If nothing else, I'm thankful for that. Time is what we both need."

"That's true." She stepped away from him. "Can you tell me more about this place?" she asked.

"Surely. And you need to know to understand." He ran his hand over his hair. "Kilmainham's exhibits gave you only the last few centuries of our history. Our story is far older. Croft-held land goes back as far as Strongbow and King Henry the Second of England. And to hear the old ones tell it, even before that. When Brian Boru sent the Danes packing from this city."

"How long ago was that? History was never my strong point."

He went over to the bar and pulled himself a beer. "Nearly a thousand years," he said. He gestured to see if she wanted a drink, but she declined. He took a long swallow and went on talking.

"The far past is legend," he said. "It's said a young woman fought with the Irish as bravely as any man and it was to her that some land fell for her gallant efforts." Another drink. "Back then, women were liberated, darlin'."

"In a way," she said. "And in some places."

"Aye. Well, seems this lass was. So she settled, took herself a husband and raised a family of numerous kiddies. So began the Crofts."

"Legend has it?" Sensing this was going to take a while, she returned to her seat. The sunlight streaming in the windows of the dining room was turning gold. Late afternoon, moving on to evening.

"Legend has it," he repeated. He drained his glass, filled it again and took a chair opposite her. "In the next century, many fortunes changed. The Normans and the English took warfare and politics to their logical conclusion and by papal decree, King Henry the Second of England was given possession of this land. Nobody bothered to ask the Irish what they thought of that." His smile was not warm. He gazed at her for a moment. Then he went on.

"Now, King Henry was a man with a sore conscience over the slaying of Thomas Becket, the archbishop of Canterbury, and with that guilty heart, fear of hellfire and the censure of Rome, he tended to think in more magnanimous terms than he might have. So the ripping up of the land was lessened, and even some previous landholders were allowed to keep a small part of what they'd once owned outright."

"Some of them being the Crofts."

"'Tis so. From then, we have documentation, and it's out of the realm of legend and into history. Our luck held on through the years and through the fortunes and misfortunes of kings and others. We sometimes had less than an acre. A scrap of land. But we had it!"

"And held it." She felt a quickening within. This man's past went further back than she could even imagine. His life, his family was traceable by a thousand years of lives! And her family had less than three hundred to its name.

"Now one thing you must already know about us," he said, going back to the bar and drawing out a third drink. "Irish men are happy as larks to die for Ireland. We seek it out with glee. The women tend to be smarter. They have children for Her."

"And so the land kept passing down through the mother's family?"

"You are right." He grinned approval and sat back down. "Sure you won't join me in a glass?"

"No, Liam. You're drinking for both of us today."

"Liam, lad." A man knocked on the dining-room doorway and entered. He was a good twenty years older than Liam, tall and thin with the same pale skin and black hair. But there the resemblance ended. He had none of the vitality Liam radiated. Life appeared to have drained him. He gave Paula a nod of his head. "There's a trunk call for ye, Liam," he said. "Overseas it is."

Liam stood. "Uncle Johnny Croft," he said to Paula, introducing the man. "Miss Dixon, Johnny. Did they say who was on the line?"

"I have no idea. Just that it's from America."

"Tottie." Paula got up. "It's about Tottie," she said, fear filling her.

"Come on."

Liam led her out of the dining room, along a dark hallway and into a den that also served as an office. The walls were paneled in gleaming wood, the drapes at the long windows were heavy and deep green, the chairs and one couch covered in oxblood leather and the desk . . .

The desk was one she would have killed for. A huge oak thing with files and drawers and plenty of space to spread work out. To the left was a long table with a computer and printer, fax and complex telephone setup.

It did not look like the office of a mere innkeeper or even the scion of an ancient family of limited means. This office belonged to a businessman of great stature and greater responsibilities. Liam sat in the chair, picked up the receiver and spoke.

Paula also took a chair. Her leg muscles were too weak to continue standing. When Liam looked up and smiled at her, relief poured in, adding to the sense of weakness. He covered the receiver for a second.

"Tottie's well. She's out of intensive care," he whispered. "They say she's going to be all right."

Paula closed her eyes and said a prayer of gratitude.

She didn't hear the rest of the conversation clearly. Liam was telling someone about the events of the day, and she preferred to block that out. She was tired, finally. Very tired. Too much all at once.

She must have dozed off, because the next thing she knew, a small hand was on her shoulder, shaking her awake. She struggled to open her eyes. When she saw who was shaking her, she smiled.

The child, not more than four or five years of age, was a duplicate of the sister she'd met earlier. Annie... something. Little snub nose, springy red hair, bright blue eyes.

"Mum says ye're to come upstairs with me," the girl said. "Mum says ye're a right mess and need some clothes." Her expression was solemn, as if Paula's condition were an indication of a major illness.

Paula laughed. "Mum's right. Take me to her." She looked around.

The office was empty. A light blanket covered her where she had slept in the chair. The drapes were drawn.

Liam had gone, thoughtfully leaving her alone to nap. Once again, she was struck by the combination of understated elegance and modern efficiency in the room. This was Liam's office? Well, Liam might deny he was a lord or aristocrat, but he was certainly a member of an elite group. The room bespoke power, pure and simple. Controlled, not raw, but power, nonetheless. Why had no one she contacted when checking on him informed her of that fact? Was he so well hidden within his family that no one in authority knew? Possible. If he held no official title or position, no "paper trail" would exist to show his strange status.

How unusual in this day and age!

How... fascinating.

"Mum's this way," the child said, tugging at Paula's hand. "This way. Don't be falling back asleep, Miss."

"Okay. I promise I won't." Paula got up and followed her out of the office. "What's your name, honey?" she asked.

"Bridget," the small one replied. "Not 'honey.' That would be a silly name. Hurry on now. Mum's waiting upstairs."

Stifling the urge to smile at her guide's brisk manner, Paula followed little Bridget up one flight of stairs and then another, down a hallway, around a corner, up another flight, another hall and finally up one more staircase into a low-ceilinged room that seemed to stretch on for a mile in either direction. "This is the attic," Bridget announced. "Where clothes and such are kept."

"I see," Paula said. She'd seen something like this once before when visiting a college friend in Charleston. The friend lived in a Southern mansion, complete with servants' quarters and too many rooms to bother counting. Among them was an attic like this where off-season and unused clothing was stored. Also toys, jewelry, scrapbooks, records and all the assorted junk any large family accumulates over the years and generations.

This attic, however, was bigger than her friend's. Obviously, the Crofts had time to do some serious accumulating.

"There ye are," Annie Purchase called out from farther down the room. "Miss Dixon, please come here. Liam told me to see ye outfitted properly."

"Call me Paula, please."

"She was asleep," Bridget announced. "I found her where Uncle told me she'd be."

"Oh, my." Annie put one hand to her cheek. "I hope Bridget didn't wake ye. I told her to fetch ye only if ye wanted to come. I know ye must be exhausted."

Paula smiled and touched the child's head. "I'm fine," she said. "I've done a lot of sleeping lately. I don't need to do more right now."

Bridget, sensing that Paula was covering for her, smiled up at her. "Want to try the dresses?" she asked.

"Liam insisted we give ye these," Annie said, indicating a rolling dress rack where a number of garments hung. "He said you'd had to leave everything of your own behind."

"I did." Paula went over to the rack. "Oh," she said. Many of the clothes were designer-made. Elegant and classic. Others were more ordinary, casual clothing made of rugged materials and clearly meant for rough wearing. Everything she could possibly need for any occasion. There was even a small hamper with underwear, panty hose and socks. Shoes were lined up along the wall.

"This is wonderful!" She turned to Annie. "And it all seems to be in my size. Where in the world did it come from?"

Annie waved a hand. "Here," she said. "Save for the undies and stockings, which Liam sent out for, it all came from storage. We've a number of young lasses in the household who were once as finely made as you." She glanced at Bridget. "Children tend to make such small sizes a thing of the past for most of us, you understand."

Paula regarded Annie's sturdy build and wondered if she had ever been petite. The woman glowed with strength, health and a kind of beauty that was not dependent on anything outside herself. "I've never been lucky enough to be married and have children," she said. "So I've stayed about the same size since I turned eighteen."

"Well." Annie put her hands on her broad hips and smiled. "A woman should have children, if she can. Even if it makes her wider here and there. Perhaps your luck'll be changing one of these fine days."

"Perhaps." Paula felt that damn blush start again. What was it about the Irish? She seemed to be blushing all the time when in their presence. Was it really them, or was she just releasing emotions long buried?

It didn't take long to select a small wardrobe from the bounty before her. Paula was then directed to a guest room downstairs where Annie and Bridget left her alone to bathe and change. Although she wasn't hungry yet, she had been informed that she was expected at the family dinner tonight.

And for Liam's sake, she knew she needed to put in an appearance. A proper one, at that. This household was like a small village, and the slightest excuse would be grist for the gossip mill. Better to let everyone see her immediately than to let them speculate about her while she hid. And better to let them see her looking good so she'd make a good impression.

She cleaned up and changed, putting on a tailored white blouse, a brown gaberdine calf-length skirt and a pair of pumps. Green silk scarf. A modest but dignified outfit she thought would fit the occasion. A little gold jewelry at the ears and throat. Then she used some of the new makeup she'd found set out on the dresser. These folks thought of everything! Hair finally in place in a relatively tidy style, she left the guest room and went to look for Liam.

Finding him in the maze of hallways and rooms was not easy. Finally, she made her way to the office and saw that a light burned inside.

But on entering, she did not find Liam hard at work on business matters.

She found his mother.

Morgan Croft looked up from her computer and smiled at her. "Good evening, Miss Dixon. Come in. I'm just going over some accounts before dinner. Increases the appetite, thinking about money."

"I'm sorry to bother you," Paula said. "I was looking for Liam."

"I thought that." Morgan indicated she take a seat. "He's asleep upstairs. Fair exhausted he was, so I ordered him to indulge in a nap before he has to trot ye out in front of all the clan."

Paula felt the blush rising again. "I don't want to be any trouble to him," she said.

Morgan regarded her. "Perhaps ye don't. But ye are, ye know."

"I'm beginning to figure that out."

"Tell me, Miss Dixon—"

"Paula."

"Tell me, Paula, when ye met, how was it between ye? I mean, he had gone to your land on important family business, so how did he come to be involved with ye?"

"He hasn't told you?"

"Why, no." Morgan folded her hands together. "Liam's not one to explain a thing. He was raised to be a king, I'm afraid. And he rather acts like it from time to time. Even to his own mother."

"I thought he said he was elected clan leader."

"It's an election when the clan changes leadership," Morgan said. "And once the lad decided against the Church as a profession, he was the clan's obvious choice." Pride that her son had been chosen leader shone on her face. "He's a king, no mistake about it. But one who seems ready to sacrifice for the kingdom at a moment's notice. That's why I'm so curious how ye were able to take him off track."

Paula hesitated. She had no idea how much of her troubles he'd told his people. No idea how much would be wise to tell. "I found Liam injured," she said. "Because of my position as a prosecuting officer of the court, I was duty-bound to help find whoever had harmed him."

"That would be Tobias?"

"Yes. They'd had a falling-out and Liam was shot."

Morgan blinked, surprised. "The old one *shot* him?"

"It was an accident. But it all landed in my jurisdictional lap, so to speak." Paula got up and began to pace the room. "Liam... Liam was difficult. Wouldn't tell us a thing. Trying to protect Tobias, he made

himself look very suspicious. But I checked him out
with Interpol and found nothing in his background to
indicate criminal activity, so I chose to believe in the
man, if not in his story."

Morgan nodded. "Believe in the man. Never believe a word any of them says, though. Irishmen have
words down to an art from the moment they enter the
world. Don't forget that it was here the word *blarney*
originated."

Paula had to smile at that. "I'm learning."

"'Twas an Irishman diplomat, Cormac Mac-
Dermot MacCarthy, used the sweet speech on Eliza the
First of England," Morgan explained. "Drove her fair
crazy with his 'saying without saying.' His family
owned Blarney Castle. But the stone and the gift itself likely go back to Druidic days."

"I'd like to see it, sometime."

Morgan shut off the computer and stood up. "I like
ye, Paula. I see why Liam's drawn to ye. Ye've the
kind of strength he's been searching for in a woman all
these years."

She gave Paula another approving smile. Then, a
strange thing happened. Her blue eyes turned chilly.
Hard as diamonds.

"But I also know ye're not telling me all the truth.
And if my son is in danger because of ye, ye'll have me
to answer to if he's harmed."

"I don't tell you everything so that no one else is put
in harm's way," Paula replied. "Liam's already involved, and there's nothing either of us can do about
it."

"Perhaps not." Morgan came around the desk.
"But I want ye to know where ye stand with me. *I* was
the clan, not my husband. I kept my name, and he

took mine. I trained as a policewoman before I married. I was clan leader before Liam, and I've made me share of hard decisions in me life."

Paula waited, fascinated.

"Ye understand my loyalties are to the family first, my son second and anyone else third. Should ye endanger him, ye will most certainly be in danger from me."

Paula stared. She'd met hostility in the mothers of some boyfriends before, but this was the first one to speak so plainly.

And the really weird thing was, she understood it completely. More than understood she approved of this kind of maternal passion! This depth of feeling. "If I had a son, I'd feel the same," she replied. "Now, you must understand that hurting him is the last thing I want. But I cannot control him. If he chooses, he'll go to hell and back, and you know it much better than I do."

Morgan nodded. "Ye're the right one," she said. "Liam's instincts are correct." She relaxed and the lines of her face faded into softness. She held out her hand. "Come, m'dear. Let's go meet the family. Not all will be at dinner tonight, but enough. Enough."

Still mystified by her response to all this strangeness, Paula took Morgan Croft's hand, and they went out of the room. They did not go to the dining room where she and Liam had eaten earlier. Morgan guided her through another series of halls and stairs until they reached a much older part of the complex. Along the way, she explained about the estate buildings.

"Liam told you a bit of our history, did he not?"

"Yes. Very... unusual, I think."

"Aye, 'tis. We held the land and built, but until the second part of this century, we did not expand. 'Twould have been unwise to draw attention to ourselves in the past. And now it seems it is still unwise."

Before Paula could inquire about that comment, Morgan went on.

"This section, however, is left from the fifteenth century," she said. "See how dark the wood is. Stained black with wood and peat smoke, and we've left it so. Reminds us of the past."

"Sure does." Paula felt she was moving back in time, herself. Kings, princes, threats from mothers regarding the well-being of their sons . . .

She was a long way from Carleton Cay. A very long way, indeed!

They turned a corner around a stone column and entered the Middle Ages.

They were in a great hall. The main dining table stretched for half a mile, it seemed. And a gigantic fireplace held the biggest fire Paula had ever seen indoors. Outside, it would be a bonfire of some note. The ceiling stretched upward into darkness, and the light fixtures were designed to look like torches. Woven hangings covered the stone walls. The room smelled of smoke and food and fresh bread.

Paula was conscious of a large number of people. Forty, fifty? She wasn't sure, and she didn't care to stop and count. They were one and all staring at her as she and Morgan made their way up to the head table that sat at a T-cross to the main one. Three big chairs were pulled up to that table. Liam sat on the center one.

The king was on his throne. A huge chair made of oak and padded with dark red velvet. Paula knew little about antiques, but she was willing to bet the chair was older than the room. Liam stood, letting her come to him. He looked magnificent in a gray tweed suit, snowy white shirt and dark tie. His hair had been cut and his face shaved close so that the usual shadow of whiskers was gone. She was very glad she'd chosen to dress up as she had. Anything less, anything more would have been wrong.

He took her hand, kissed her cheek in a formal manner and showed her to the chair on his left. His mother received a similar kiss and was given the chair to his right.

The king and the queen mother.

And what was she? Paula felt as if she were in some sort of strange dream. From the long table below, dozens of pairs of eyes regarded and dissected her, inch by inch. She didn't feel hostility from them, however.

Just intense curiosity.

Liam remained standing. He said nothing. Just waited until the young people serving had finished distributing tankards of ale to everyone.

He waited. The silence was thick as smoke.

Then, he raised his own tankard and shouted, "The Croft!"

Chairs scraped back, people stood and voices responded, deep and high, young and old, "The Croft!" The sound was almost a roar.

Paula sat still, uncertain what to do. Morgan hadn't stood up, either. Liam's mother gazed serenely down on the crowd of family, a queen surveying the nation she had once ruled and that was now ruled by her son. A woman of accomplishment, strong and successful.

A faint smile turned up the corners of her mouth, but otherwise she was the picture of dignity.

Paula wished she could imitate her, but she knew her face was displaying her emotions. She was confused and suddenly very frightened. She wished she could understand all this.

Liam turned to his mother, raised his tankard...

But didn't toast. Instead, he turned around to Paula and said, "To the women, to the life of the Croft!"

"The life of the Croft!" shouted the throng. The yell echoed off the vast ceiling and around the hall. "The life! Life...life...life."

And Paula knew she was in way, way over her head!

CHAPTER TWELVE

ALL THROUGH the feast—it was much more than just dinner—Paula picked at her food, her appetite nonexistent.

No one else was having a similar problem, however. The crowd below was having a fine old time from what she could see. The merrymaking never got out of hand, but it was extensive. People laughed and joked and shouted at one another. Occasionally, a comment would wing Liam's way and he would respond with apparent pleasure and cheerfulness, but much of it was in Gaelic, and any English was spoken with such a heavy brogue, Paula couldn't understand a single word.

It wasn't until after dessert and coffee had been served that he leaned toward her, fixing her with his gaze and smiling.

"Bit much for you?" he asked.

"Sort of."

"Please. Just trust me."

"I don't know that I do. Or if I ever did."

He grinned, showing white teeth. "But you're here, aren't you? That's what matters."

Paula had no reply to that.

Liam turned back to speak to his mother. They conversed in tones too low for her to hear. Paula considered what Liam had said.

She *was* here. And, it seemed, she was going to be here for a while.

In a very real sense, Liam's prisoner.

Just as he had been hers not so very long ago. She was dwelling on the irony of that when he stood up and banged his fist on the table for attention and silence.

The throng quieted.

"Brothers and sisters," Liam began, "I'm reporting to you tonight about my failure to complete the mission you sent me on two months ago."

There was no buzz of comment from the audience. They were rapt, concentrating on Liam's words.

As was Paula. With the gold glow of firelight and artificial torchlight on him, standing tall at the table as he was, even in modern dress, Liam Croft did look every bit a king. She wondered how she missed it before. He had a kind of bearing and dignity that he had hidden completely during the time he was in America. He'd behaved charmingly, bravely, foolishly, but never like this. Never had he seemed a man of true power, one who ruled and commanded respect to this degree.

Liam went on. "I failed," he repeated. "But the task is far from over. Tobias Croft is in good health and in excellent care for the time being. I will, when the time is right, return and complete my mission."

She waited for at least a rumble of objection.

No one said a thing.

Did no one dare impugn this "King's" authority?

"Meanwhile," he said after a moment, "I have brought with me this woman, Paula Dixon. She is our guest, to be made welcome and cared for as one of our own. She..." He hesitated, glancing over at her, and...

And Paula saw his heart in his eyes. The strangeness, the majesty fell away like an old cloak. This was still Liam! Brave, resourceful, unpredictable Liam.

"And I hope she will learn to like it here among us," he finished.

He sat. Morgan stood. She raised her wineglass. "To Paula Dixon," she said loudly.

And they all saluted Paula with wine and cheers.

After that, the festivities took off in earnest. Some of the younger children were herded out by their mothers, tomorrow being a school day, she was informed. But most of the people, young and old, stayed. Someone produced a fiddle, another a drum and a third came up with a small whistle, and music filled the hall.

Dancing began. Liam leaned over and explained the style was "set" dancing. "'Tis very ancient," he said, raising his voice to be heard over the noise.

"It looks like fun."

"It is." He reached for her hand. "Let me show you just how much."

HOURS LATER, Paula lay back exhausted on the bed in the guest room. They had danced and sang until midnight, and she had enjoyed every minute of it. She had met so many Crofts, she couldn't remember all the faces, much less the names. But she found them a hospitable, cheerful group, intent on caring for one another and now, for her, as Liam's special guest.

More important, she had enjoyed Liam. All the strangeness and alien behavior had disappeared. Once off the head table, he was just one of the group, set on having a wonderful time.

She'd had no problem at all feeling part of things.

This required some serious thought, she decided.

Before he'd left her to go to his own room, Liam had asked her what she'd thought of the night. Paula had been honest.

"I found it really weird," she said, looking directly at him. "Until we started dancing and singing, I felt like you were a total stranger. Someone I'd never met before."

One black eyebrow rose.

She tried to explain. "You had a...manner I haven't seen before," she said. "It was...alien to me."

"I think I understand."

"I don't."

"Paula, when you go into court to prosecute someone in the name of the state, do you act as you do in everyday life?"

"No, of course not."

"You put on a persona, don't you? The prosecutor."

"It's part of my job," she replied, beginning to catch his drift.

"Clan leadership's part of *my* job," he said. "All that tradition and ritual *is* the job. The role goes back so far in time, much of the reason for things is lost. We just have to take on faith that a clan leader is to behave a certain way for the benefit of the clan. Not for himself, understand." He reached out and touched her cheek with his fingertips. "I know it must be a lot to take in at once," he said. "And I expect my mum probably gave you the dickens about me, too, didn't she?"

"We talked."

"I imagine you did." He leaned down and kissed her gently. "Go to sleep now, Paula Dixon. We have time to get used to each other, now. And for the others to get used to us." Another kiss, light enough to pass as a friendly caress, warm enough to stir her blood. "Good night, darlin'."

"Good night," she said.

And he was gone.

That had been a while ago. Now she tried to sleep, but found it elusive. She looked at the clock on the bedside table. Two in the morning. Seven o'clock at night at home. Was she still on South Carolina time?

Or was she just too overloaded mentally to rest?

She was hungry, in any event. Picking at dinner had done nothing to fill her up, and the dancing had burned up a lot of calories. Maybe the main kitchen would have ingredients she could put together for a snack. That sounded so good, she decided to take the chance. She got up, dragged on a pair of slacks and a sweater, found shoes and went out of the room.

The halls were silent and lighted only here and there by small lamps set on narrow tables, but she wasn't nervous. The aroma of the fireplace and the festivities still lingered in the air, and smelling that, she couldn't be afraid.

She found the kitchen without any difficulty. It was almost as big as the great hall and located just beyond that room. At the end of it, a wide cooking hearth contained a fire that burned embers. Someone sat on a rocking chair in front of the fire.

Morgan Croft.

"Could ye not sleep?" the older woman asked, not turning around to see who it was. Just knowing.

"No," Paula said. "And I'm hungry."

"Fruit and cheese out on the counter there. Some bread, as well." Paula found a plate and piled it high.

She then went to the hearth and took a seat on the warm tiles. "How come you're still up, too?" she asked.

Morgan smiled. "I'm getting old. Old women don't sleep."

"Um." Paula bit into a pear, savoring the sweetness. "You are not exactly ancient, Mrs. Croft. And I usually don't have any trouble," she said. "I think I'm still on South Carolina time."

"Ye looked Irish tonight," Morgan said.

"But I'm not."

"Your ancestors . . . ?"

Paula shrugged. "English, I think. My family's been in the States for almost three hundred years. They don't bother going back much further than that in our part of the country. Embarrassing details might turn up that a prominent family would rather not know. So, we Dixons and the other side, the Morrises, claim to be English."

Morgan chuckled. "Ye're a Celt, child. No matter what your people say. Ye moved and smiled and glowed tonight like a Celtic princess. The blood will not be denied."

Paula said nothing.

"He wants to wed ye, ye know," Morgan said. "To place ye by his left side at table like that tells the clan that's what he wants to do."

"I . . . see."

"Do ye? Do ye understand what it meant?"

"Maybe. Maybe not. I guess not."

"He put ye to his left. His heart side. Did ye not wonder why, with a roomful of curious Irish who love to gossip and argue more than to breathe, no one, not one soul questioned you?"

"I—"

"Ye share his power. His authority. They would never question ye, now."

Paula set down her plate. "Where is he?"

Morgan did not answer.

"Mrs. Croft, where's Liam tonight?"

Nothing. Just a look from eyes as wise as time.

Paula swore softly. "He went back to the flat, didn't he? He went to wait for whoever's after me."

Morgan regarded her. "He did. Now, what will ye do?"

Paula stared back steadily. "Go to him."

And Morgan Croft nodded. Approvingly. "'Tis chilly out this night," she said. "Take the sweater and the mackintosh over by the doorway. It'll keep the damp from ye."

SHE DROVE Liam's car. At that time of night, the streets were virtually empty, so the right-hand system didn't throw her too much. It was only a short distance to the flat, and she pulled up and parked less than fifteen minutes after receiving the keys and whispered instructions from Morgan.

The older woman's motives confused her. At home, in the South, for a potential mother-in-law to be so blunt with a son's girlfriend would be unheard of. Much less for the mother to put the girlfriend at risk by encouraging her to venture out in a strange city in the middle of the night to be with her...

Her lover.

Paula shut the car door as quietly as she could. She had a key and knew how to dismantle the alarm. She'd go in and stay on the sofa in the front room until morning when Liam woke. Then, she'd get him to talk to her. *Make* him talk.

She went up the walk, opened the gate and readied the key.

She screamed in terror as an iron arm went around her neck and a huge hand clamped over her mouth. She was dragged, kicking and fighting silently but ferociously to the side of the building and then into a doorway in the back. She scored at least one blow on her captor's shin. He grunted in pain and anger, and his grip on her tightened to the point of real pain. Dizzy, almost blacking out, she went limp for a moment. The man holding her took that opportunity to open a door and thrust her into a dark room.

Paula hit the far wall hard and fell to the cold floor, swearing at her assailant with what little breath she had left. When she called him a rotten, carpetbagging skunk-son-of-a-bitch, she got his attention.

"Paula?" he said. "Paula, that can't be you!"

"Liam?" She sat up. Pure darkness surrounded her. "Liam Croft, if that's you, I swear, I'll—"

"How the bloody hell did you get here?"

"Your mother sent me!"

"Shh. Mum? Why would she do that? She knows I'm—"

"What? Staking this place out? Waiting for trouble?"

"Ah. You're upset." Hands reached for her.

She batted them away. "Damn right I'm upset," she said. "It's my trouble that's the problem, so I should be involved. I come here, looking for you, and what happens? I get mugged!"

"I thought you were someone else. Paula, I'm sorry. I couldn't tell it was you, all buried as you are in that sweater and coat. You're lean enough that I thought you might be a young man with those trousers on. I am a bloody idiot.''

She felt a sob rising in her throat. "You hurt me. Scared me.''

''Ah, I'm sorry. Darlin', come here.'' He reached again, and this time, she didn't resist. She went to him. In the darkness, his arms felt even stronger than usual.

''What else did Alex say to you this afternoon?'' she asked, her voice muffled against his chest. ''What made you decide to come here tonight?''

''Nothing.''

''Tell me!'' She tried to pull away, but couldn't. ''Liam, tell me!''

He released her. ''Let's go inside,'' he said, his tone flat and dull. ''I forget you aren't one to be babied or protected.'' He helped her to her feet. ''I'll tell you everything,'' he added, an odd new note in that voice. ''You deserve it. I was wrong to keep still tonight.''

A few minutes later, they were seated at the kitchen table.

Liam looked drawn and tired. He'd been so full of energy earlier that night, but now he looked drained. His pallor was pronounced, and the smudged blackness of his whiskers on cheek and jaw even darker than usual.

She reached over and covered his hands with hers. ''Okay, out with it,'' she said. ''This is me, as you said, not some fragile princess you have to protect.''

He looked a little surprised at her words, but he smiled. ''True. It is a fact I keep forgetting.''

''What's going on at home?''

Liam sighed and pulled away from her touch. ''A good deal, I'm afraid. Sheriff Reynolds is getting better. Well on the road to recovery. That's all that's positive."

"Well, that is terrific news. What about Sears?"

"Still likes his role as outside investigator, according to Alex." Liam stood up and started to walk around. "He's now working on a conspiracy theory. One that involves you, me and Father Sheridan."

"What? Have they found Father Sheridan? Talked to him?"

"Yes, they have."

"Well?"

"He won't say a word. Says he had heard a confession that disturbs him and may have bearing on your case, but he claims clerical rights and refuses to divulge a breath of it."

"What's Sears's problem with that? It's an ancient rite of priests to keep silent about confession."

"Sears is sure it's you told him something."

"Me? I'm a lousy Catholic, Liam. I can't remember when I did my last confession."

"Um." Liam looked slightly disapproving.

"It's the truth. You might not like it, but it's the way I am."

He went on. "And now, Sears also believes your boss and secretary, though why, I cannot for the life of me figure out. They insist the stalkings are all in your imagination, if not of your own doing."

Paula considered that. "Charlie can be convincing. That's why he's a good prosecutor. He's persuasive. But why?" She spread out her hands, palms up and open. "Why would I pretend someone is after me? Why would I set a bomb in my own office? What's my motive, for goodness sake?"

"Political."

"What?"

"It's Sears's notion that you're doing all this to draw political attention to yourself. You yourself have never been hurt, except when that scoundrel Gradon hit you. Alex says that the man believes you to be an ambitious, conniving woman from a powerful old family. That your goal is to beat Charlie in the next election, take over the office and go on from there."

"That's just nuts!"

"Nevertheless . . ."

"I hate politics. I like the job, but not the campaigning. If I didn't like prosecuting so much, I'd head into private practice. And I'd make a heck of a lot more money. Has Sears considered that?"

"I am only reporting what your friend told me."

She tapped her fingers on the table. "I've got to go back. Defend myself. I have to—"

"No! That's why I didn't tell you any of this before. If you go back, you play right into the hands of your enemy. If I were after you, I'd start the same kind of whisper campaign against you. It is designed to draw you out. Make you return home. Can't you see that?"

"But...this morning...the disabled alarm... Isn't it possible . . ."

"That someone's already here? Yes. That's why I'm staying in the flat."

"Liam, you can't take on my battle. Not without me!"

He regarded her, his gaze intense. "Nothing would please me more than to have you with me. And you know it. Is that really why you came here tonight?"

She sat still. "Maybe it is. I'm very confused."

"I'm not. If I had doubts, the sight of you dancing with my people this evening took them all away."

"I...I can't be—"

"Don't say the word." He leaned over and touched her lips with his fingertip. "Give us time."

"I'm in love with you," she said. "And it scares me to death."

His smile was tender. "Worse than the bomb threat?"

"Much worse." She started to shake. The tremors made her teeth chatter.

"Come to me, then," he said, holding out his hand. "I'll take your fears from you."

Slowly, she rose from her chair. In two steps, she was in his arms. And two seconds later, she was no longer afraid.

He carried her from the kitchen, down the short hallway and into the bedroom. He shut the door with a kick, leaving them in relative darkness. The only light in the room was from the street lamps outside, shining through the lace curtain.

He laid her down on the bed. "Last chance to run, Paula Dixon," he whispered. "Say the word, and I'll take you back to the compound."

"I'll stay." She reached up for him. "I'm tired of running, Liam Croft."

His chuckle was warm. And triumphant.

For a while, he lay with her, just kissing and touching. Doing nothing beyond slowly arousing her senses with his hands and voice and mouth. Paula explored his lips, his face, hands and hair, delighting in the smell and texture of him—smoke and spice and maleness. His hair was thick and soft, meant to be caressed with her fingers. His whiskers were rough against her skin, but pleasantly so. The abrasion made her nerves tingle with excitement. But it was his voice that seduced her completely. Full of dark mystery and husky, passionate promise, his voice was the sound of a lover who was completely devoted to her pleasure. He whispered, murmured and spoke aloud, praising her beauty in at least two languages that she could tell. He made love to her with words before he ever reached beneath her clothing.

Then, his hand slid up under her sweater. He found only bare skin. Paula sighed with pleasure and lifted her body to his touch.

"Ah, lovely," he murmured, his mouth against her throat. "Please tell me you planned to come to me when you didn't dress this night."

"I . . . just didn't bother with underwear," she said breathlessly.

He slipped her sweater off, and stripped off his own.

And he began to make love to her.

Paula was not a stranger to love, but this was like nothing she'd experienced before. Liam loved her with far more than his fine, strong body. He kissed and worshiped every inch of her, driving her crazy with desire with the gentleness of his caresses. His method was as madly teasing as it was deeply passionate. When they were both finally naked and he filled her with himself, slowly, maddeningly slow, he drove into her again and again, bringing her unbelievable ecstasy as wave after wave of sensation took her body beyond anything she had known possible.

Took her body and took her heart. When he cried out, "Do you love me, Paula?" she answered, "Yes!"

And then he said, "Marry me. Will you have my children?"

And she answered yes again.

And then he let himself go. Right then, Paula knew whatever happened, she could not go home again.

MUCH LATER, pale dawn began to tint the small bedroom with blue-gray light. Paula lay quietly by her sleeping lover. He had exhausted himself, giving pleasure to her. She had never dreamed her body was capable of so much sensation.

He really loved her.

She felt the same about him.

Now, she'd have to deal with the reality of a promise made in the heat of passion. To marry and have children.

She rolled over and looked at him. Lord, he was a beautiful man! Sleep eased the tension on his face, giving him a younger, boyish look. But the body, muscular and patterned with silky black hair, was fully male. Yes, indeed. Very male.

And he wasn't likely to let go of what he wanted. Was that a problem? Only if she wanted out. Right now, that was the furthest thing from her heart. She wanted to stay. To stay and be queen by his side. The prospect was romantic and mystical and exotic.

And very likely a trap. She knew herself well enough to know she would never be willing to be just a fixture in a man's life, no matter how much she might care for him. She had to have her own path, as well.

If she did stay here, what would her life be like?

Maybe the question was, what did she want to do? He sighed, stirred and opened his eyes.

She *wanted* to be with Liam. Paula reached for him. But he took hold of her wrists. *Don't move,* his lips said. *Someone's in the kitchen.*

CHAPTER THIRTEEN

PAULA FROZE. She heard nothing, but she didn't doubt Liam's keen senses. Silent as a shadow, he slipped from under the sheet and pulled on his pants. She started to get up, but he signaled her to stay put with a warning gesture of his hand.

Then he reached under the bed and took out a shotgun.

Before she could recover from the shock of seeing him, weapon in hand, he went to the door. Paula watched him check the gun with a familiarity that bespoke skill and practice. He knew the thing well, she realized. Liam held it as though it were second nature.

He opened the door without making a sound and moved into the hallway, closing the door behind him. Paula hardly dared breathe.

But she couldn't just sit and wait. She eased out of the bed and stepped silently into her clothes. Dressed, she hunted for some kind of weapon for herself. The light in the room was dim, but she could see well enough. Over by the door was a cane like the one Tobias had used. Paula picked it up.

It had a good, sturdy heft, like a baseball bat. She gripped it, stood by the door.

And waited.

A few seconds later, all hell broke loose. She heard Liam shout, then a deep-voiced yell, and a higher-voiced scream, the noise of breaking glass and dishes . . .

But no boom of the shotgun. She opened the door and stepped into the hall. It was much darker there, and she could barely see a thing, until a shape came running toward her, yelling like a steam whistle. It reached out with talonlike hands to grab her.

So she swung the cane at it. The head of the weapon drove into the figure's midsection, and it made a swooshing sound, like air going out of a tire. Then it went down for the count. Dead out on the floor. From the front room, Liam yelled, and more glass and crockery broke.

Paula hunched down, cane ready. The noise from the fight in the front room rose in volume, then suddenly silence fell. She began to shiver. The figure at her feet groaned, but didn't stir.

The lights went on.

"I told you to stay put!" Liam loomed in the hallway. Blood ran down his face from a cut just over his left eye. He looked at the body on the floor. "But bloody damned good work, anyway," he said. He grinned. "You're a fighter, Paula Dixon, as well as a grand and glorious lover."

She stood, knees trembling. "Who are they?" she asked.

"I don't know," he said, moving toward her. "Yet." He gave her a quick hug. "Are you all right? Really?"

Paula nodded. "He never touched me."

He reached down and turned the body over. A youthful face, eyes closed. A boy of not more than fourteen years. Paula made a sound of deep regret.

"Don't be feeling for this one," Liam cautioned, toeing the boy with his bare foot. "He and his mate were setting up a right nasty surprise for us in the kitchen."

"His...mate?"

"The other kid." He indicated the front room. "Bit huskier than this'n." He touched his forehead. "Near laid me out before I took him. Damn, but I'm getting sorely weary of being hit on the head."

"Call the police," she said, beginning to shake all over.

"In a while." Liam bent down and lifted the boy by his trouser belt. "First, I want some answers to some questions." He hauled the limp form into the front room, the muscles in his back and shoulders scarcely straining with the effort.

Paula followed. "You can't question them yourself," she said. "It's illegal. It's wrong."

"Aye. 'Tis." He tossed the boy onto the sofa. Another, larger youth lay sprawled out on the carpet. "So if you don't wish to be involved, just go back to bed," he added.

"No." She crossed her arms. "I'll stay."

"Look in the kitchen, then," he said, turning on the overhead light. "In the oven, if you will. Then tell me how much sympathy you have for these lads."

Paula hesitated, then went over to the kitchen alcove. The oven door was open. Inside was a strange-looking device that she couldn't identify at first. Then, it hit her.

"Another bomb," she said, fear gripping her insides and turning her heart to ice. "It looks homemade, but it's big enough to be lethal."

"Indeed. And we would not be the only ones blown to glory. That's plastique, love. If you lit the oven, the entire block would go. Every man, woman and child."

Nausea rose in her throat. She choked it down and turned back to him. "Do what you have to," she said, all pity for the young men gone. "This is war."

It didn't take long. Nor did Liam have to get overly unpleasant. Amazingly, once the two returned to full consciousness, just his baleful, bloodied, half-naked presence and apparent willingness to inflict bodily harm was enough to intimidate them into confessing. In an argot Paula barely understood, they spilled it all.

They'd been hired to do the job.

But they didn't know who had done the hiring nor who was paying the money.

"It were delivered by the post," the older one whined. He was a brawny, red-haired boy with heavy features and a thick body, muscled beyond his years. Paula was thankful it had not been him who had run at her in the hall. She doubted if her baseball swing would have sufficed to bring that one down.

It had done well enough on the smaller teen, however. He spent most of the interrogation huddled into a ball, clutching his middle and moaning. She would have felt sorry for him if his sharp, feral features hadn't also been twisted with hate every time he looked at her.

"And what did the post tell you?" Liam asked, handling the shotgun as if he was ready to use it at any moment.

The youth stared. "I got no—"

"Was there a mark to indicate where the stuff came from?"

"I didn't look at the box. Just at the money."

"I hope you saved the box."

"Nah, we—"

"It was local." The thin boy spoke up. He sounded more than eager to discuss the matter. "A local post."

"Shut it," the bigger boy snarled to the smaller. "I don't have no bloody truck with squealers."

Liam cocked the shotgun with a crashing sound. "Squeal away," he suggested.

The boy did. But when he was done, Liam and Paula were not much the wiser. The hiring and money had been done by mail from a Dublin drop, but that meant nothing. Anyone could have sent the goods from anywhere in the world and ordered them reposted from a neighborhood box.

"Phone," Liam said to Paula, his manner and demeanor back to normal. "Now, we call the garda." And he gave her the superintendent's home number.

"WELL, I'll give you this was no false alarm, Liam," Superintendent Creedon said. "That's as vile a piece of bombing work as I've seen in a while." They were still in the flat, but hours had passed, and the bomb squad had removed all traces of the explosive device. Before they appeared, Liam had also hidden all traces of the shotgun, and the young thugs' claims that they had been threatened with such a weapon went unheeded by the police.

Paula was impressed, though uneasy about Liam's obvious familiarity with the gun and his apparent willingness to use violence if necessary. He'd looked like a soldier, or even a criminal, himself. That role, like the one of king of the clan, was over for the moment. Now, he looked like an innocent, helpless, wounded citizen who had defended his territory against the intruders with only his fists and a cane.

"They're teaching the lads young these days," Liam agreed dolefully. "You say these two were into the drug trade?"

"Aye. Young they are, but not in experience." Creedon looked sorrowful and angry at the same time. "You two are lucky they didn't just burst in and knife you both or shoot you dead as you slept. I'm surprised, in fact. It's more true to their style."

Paula concealed another shudder.

Liam seemed unimpressed with the thought of bloody death. "I'm not surprised," he said conversationally. "They were under orders and paid to do it a certain way. *Ouch!*"

"Hold still," Paula said, dabbing at the cut on his head with an antiseptic solution. "This really ought to have some stitches, I think."

"Miss Dixon," Creedon said, "we aren't sure there's a connection, of course. But I've been in touch with the authorities in South Carolina regarding this and yourself. They are understandably quite upset."

Paula dabbed and patched. "I just bet they are," she said.

"Tell me, please," Creedon went on. "Am I missing something here? Did you not tell me everything when you were in my office?"

"No."

"Then, please." He spread out his hands. "Do so now."

Paula sighed. "From the start, then. With the threat here, you're entitled to know everything." Quickly, but leaving out no detail, she outlined what had been happening in her life before and since she found Liam Croft lying bleeding in the South Carolina ditch.

Liam added nothing.

Creedon considered what he'd heard. And then he dropped a verbal bomb. "Perhaps, Miss Dixon, you are now not the main target."

"What?" She stopped putting away the first-aid equipment she'd been using to patch up Liam. "Of course I am."

"Liam, tell me more about your mission to gather in the old man to the family hearth," Creedon said, addressing the Irishman.

Liam cleared his throat. "'Tis no secret. We need Tobias's signature on a document."

"What sort of document, lad?"

"For the land, y'know. The old land grant dictates that the eldest male in the clan sign the parchment once every fifty years, or..."

"Or what?" Paula asked. She'd heard reference to this often enough. Now she wanted details. "What happens if Tobias doesn't sign, Liam?"

He shifted in his chair, clearly uncomfortable with the topic. "It's debatable, love," he said. "According to our solicitor, nothing. We hold it by right of long-time occupancy. But by ancient tradition, without the twice-a-century signing, we'll forfeit the land. It'll be open to public bid. At best, the right of our holding it as a family trust could be challenged. At worst, someone could convince a judge to open the land for bids."

"Good Lord!" The implication of his words sank in. "That's a lot of valuable real estate, isn't it?"

"Aye."

"And it's a lot of motivation," Creedon declared.

"I suppose." Liam scowled and turned to Paula. "Would you mind fixing some tea, love?" he asked. "I need a cup, meself."

"Answer the man, Liam," she said, not moving from her chair. "Someone in your family could be—"

"No!" He slammed his hand down on the table. "No Croft would betray the clan. Not even—"

"Not even for great wealth and fortune?" Creedon sat back. "Come on, laddie. You know better."

Liam shook his head. "I'll not believe one of ours has done this."

"No family is perfect," Paula said. "Maybe you have a rotten apple in the bunch. A greedy—"

"You find him, then," Liam leaned over and glared at her. "I will not believe we have a traitor. So, if you do, Miss Prosecutor, you find him for me!"

"Easy, Liam," Creedon said. "She's only trying to help you."

"Then find the bloody bastard!" Liam roared at her. He stood up. "And when you do, you'd best take the information direct to Superintendent Creedon, here. For if I know of it first, I will give out clan justice."

"That'd be murder, Liam Croft," Creedon said calmly. "And you've better sense than that. Now, take some tea, several deep breaths and settle yourself. If we're to win this, we'd best think and act together. We are not your problem, lad."

Liam sat, but Paula sensed his fury was far from gone. She got up and started tea, moving automatically while she thought. Thought carefully. At the table, Liam and Creedon spoke softly.

This was big-time trouble. If there was a traitor in his family, she could just imagine what kind of justice would be delivered to the betrayer. She'd seen too many sides of Liam Croft to believe he would just gently pass the person on to the authorities. He was quite capable of killing one who turned against his own blood.

She had to find the traitor before Liam did. For Liam's sake.

And for her own.

LATE THAT AFTERNOON, she sat in the office with Morgan Croft, making plans. She and Liam had moved back into the compound. Staying in the flat was too dangerous. In fact, just about anywhere else was likely to be too dangerous.

Soon after they returned to the compound, Superintendent Creedon had held a meeting with Liam, Morgan and several of the other Crofts, regarding security and the safety of their clan leader and Paula. That was taken care of easily enough, though Paula knew her movements would be restricted to the immediate locale. No one but family would be allowed within the doors of the compound for the time being.

But there was more to consider. No one was convinced that the bombing of Paula's office back in Carleton Cay and the abortive bombing of the flat were connected, but no one was willing to take the chance they were not. The best suggestion came from Niall Croft, Liam's youngest brother.

"If it's the land the bastard's after, shouldn't Tobias be contacted and protected, as well?" the young man asked. "Seems logical he'd also be a target, if his signature is so necessary."

Everyone agreed with that.

Immediately, Paula had made a call to Tinsley and Alex and had been assured that not one unauthorized person would be allowed to set foot on the island until it was known that the culprits were in jail and everyone else was safe.

Then, Alex had made another suggestion. "Paula, while you're holed up in that clan complex, worrying about everyone but yourself, why don't you do some research on this land thing of Liam's?"

"How? The legal system here is so much different from ours. I wouldn't know where to begin."

"Go back," he advised. "Get access to old books, ancient documents and search as far back in legal history as you can. Go back before Christianization. The original laws in Ireland were drawn up by a professional legal tribe called *brehons*. I think the base of the code was the extended family. And women had much higher status under Irish law than they did under English common law. I see a pattern, don't you? Listening to what you say about the Crofts, I'm willing to bet it's tied in back that far."

Paula considered this. Alex was a walking encyclopedia, and while years before she had found that characteristic tedious in a lover, in a friend, it was a great trait. Especially now. "I'll try," she said. "And Alex, thanks. I owe both you and Tinsley."

"Hey, don't mention it."

"Is Tottie getting better?" she asked.

"She is. In a few days, you can talk to her yourself. She's coming out here to recuperate when Jim discharges her from the hospital."

"Call me."

"Will do."

After hanging up, she reported her conversation to the Crofts. Morgan liked the idea of her working on the old documents. Liam seemed to think it would be a waste of time, but it would keep Paula busy, so he supported her request for material. She found his attitude annoying, but said nothing to him. Until they had real privacy once more, there was a lot that would go unsaid between them, she realized.

Including discussion of promises made in the heat of passion.

So here she was with Morgan, preparing to explore the legal past just as she explored a modern criminal case. No stone would be unturned.

"We can have computer access to law libraries across the country," Morgan said, showing her how the network operated. "And with a word in the right ear, I can get you into any rare document collection you need to see."

"But I'm under strict orders to stay put behind the compound doors," Paula complained. "Liam'll have my hide if I try going out." She frowned. "I don't like it, but he gets that look, and frankly, I'd rather not buck his authority right now. I wouldn't put it past him to lock me up, if he thought it was the right thing to do."

"What my son doesn't know won't cause him harm," Morgan said, a twinkle in her blue eyes. "I doubt ye're as delicate as he thinks, m'dear. And I know I'm not."

"You'd sneak me out?"

"Indeed. If ye were working for the good of the family, I would do so without hesitation. Liam worries for ye. However, I don't see ye much worried for yourself. Ye're a woman who can care for herself, if necessary, I believe.''

Paula smiled, delighted. "Mrs. Croft, I think we're going to get along, after all."

"Then call me Morgan, Paula. For I agree."

And a conspiratorial bond was forged.

TIME PASSED, days and nights. In the office set up for her down the hall from Liam's, Paula stayed busy with her research and had no reason to leave the compound. Enough material was available by modem, fax or messenger to keep her buried in ancient paper for hours every day. Gradually, she began to understand the legal background and traditions of the Irish nation. It was alien to everything she'd studied in college and law school, but once explored, it made sense to her.

And she found she rather liked it. Left alone, without English interference, it would have turned out to be a remarkable system of jurisprudence. As it was, it contained elements of so many traditions that some tended to cancel out others. It seemed relatively easy to argue one tradition at the expense of another and win. At least for a time.

Interesting. And very Irish. She had discovered that debate and argument and winning were part and parcel of everyday life with the Crofts. Often over the past few days, she would hear Liam's voice raised in roaring form against one of his uncles or brothers or even his mother and sisters, only to discover a few minutes later, that the combatants were laughing and sharing a glass of ale or a cup of tea. They *liked* to fight. Paula filed that fact for the future.

She fell into a pattern of rising at dawn with most of the family, sharing a communal breakfast in the great hall, and then heading off to work in her office. Lunch was taken off a tray there. Dinner was usually in one of the smaller dining rooms with just a few people present. Liam frequently was gone. Off on family business, she was told, or working down the street in the pub, Croft's Loft. For the first week, she was too weary in the evening to ask if she could go there.

The Croft household fascinated her, however, and when she wasn't working, she was taking note of the mechanics and operations of an extended family. She got information during meals, just by listening to conversations, which, when she was around, were politely held in English, and by asking a question here and there and by directly quizzing Morgan Croft, who seemed more than pleased to fill her in.

The estate was laid out in a haphazard manner. It covered a section of approximately one square mile of land at this point in history. There had been more and there had been less, depending on the family fortune in business, war and politics. The main house, the one she lived in, built in the first half of the twentieth century, connected to the great hall and the oldest section, dating from the Middle Ages. Near the house were smaller buildings, dwellings and offices. Along the streets on all four sides were businesses, enterprises and shops run by family members or close relations. Many lived in flats above the shops. Prosperous and busy, the area would attract anyone looking for business opportunities almost immediately, Paula realized.

What that sort of person might miss, however, was that all the prosperity and enterprise depended on family bonds and loyalty. Everyone had a job, everyone was well paid and everyone cared for everyone else. While the area might be valuable just as bare real estate, the real wealth came from the cohesiveness of the clan.

Paula was rarely alone. She also had no opportunity to be alone with Liam. While that bothered her, she understood the need for propriety within the family territory. Traditional values were strong here, and for them to behave as lovers would undermine his authority and her welcome.

But there were good aspects to communal living, too.

When she made a comment about needing a secretary, Noreen Croft, Johnny Croft's daughter, nineteen, serious and skilled, appeared in her office, eager, ready and willing to work. The teenager was attractive and neat, with dark hair and the pale Croft complexion and eyes that missed nothing.

Noreen had been laid off from her previous job, she told Paula, and was weary of hunting for a new position outside the clan. Paula's work had the added dimension of being clan business, and that made Noreen dedicated to the extreme, she claimed. If she seemed a little intense about it all, her attitude didn't bother Paula. Whatever her motives, the girl was the best secretary Paula had ever had.

By the close of the week, Paula had studied the Irish legal system, outlined the pattern in which the Croft lands were passed on from generation to generation over almost a thousand years and discovered a possible loophole to the need for Tobias's signature.

More remained to be done before she was ready to report to the family on this. But she felt she was definitely on the right track.

Friday, she spoke briefly to Tottie. Her friend's voice was weak, but she sounded in good spirits and said the Berringers were spoiling her rotten.

"You're loving it," Paula said, teasing, tears in her eyes at the joy she felt hearing Tottie joke, however feebly. "You just rest and get back to work," she added. "Without the two of us, things may fall apart in the Cay."

"Don't worry," Tottie said. "Some things are going all right."

Paula then asked about Casey Sears's plan to use a decoy in her place. "Has that accomplished anything?"

"No." Tottie hesitated. "Not a thing. But, please, Paula. Don't worry. Trust me. Things are in good hands."

"It's not easy, being so far away from my own investigation."

"I understand. Paula?"

"Yes?"

"What's it like there?"

Paula considered her answer. "Good," she finally said. "Good. In fact, better than good. If it weren't for the person after me, I think I might find I was happy."

Now Tottie laughed and sounded like her old self. "Girl, if it weren't for the creep after you, you wouldn't be there."

"True enough. Tottie, level with me. Are there any clear leads?"

"I wish."

Although she was sure Tottie knew more than she was telling, Paula left it at that. She was cut out of the loop for now. Just as well. She had enough to keep her busy right where she was.

Saturday, she continued working, loading information into the computer, designing a streamlined system for the ponderous caseload evaluation and keeping Noreen jumping even through the dinner hour, until the young woman rebelled.

"'Tis time for a break," Noreen declared. "You cannot keep your wits and work this way."

"I always have," Paula snapped. "When I worked on a case at home, I buried myself in it."

"You're not there. You're here." Noreen reached over and shut off the computer. "And I've orders to get you out of this room this evening."

Liam. Paula hadn't seen him for two days, except at breakfast. "Whose orders?" she asked.

Noreen smiled. "Himself and you know who. Now off to your room and get yourself pretty, Paula Dixon. For you're going out tonight."

CHAPTER FOURTEEN

IN HER ROOM, Paula found a pleasant surprise. A vase of fresh roses stood on her dresser. The attached note was from Liam.

"The pleasure of your company tonight?" it read.

Paula smiled. He might be a "king," and she might be his "princess-prisoner," but at least he had the good sense and tact not to rub the point in. Roses and notes were a nice touch, easing the situation considerably. She bathed and dressed, wondering where they would go.

Where they *could* go.

She soon found out. Less than an hour after she had left her office, Liam was knocking on her bedroom door. She opened it quickly. "Hello, love," he said, softly, his gaze taking her in from the top of her head to her feet. "You look wonderful. My, it seems a century since we were alone together, doesn't it?"

"Yes, it does." She swung the door wider. The sight of him literally made her heart beat faster, just like a teenager with a crush. What she felt, however, was far deeper than any crush. "Come on in."

He stayed outside. "It isn't that I don't want to, understand." He glanced down the hall. "But..."

"Okay. I understand. Where're we going? Am I dressed all right?"

"You're dressed fine," he replied. "And we're just going over to Croft's Loft. It's safe enough there. We'll be attended and surrounded by my own bully boys and if anyone tries to start trouble, they'll be quick to handle it. We can relax and have some fun." He held out his hand. "I don't know about you, but I'm ready for it, myself."

"Sounds good to me." She wasn't sure about the "bully boys" bit, but she knew they did need to be careful, and she would have to trust Liam's judgment. This was his world, and even if she was beginning to get used to it, he still knew it best.

She took his hand.

A short while later, she found herself in another world entirely.

Liam's pub. He was king here, too, but in a very different way. Here, he was a king who served, who entertained and who made his customers feel as welcome as if they were in his home.

To get there, he'd led her from the main house out onto the estate grounds. The May night was warm and soft, and she smelled a heady combination of flowers, freshly mown grass, wood smoke and beer. She commented on it.

"The sweet perfume of Dublin," Liam said, his voice low so that no one but Paula could hear him. The path they walked was crowded with other Crofts and their friends. "Beer and flowers," he added.

"That's very Irish," she said. "Something sweet and pretty, something plain and good."

He didn't reply for a moment. Then, "You're starting to understand us," he said. His arm went around her shoulders.

Before she could respond, they were at the back door of the pub. Noise and music enveloped them like a rough, warm blanket when he opened it.

The room was huge, not as large as the great hall, but big enough to hold a crowd of several hundred people seated at long wooden tables. The ceiling was low and raftered, stained black with smoke from the fire that blazed in the hearth on the south wall. The walls were whitewashed and glowed with a patina that had come from over a century of occupancy. Light came from wall sconces similar to those in the hall, from the fireplace and from a spotlight on the stage. A group of musicians sat up there, not playing at the moment, but talking among themselves and drinking pints of beer. The music she had heard was recorded and piped in through a sophisticated sound system at just the right level for the room. Not loud enough to stifle conversation, but clear enough to be heard. No windows to the outside from what Paula could see. A world self-contained and dedicated to a good time. When Liam was spotted, people called out his name. Soon the room reverberated with the sound. He waved cheerfully, guided Paula to a small table set near the band and signaled drinks for both of them. The pints appeared as if by magic.

Liam lifted his glass. "To us," he said, pitching his voice so that only she could hear. "To the present, the past, but most of all, to the future."

Paula picked up her glass. "That's a good toast," she said. "To the future. To the end of our troubles." She clicked her glass against his. "To the end of troubles," he said. "And to the start of happiness." He leaned over and kissed her full on the lips, a loving, warm, possessive kiss. She loved it!

They twined arms and drank.

And the evening began.

Since Liam was there that night as a reveler instead of a host, he wasn't called on to serve. But his status didn't exempt him from singing. A few pints, and he was up with the band, playing skillfully on his banjo and singing ballads and drinking songs.

And all the while, he was courting Paula.

She could see it in his eyes, hear it in his voice, feel it in his touch. He had chosen this time and this place to play the suitor. He was in pursuit of her heart tonight, no doubt about it.

She was more than willing to be chased! Whether or not she would allow herself to be caught remained to be seen. So many things stood in the way of any future they might have.

Could they possibly make it work?

BACK IN South Carolina, another schemer-dreamer railed at fate. Luck was not dealing out the cards the way he wanted, and it made him furious.

At first the opposition's ridiculous attempt to draw him out with that ludicrous decoy living at *her* house had only amused him. Now, it infuriated him to see the pretend-target sashay in and out of her home daily. Enraged and hurt him. For it meant the game was really and truly changed. *She* was no longer here, and it took no genius to figure out she'd gone to Ireland with that cartoon hero of hers. Escaped to temporary safety.

The opportunity to stalk and injure and kill at leisure was gone. Disappointment became rage, causing him to run through his house, destroying things. As morning blossomed from dawn, he sat in the wreckage of the den, crying.

Momma would be furious!

Unless he could come up with a plan to get at her in Ireland where she hid from him.

Then, he could kill her, and Momma wouldn't mind the mess in the house.

Feeling more in control, he rose from the debris and went into the kitchen. He fixed himself some breakfast, drank some coffee.

And made plans.

Before he left for work—he did have a job and had to earn his living, for Momma was now unable to help with the mundane details of his life—he'd made some decisions. Among them was the possibility of again taking the war to *her*. Over to Ireland where she must think she was safe. Over to Ireland where that huge dolt of a lover must think he had her now, all to himself. Over to Ireland, where all manner of possible tricks could be played.

And murder done in the name of revenge!

LIAM AND PAULA made their way back to the main house in the dark. Both had consumed a fair amount of ale, but the drink made them energetic rather than tired.

Or, maybe, it was just being together that did it.

"I hate the thought of going to my room alone," she said, desire for him overcoming her sense of propriety. "Can't we sneak off somewhere tonight?"

"Why, is this passion I hear?" Liam chuckled, stopping on the path and pulling her close. "Or perhaps just the pints that went down your pretty throat tonight."

"I didn't drink that much, Liam. I know full well what I'm saying. And I want to be with you." She moved against him. "Don't tease me. I'm serious."

"Who's teasing whom?" He cupped the back of her head with one hand, the curve of her hip with the other. "I'm noticing a considerable amount of teasin' bein' done to meself right at the moment." His lips grazed hers. Barely. "But we both have to wait, darlin'. 'Tis the right thing to do."

"Damn you," she whispered, wanting him so badly she felt on fire. "You're right, as usual." She stepped away from him. "But that doesn't mean I have to like it."

"Nor would I have you like not bein' in me bed," he said, putting his arm across her shoulders and beginning to walk again. "For that's where you belong, love. We proved that the other night in the flat for once and for all. And that's where you'll be, when time, events and fortune permit."

"Hmm." She fell into step with him. "You sound confident."

"I forgot to mention my best assurance."

"What's that?"

"My faith," he said, turning her face and kissing her with such tenderness and suppressed passion that tears came to her eyes at the emotions he caused in her. "You were born to be my wife, I, to be your husband. I believe God wants us together forever, don't you?"

Paula didn't answer. With that kind of conviction, she had no grounds for argument.

They went home and slept in separate beds.

THE NEXT MORNING, she was awakened by a gentle but persistent tapping on her door. Morgan's voice called to her. "Paula? Paula, m'dear. Are ye there? Are ye all right?"

"Just a minute." Paula sat up and groped for full awareness. She felt nauseated for a second, but that passed. Getting out of bed took some doing, however. She felt dizzy and weak. Her legs trembled as if she'd been running all night.

Running. Or making love.

"Church in two hours," Morgan said when Paula opened the door. "Sorry to waken ye, since I know ye and Liam had a fine time last night, but it's important to him ye come with us to Mass this morning."

"Okay." Paula leaned against the door frame. "Somehow, I'll make it."

"Too much spirit last night, m'dear?" Morgan looked concerned. "If ye're not used to Irish drink, it might tend to do ye harm for the first few times."

Paula tried a smile. Her head did feel heavy. "I guess so," she said ruefully. "I've always had a good head for liquor, but you may be right. The local stuff takes some getting used to."

"I'll send up tea." Morgan patted her arm. "Good strong stuff. That'll cure ye."

"Thanks. I hope so."

The tea hadn't been much help, though the dry toast had calmed her stomach, Paula reflected later as she sat on the wooden pew beside Liam and Morgan Croft. Over a hundred other members of the clan were crowded into the small church. The air was hot and smelled of incense, soap, sweat and wool. She had to struggle to stay awake, fight not to get sick and exercise tight self-control not to reach out for Liam's hand.

Not that he was likely to notice, so wrapped up he was in his world of faith and ritual. The worshiping went on around her, Liam caught up as she had seen him back in Carleton Cay. Morgan had been right—it was important to him that she be beside him here. And somehow, his religious ardor touched her. She realized she could no longer help herself when it came to her feelings and Liam Croft.

She was in love. Finally. No questioning that. Not anymore.

After service, she met the priest, who greeted her with warmth. Father Connelly shook her hand and smiled. "You're welcome here, Miss Dixon," he said. "Liam, me boy, you'd best get the lass out in the fresh air. She looks quite pale."

"I . . . I am kind of shaky," she admitted. She said goodbye to Father Connelly and let Liam lead her out of the church. The outdoor air helped restore her almost immediately.

"Ah," she said. "That's better."

"Nothing like a hangover to make Mass a trial," Liam said. "Mum explained you were a bit under the weather this morning. I'm sorry I led you into too much carousing."

"You didn't lead me into a thing," she replied. "And I don't think I drank that much. I guess I'm not used to the stuff here, that's all."

"We'll change that," he said.

"I'm sure you will."

He looked at her sharply, but didn't follow up on her comment. The rest of the attendees were beginning to emerge onto the sidewalk, and private conversation was once again stifled.

They were less than two blocks away from the compound, and no one had taken a car. The day was perfect for walking. Liam took her arm. "I have a surprise for you," he said. "One I believe you'll find welcome after this week."

"I just hope it involves food."

Surrounded by family, they began to walk. "Hungry, are you, love?"

"Famished."

"Then, this'll please you all the more."

"That's good to hear."

Liam slowed, allowing most of the family to move ahead of them. He held Paula's hand in the crook of his arm, keeping her to his pace. "What's the matter?" he asked softly. "Have we done something to upset you? Have I?"

"No, I... Yes, I..." She looked away from him.

"Which is it, Paula? I won't have you unhappy."

"You can't help it." She stopped. "No one's done a thing. It's the situation. I feel... hedged in."

"I'd be amazed if you didn't." He started walking again, and she moved with him. "I would feel the same way if our roles were reversed."

"You did, as I recall. And you took off."

"That was for a purpose. And there seemed no real danger for me in the action." He patted her hand. "Here we go," he said. They turned off the main road, leaving the flock of family behind and heading up a narrow cobblestoned path. The buildings were set right at the path, giving the area a medieval flavor.

"Is this safe to do?" she asked.

"I'd say so, otherwise we wouldn't do it. The place we're going isn't in the family, but the owner is an old friend. And not even he expects us today, so no one could have set up any sort of trouble for us. I had a sense you would enjoy a bit of time on our own."

"Liam, how did you know I needed a break from your people?"

"Because, love, now and then, so do I. It's only natural."

He couldn't possibly have come up with a better answer. Paula felt the tension leaving her and the joy reentering her soul.

The surprise was a ten-minute walk up the cobble-stoned path. As the angle of the path rose, the age of the buildings increased until she was certain they actually were in an area established at least five hundred years before. Once again, that sense of alienness settled on her, and she was a stranger in a strange place.

But the negative feeling was gone. This had an edge of adventure and intrigue. Not danger. Just . . . fun.

"Goodness," she said. "We walk to church. Now we're up here. I feel more like a character out of a historical novel than a real person."

"You're real, m'dear," he said. "But you're right. A little playing is what we're about here." He pointed along the path, upward where the shops signaled their wares and specialties by artful and archaic signs. "We've gone back in time," he said. "And now we're about to embark on a truly fine and ancient Irish tradition—that of stuffing our faces with fine food." He led her around a corner and into a cul-de-sac.

"Oh!" Paula stood stock-still. The courtyard and building was set up like a medieval castle with the yard acting as the central bailey and the structure behind it, towered and turreted just like the real thing. The waiters and waitresses were in costume. In the center of the bailey was a welled cooking fire, tended by folk in fifteenth-century garb. Meat was roasting slowly over the fire. Paula's nostrils filled with the tantalizing aroma. Suddenly she was ravenous. Pots boiled out the sweet and spicy odor of vegetables and the heady scent of fresh bread permeated the air. Along the inner wall were long tables, accommodating diners in modern clothing. Everyone was eating and apparently having a great time.

"Join me at a table, fair damsel?" Liam teased.

"I'd be honored, sir," she replied, delighted with his surprise. And with him.

The meal was sumptuous and endless. They ate for hours. Seated at one of the long tables, in the company of complete strangers, they were able to relax and just enjoy the unique experience. The others at the tables were tourists, mostly from Europe, but there were a few Americans scattered around.

They were finishing dessert and coffee when the proprietor appeared. When the big blond, bearded man saw them, he let out a roar of welcome, grabbed Liam off his bench and pulled him into a bear-hug embrace.

"Croft, ye old cattle thief," the man hollered. "Where've ye been keeping yeself?"

"Right under your bloody nose, Tim Donovan," Liam replied. "I've been at home for near a fortnight's time now."

"Ye liar." Donovan's gaze shifted to Paula. "Or perhaps not. Who's the colleen? One of your sisters or cousins? Introduce me, boyo. I'll be showin' her a better time than you." He leered at her cheerfully.

Paula smiled, but only slightly. She wasn't sure just how this was going to go.

"Oh, Timmy," Liam said, ducking his head and shaking it. "I'm thinkin' you're makin' a mistake."

"Oh, I think not." The blond giant moved around Liam and reached for Paula's hand. "Hello, darlin'," he said, drawing her off her place on the bench. "Come with me and I'll be takin' ye places in my castle this fine laddie won't dare to go. He's frightened of high places, is Liam Croft."

She twisted away. "Thanks," she said. "But I'll stay with Liam."

"Oh-ho." Donovan regarded Liam. "That's how it is, is it? Not a cousin or a sister, now I'm thinkin'."

"Miss Paula Dixon," Liam said, suppressing a smile. "This rogue is my friend, Timothy Donovan. And if he didn't set out such a grand feast at this pest-ridden establishment, I'd never have brought you here to be so insulted by the likes of him. Donovan, this is the woman I shall marry."

"Oh." Tim Donovan turned red. "Oh, my. I have overstepped meself this time, have I not?"

"Aye." Liam put his arm across Paula's shoulders. "That you have. But I'll forgive you this once, because you did not know."

"I'm truly embarrassed and pleased at the same time," Donovan declared. "You'll be comin' inside and sharin' a bottle of champagne with me by way of celebration?"

"It's not exactly official yet," Paula said.

"So we'll hold off on the champagne for a while," Liam added. "But we'll keep you to the offer."

"Grand!" Donovan winked at Paula. "Then how about my suggestion ye come wi' me and see the tower to the castle, Miss Dixon. Dear old Liam here gets all weak in the knees up so high."

Liam's smile became tight. "I do. She knows that. Go on with him, Paula. The view's worth the climb."

"I really don't..."

"It's all right, love," he said, releasing her hand. "I recommend it, though I cannot do it, myself. Nothing on this green earth could get me up there, so you go with Timmy."

She looked at him.

"Really," he said.

Donovan took her inside. The interior was exactly what she would imagine a castle to be like—stone walls, large banners and wicked weapons hanging on them. Stone floor.

"Do you use this?" she asked. "For the restaurant?"

"Aye. When it rains and in the winter," Donovan said. "I know it seems dreary right now, but with a great roaring fire to drive out the damp, it's quite cosy. Ye're American, are ye?"

"Yes."

He led her along the side of the huge room to a narrow passageway. "How did ye come to meet Liam Croft, then?" he asked.

"I found him," Paula said, adding nothing else. Liam seemed to trust this old friend, but something about the big man bothered her. Maybe it meant nothing. But she had learned to trust her instincts, sometimes in defiance of concrete evidence. More often than not, her feelings were correct.

"What was the lad doing in your country?" Donovan asked. "Looking for that old uncle everyone says is still alive?"

"I wouldn't know." She followed him along the corridor until they reached a niche in the wall. A winding staircase led upward from there. "We ... just got to be friends, and now here I am," she added. They started up the stairs.

Donovan paused. "Ye don't look to me like the kind of woman who just follows after a man you just met, Miss Dixon. If you'll pardon my saying."

"Say whatever you want. I was there. Now, I'm here. With Liam."

Tim Donovan grinned. "Are all American women as spare with words as yourself? If so, I'd be wantin' to look for a bride there, I think. A lass who'll keep silent and listen to me, day and night. 'Twould be a dream come true for any Irishman!"

Paula smiled back at him. "I'm a prosecuting attorney, Mr. Donovan. I can talk a blue streak when it's necessary."

"You're a solicitor?"

"A prosecutor. I don't know what we're called here."

A strange expression came over his face. "Perhaps ye don't want to know," he said.

He led the rest of the way to the top of the staircase without making another comment.

When they reached the top, Donovan opened a trapdoor set in the ceiling. Daylight streamed in, making Paula squint. "This is the roof of the tower," he said. "When we restored the castle, the pilings under the ground were still in place and able to provide plenty of support for the structural weight. But the original probably was only two stories high and—''

''You're telling me this is a castle site? And you rebuilt over it?''

''That I am, Miss Dixon.'' He climbed out onto the roof and held down his hand. ''Come up and see Dublin.''

She did. The view was spectacular.

The tower was at least one story higher than any of the surrounding buildings, so she could see for miles. Dublin spread out along the river, the greenery of trees and grass shining under the spring sun. She moved over to the waist-high parapet and looked down. In the courtyard below, Liam stood, looking up. Paula waved. He continued to look at her, but did not wave back.

''Over here's Liam's land,'' Donovan said, pointing to the other side. ''Look and ye'll see the finest single holding in all of the city.''

Paula went over. ''So your castle really overlooks Croft property,'' she said. ''It abuts right onto the estate.''

''That it does,'' Donovan said, an odd tone in his voice. ''I've been after Liam for ten years to sell me some of the land for expansion, but friendship doesn't include business where that lad's concerned.''

''You want to buy Croft property?''

''Wouldn't ye? If ye stood where I stand?'' He pointed. ''Look how the river flows to your left, how the land rises to your right, full to brimming with flats and townhouses. Hardly a one with a yard to brag about, much less a garden. Development's too close here for one extra scrap of land to come on the market in me lifetime. The only way I could get more space is out of the Croft holding."

"But Liam can't sell. He doesn't own it. The family—"

"Ah, don't give me that about the sacred family! He's the one with his finger on the bank accounts and the title to the land. He could sell, if he chose."

"Mr. Donovan, I don't think you understand. The Crofts have a unique—"

"*I* don't understand?" The man looked angry. "I'm Irish. How long have you known Liam? A month? Two? How long have you been here among us? A week? Two? Listen, Miss Dixon, I—"

"How did you know that?"

"Know what?"

"How long I've been here?"

Donovan smiled. "Why, local chat, of course. You don't think a lad like Liam could bring home a lovely lass like yourself without word gettin' about, do ye?"

She nodded. His answer made sense. As large a city as this was, it was also very much like a small town in some respects. Yes, people would have noted Liam's situation, what with the excitement of the bomb in the flat and the arrest of the two youthful offenders.

She looked over the edge again and noticed an ugly detail she had missed before. This side of the castle tower had iron rings set into the stone. Between them jutted an iron gibbet, its triangular form casting a forbidding shadow on the grassy ground four stories below.

"For hangin' the losers in a fight or rebellion," Donovan said, grinning at her. "As an object lesson, I'm told. Ye could see the execution for miles around. Made folks pay attention."

"I'm sure it served its purpose well." Paula shuddered and moved away from the sight.

"He was intended to be a priest, ye know," Donovan said, referring to Liam, his tone friendly and conspiratorial. "But he kicked over those traces early enough. He's had enough lady-friends to fill a stage. Ye're the first he's claimed as his own, though."

"Is that so?"

"Indeed it is."

"Then, I expect I'd better get back to him, don't you think?"

"If that's what ye want, Miss Dixon. If that's what ye truly want."

"It is," she replied. "It is."

CHAPTER FIFTEEN

"So, what did you think of our local castle?" Liam asked as they walked back to the Croft compound. He had said little to her when she returned from the tower with Donovan, but he had been pleasant enough to his friend. Even though Donovan had continued to tease him about his fear of heights, Liam had kept his smile in place and his temper in check.

She didn't sense it had taken much effort. He seemed in a fine mood.

"It's different," she said. "We don't have anything like it in Carleton Cay."

"And the castle holder?"

"He scares me."

"I don't believe that. Not for one moment. You don't frighten that easily."

"It's not myself I'm frightened about. It's for you. Liam, if he thought by poking one of those nasty medieval weapons through you or by hanging you on that awful gallows attached to the outer wall he could get access to some of your land, Timothy Donovan wouldn't hesitate a moment. That's what I think."

Liam laughed.

"I don't see anything funny about it," she said. "I see some real problems for you."

"You're quite right, of course."

"I am?"

"Aye."

She stopped walking. "I don't get it. Why are you so damn cheerful, then? I just spent a quarter of an hour on top of a tower with a guy who might be involved in trying to harm you. He could be the one who hired those two little thugs to blow you up! That's hardly a laughing matter."

"I don't think he's guilty."

"Why not?"

"Paula, darlin', Timmy Donovan and I have been trying to kill each other since we were in nappies. Our mothers swear when they first met, walking us in prams, Timmy lobbed a rattle at me, and I returned the favor with another toy. Gave him a black eye, I'm told."

Paula had to laugh at that image. "Little terrors, were you?"

Liam went on. "The sisters at the school we attended consigned both of our immortal souls to hell everlasting by the time we were ten because we couldn't help fighting with each other over every little thing. It's in Tim's blood and bones to fight with me. I like to think I've outgrown the urge, but perhaps I haven't at that. I confess I quite deliberately flaunted you at him. I'm actually surprised he didn't make a move in your direction. 'Tis no news to me he's wanting Croft land."

"But why...?"

"Why did I let you go off with the scoundrel? Not because I thought you might be in danger, for I did not. I did it simply to see what you'd say about him. He's not a bad man, is old Timothy. Oh, a bit on the greedy side, perhaps. But he isn't strong, and—"

"Seems strong enough to me. He's big as a house, Liam."

"In body size, perhaps. Not in spirit, darlin'. There's a big difference. Timmy's not a fighter, for all his bulk and bluster. For many years, he outweighed me by several stone, but I was still the one sent home, whipped by the good sisters for winnin', and he was the one with the blackened eye and the bloodied nose and cryin' like a banshee had hold of his soul. The whippings I received hurt far less, let me assure you. 'Twas a matter of pride to win those small battles."

"All the more reason for him to harbor resentment."

Liam grinned. "That's what I find so endearing about you, love. No one is safe from your fine, suspicious mind."

"Just so you remember that."

"I will." He kissed her hand and continued on their walk. "That I will."

THEY RETURNED to the compound and joined a group that was heading out to the park for a late-afternoon picnic. They would, he said, be quite safe with such a mob. When she protested briefly, claiming that a pile of work waited for her in her office, Liam reminded her that it was Sunday, a day of rest, and that she should respect that tradition, even if other Americans did not.

"There's a saneness in resting one day out of seven," he said. "Even if you don't believe in all the rules."

He was right. She did need a break. So she agreed.

Liam then took the part of tour guide. "Phoenix Park," he told her as they crossed the street and walked through the entrance, "is the largest public park in Europe. In here is a fine zoo, the president's palace, the American ambassador's residence, a freely wandering herd of fallow deer and the People's Garden. Also, the headquarters of the Garda Siochana, which you have already visited. All on over seventeen-hundred-plus acres of land."

"And you live right next door."

"Indeed we do," Annie Purchase chimed in. Liam's sister had moved near while they walked. "And that makes our land all the more dear."

"All the more desirable to developers," her husband, Danny, said.

Paula looked at Danny. He was a dark, quiet man and had said little to her since she'd moved into the main house. He and Annie seemed deeply in love, and from what she knew of Annie, no man without some strong, positive virtues could hold her affections. "Are there speculators who've expressed interest in the property?" she asked.

Danny nodded. "Mostly foreigners," he said.

"What sort of foreigners?" she asked.

Liam put his arm across Paula's shoulders. "No work today, love," he said. "Rest, remember?"

She started to challenge him, to suggest that his lunch date at the castle amounted to a kind of work, sneaky though it was, but she kept silent. Liam was up to something. From experience, she knew it was best to wait and see what developed.

What did develop, however, was just a lovely afternoon spent in his company.

And that of his family.

Kids ran around, shouting and kicking soccer balls. Teenagers and young adult males played a real match

over in a nearby field. Babies cried and cooed and
were held and loved and fed. Some of the men played
ball with the boys. Several women knitted while they
visited and talked. Little girls played jump rope on the
fresh green grass. Over in a large gazebo, a band
practiced folk music. Some couples moved to the edge
of the family group so they could talk alone.

She and Liam stayed central and surrounded, however. Too many family members were within earshot
for them to hold any private conversation, but Paula
had a good time and found herself more relaxed than
she had been in weeks. Somehow, the surrounding
relatives helped, she realized.

She mentioned it to Liam. "I'm an only child," she
said. "My immediate family has little to do with relatives, near or far. I've never been in a home situation like yours."

"While it's not common anymore, throughout history this was the norm," he said, gazing around at his
relatives. "We've abandoned a good thing in the interest of modern life. It's natural for related folk to
stay together." A soccer ball bounced by. He reached
out and caught it with one hand and threw it back to
the child who had kicked it astray. He shouted en-
couragement to the boy. The child grinned and when
he kicked the ball again, it was right to the target.
Liam whistled in appreciation.

He liked kids. Paula remembered how he'd taken to
the island children so easily. "Tinsley and Alex have
the same thing, but not with relatives," she said.

"True. They've found their own tribe out there on
the island. But mine's right here. And here is where I
belong." He looked at her. "It's where I have to stay,"
he added.

"I know that." She reached for his hand. "Believe me, I do know that."

They continued to hold hands and enjoy each other without speaking as the sunlight faded and dusk settled on the city. Then twilight signaled the end to the outing. One by one, the Crofts began to pack up, ready to head back home. They all moved slowly, as if regretting to leave the beauty and peace of the park in order to return to the regular world.

But they went, and Liam and Paula went with them.

LATE THAT NIGHT, Morgan Croft found her son sitting at his desk in his office. He wasn't working. He was staring at the blank face of his computer screen.

"Is Paula asleep?" she asked, coming in and taking a seat, uninvited.

"I suppose. She was quite tired."

"She's well?"

"Of course. And yourself?"

"I'm fine, Mother." He gave her his attention. "What do you want?"

"Information." Morgan settled in her chair. "Have ye declared your intentions to Paula Dixon?"

Liam actually blushed. "Yes, I have," he said, remembering the moment he'd done so.

"Soberly and without passion, but with earnest love and the promise to be with her all your life?"

He shifted on his chair. "Uh...not exactly in those words, but—"

"Then ye'd best be doin' it."

"And I shall. But the time is not—"

"The time's never right, Liam. Not for a man. Ye've slept with her, and now ye believe she's yours. Sorry to tell ye, but it doesn't work that way. Just because ye made her feel grand in bed, doesn't mean she belongs to ye forever. Don't be making such a silly mistake, me lad."

Now Liam was sure his face was a bright red. For his own mother to speak of such things was unheard of!

"She said yes to me," he sputtered.

"Of course she did. And ye? Wouldn't ye have said yes to anything she asked at that moment?" Morgan rose from her chair. "Put aside what has happened between ye. Each day is a new one, and ye must court her afresh every morning." She smiled. "As your father did with me."

Liam felt the sting of tears in his eyes for the first time in many years at the mention of his father. "I remember how the two of you were," he said, his voice catching. "So in love, even through his illness. I've longed for the same for meself."

"And ye've found her," Morgan replied, coming over and touching his hair. "Make sure she knows that, is all I'm sayin'."

"I will," he replied fervently.

She said one more thing. "Ye must also see to it that she has something more here than your love to keep her. She has lived independently and successfully for over ten years. She'll not surrender that easily, no matter how much she may love ye. She must have a place here. A genuine place. A reason for stayin', aside from ye."

"I agree. And I've been thinking about it."

"Good." She kissed his forehead. "Then ye'll be fine, me son. Ye'll both be fine."

But after Morgan left his office, Liam clicked on his computer screen again, and his attention was lost in the data displayed there.

And he put his mother's advice out of his mind. For the time being. Paula was late for breakfast the next morning. She'd made a stop by her office before coming into the small dining room, and she had a few pages of printout with her. She put the paper down on the table by Morgan and went over to pour herself tea from the serving center on the sideboard. Morgan picked up the pages. "What's this?"

"I need to go to Trinity's library," Paula said, coming back over and sitting down, a cup of steaming tea in front of her. "They have archival documents that I have to see. Can you arrange it?" She sipped at her tea, made a face, put it back down.

"I can." Morgan checked to see they were alone. "Liam's out this morning. Left with the sunrise without telling a soul what he was about. I think we're safe from his disapproval if we—"

"I don't think we need to worry," Paula said. "He took me to that castle place yesterday deliberately. For all he knew, it was dangerous to leave me alone with that Donovan character."

Morgan smiled. "Tim? Oh, there's no harm in him."

"Maybe. Maybe not." Paula stared at the tea. "But I'm ready to get on with this. I'm ready to quit hiding."

"Are ye, now?"

"Yes." Paula got up and stood in front of the sideboard, regarding the food. "I'm also hungry as a horse."

"Try the oatmeal."

Paula did. It was great. She had three large helpings.

Morgan watched her, thoughtfully.

An hour later, she and Morgan were on their way downtown.

They went by Dublin Bus, catching the ride into town at a stop down the street from the entrance to the compound just like any pair of housewives out for a day of shopping. Except that instead of a shopping bag or purse, Paula carried a briefcase. Before they left the compound, Morgan had made two phone calls to "important people" she knew at the college, insuring them access to the documents Paula wished to view.

Spring had turned out with all its fair promise that morning, and as she rode to the city center, Paula watched Dublin go by. Shopkeepers tidied the sidewalks in front of their stores, housewives set out window boxes already full of blooming flowers, and all the way, the river Liffey flowed dreamily along to her right. She closed her eyes and breathed in the smells—fuel fumes from the bus, water and fertile mud from the river, earthy wool and soap and sweat from the people around her. And over it all, the sweet-musty, organic odor of the huge Guinness brewery that dominated the approach to the city center.

Once they reached the last stop, she and Morgan got off and walked across O'Connell Bridge with the midday crowd. From there, they took the few blocks farther to the entrance to Trinity College.

"You seem to know your path," Morgan commented as they walked through the entrance. "Have ye really not been in the city before?"

"I ran city maps up on the computer," Paula confessed. "Memorized them. I'm very good at orienting, once I have a map down in my mind."

"It's a gift ye have," Morgan said. "I get lost the moment I step outside county bounds. But I know Trinity well. My late husband, Liam's father, and I studied here." She led the way across the campus to the Old Library. A crowd stood in line to view the Book of Kells, but Morgan spoke to the guard and they were let inside immediately. Another guard took them past the exhibits and up the staircase to the Long Room where the Book was displayed.

The Long Room was a shrine to the Book, but it was also gorgeous and worthy of attention in and of itself. It held the same sort of mystical sanctity as a church. She yearned to linger and absorb the atmosphere, but she had other work to do.

The guard took them into a smaller reading room, and a librarian appeared with the documents Paula had requested. Morgan made herself comfortable over in a corner chair and prepared to rest while Paula settled in at a desk and read, her every move monitored closely by the nervous archivist.

And there, a few hours later, Paula found everything she needed. She made notes and took some pictures. She woke Morgan from her doze and briefly explained what she'd found. Morgan's eyes filled with tears of joy and gratitude.

"Ye've saved us," she said, embracing Paula. "We sent Liam for Tobias, and the good Lord sent us ye, instead."

"It's not over until a challenge comes," Paula reminded her. "But this should stand up in any court in any land." She made a few more notes, asked for two more documents and then declared the search over and successful.

And when she was done, she could hardly wait to see Liam and tell him!

LIAM'S DAY had begun before dawn. He'd stayed awake until almost two in the morning, studying and worrying over what he'd discovered by merging data on his computer. Analysis would take some time, he knew, but the pattern was emerging, clear as glass.

A traitor did dwell among them. What remained to be seen was if the bastard was family by blood or only by marriage.

Either way, it was a shame and a disgrace. He'd located and tracked the person's activities by looking into family financial records over the past three months. Since he'd been gone, unable to oversee matters closely as he usually did, funds were misplaced, trunk calls made to several American cities and other discrepancies in the data kept for the Croft holdings. He had no way to see individual accounts or records, for that would violate privacy rules and laws, but anything done in the name of and for the family was open to him as leader.

If he hadn't been leader, he could never have discovered the trail, much less followed it. But he was, and the path now led him to a remote village up the coast. Many of the calls from the main house in the compound had been made to a number with an exchange there. And there, he hoped to find answers. Answers and a name.

The farther north he drove, the gloomier the weather. From the sea, a heavy mist moved in, slicking the road and making a salty mess of his car windows and obscuring the view out his windscreen. He slowed, moving the gear lever down, and continuing on at a snail's pace.

As he drove, he thought. Not pleasant thoughts, but ones that needed to be considered and dealt with. Paula and the future were not on his mind at all. In spite of his mother's advice, he had decided to put thinking about that off until all the rest of the trouble was cleared up. Then, he could concentrate on good things. He reached the village a little after noon. Pulling up to the only pub in sight, he got out of his car, drew his coat close against the damp and chill and went inside. If there was anything at all to be learned here, it would be found inside the local drinking establishment.

A peat fire blazed in the hearth, driving away the springtime cold, and the familiar aroma of hops welcomed him. Which was more than the patrons did. Half a dozen men sat in the pub and met his entrance with hostile stares.

"'Day to ye," Liam said, smiling and shaking moisture out of his hair. "Right foul outside."

No one said a word. Keeping the smile going with an effort, he went to the publican and ordered a pint. He'd have a few, get on speaking terms with the locals and then ask his questions.

PAULA PACED AROUND in a circle in her office. Nearly ten o'clock at night and Liam still wasn't back. Her eagerness to speak to him had now faded to a combination of worry and anger. Where was he? She had intended to present her findings at a family meeting tonight, but without him in attendance, there was no point to it.

Whatever he was doing, she hoped it was extremely important. Important enough for him to go off without leaving a word to anyone regarding his destination. She paced some more.

A knock on the door frame stopped her. She turned to see Johnny Croft standing at the entrance. "Evening, Johnny," she said. "Any news?"

"None. Morgan sent me to ask if ye needed anything?"

"No. Just to see Liam."

"Well, then. I'll be saying good-night."

"Good night, Johnny."

He left, shutting the door partway. She continued pacing. After a while, she stopped and looked at her watch.

She couldn't wait up much longer. Ought to just give up and go to bed. She was weary from the long day and needed sleep.

But her anxiety level was too high right now.

She went to her desk. The computer was still on, though Liam's special screen-saver program was running, sending tiny gold harps skipping across the blackness. She tapped the enter key and the harps disappeared.

What had Liam been working on the night before? Morgan had said at dinner that one reason he might be out late this night was that he'd been up all hours at his computer last night.

What had been so interesting? Paula tapped keys. The computers here were all connected into a central storage unit. If she could access Liam's files, she might be able to figure out what he was doing and where he was doing it. She settled in and went to work.

A few hours later, she threw up her hands and groaned. Whatever system Liam used, it was too much for her to figure out. She needed help, and she needed the best. Consulting her watch once more, she figured it was early evening on Berringer's Island.

The phone on the island rang almost ten times, and Paula was about ready to give up and hang up, when Tinsley finally answered. She sounded out of breath.

"Tinsley, it's Paula. Sorry to bother you but—"

"Paula?" The connection was good. Tinsley sounded as if she were right next door. "Paula, what are you doing calling me?" She also sounded angry.

"Nice to hear your voice, too, Tinsley. Actually, I want to talk to Alex about computers. Is he—?"

"Paula, is Liam there?"

"No, that's why I'm calling."

"Paula, where are you?"

"Ireland. Tinsley, what's wrong?"

Instead of answering, Tinsley Berringer swore. "Are you protected? Exactly where are you?" she asked. "Are the cops there?"

"No. I'm inside the Croft compound, as safe as I'd be anywhere. No cops, though. What's going on?"

Tinsley took a deep breath. "Lots. Paula, whatever you do, stay where it's safe. Don't go out. Don't trust anyone."

"What's going on!"

"I can't tell you. Just stay put, okay?"

"Tinsley, is Tottie there?"

"Yes."

"Put her on."

A pause. Then Tottie's voice. Weak. "Hey there, Paula. You behavin' yourself?"

"No, I'm not. Tottie, how are you?"

"Been better." Pause. "But I'm going to be all right."

"Thank goodness! Can you give me any idea what's up?"

"Just do what Tinsley said, girl. Stay with Liam's people and lay low. Casey's flushed out the bad guy for us and—"

"Casey?"

"Agent Sears." Tottie's tone changed. "He is a good man, Paula."

"Okay. I'll take your word for that. So who's the bad guy?" She asked the question casually, but Paula tensed, waiting for the answer.

"Just lay low like I told you, Paula. Stay out of the way and let the police handle this one."

"Who is it?"

"Charlie, we think. Someone using his passport left for Ireland days ago. We just found out. But don't you dare—"

"What? Charlie! That makes no sense. Why would he . . . ?"

"Blow up the courthouse? Think. You're a political threat. The publicity was outstanding, and . . ." Tottie's voice faded.

The phone line went dead.

Paula tapped at it for a moment, then tried calling back.

Nothing.

Damn. Overseas connection must have gone off. She looked at her watch again. Almost one. Too late to call anyone, even if the phone did work. She should just do what Tottie said. Stay put and wait. If the phone was out of order, she'd have to wait until morning to send someone to report it, anyway. She hadn't gotten what she was after regarding the computer, but the information Tottie had given her more than made up for it. But *Charlie?* She just couldn't believe he was the one responsible. Even if you took in the political factor, it made no sense.

No. It did make sense. What it didn't do was sit right with her. Instinct, Paula, she told herself. Listen to that old inner voice.

It's not Charlie.

Who, then? And why did Sears think it was her boss? And what was being done? And how much danger was she...

She heard the sound of a phone ringing somewhere in the house. She picked the receiver up.

It still didn't work.

Paula stood. Something was wrong. Her inner alarms went off, clanging danger.

Someone was approaching her office. Footsteps in the hall outside... Moving carefully, so as not to be heard... She switched off the light, leaving the room in darkness.

"Miss Dixon?" Knock on the door. "Are ye there?"

"Noreen?" Paula turned the light back on. Her young secretary stood in the doorway. "What in the world are you doing up so late?"

Noreen stepped inside the door and shut it behind her. "I was waiting for a call," she said. She took a gun out of her skirt pocket and pointed it at Paula. "The call just came. Sorry."

"Liam?"

"No. But it was about him. His car's been found abandoned on the coast road. I don't think he's dead, though. More's the pity."

Paula kept her body very still, her emotions tight under control. "Why's that?" she asked.

"I'd get me money sooner, of course. Ye silly bitch, don't ye understand?"

"No." Paula's hand was still on the light switch. She hadn't moved, yet. "I guess I don't get it. Any of it."

Noreen smiled. "It doesn't matter if ye don't," she said. "First, ye have to come with us. We're going to use ye to lure him into a fatal trap. Then it's goodbye to ye both. Because ye have to die, too. Carryin' his child and all, ye—"

"What?" Now her hand trembled. But she didn't move it. "His child?"

"Don't be acting innocent. I've seen you of a morning since you were with himself in the flat that night. Sick, ye are. Then, ye're fine. Ye eat like three men. Ye're carryin', that's for certain. And it has to be Liam's, I'm sure. With his babe in ye, even with him dead, Morgan'd have reason to keep on," Noreen said. "So, ye have to go. Sorry. I rather liked ye, Paula Dixon."

"Are you doing this in order to force Morgan to sell the land?"

"Of course. And I didn't do it alone." Noreen started to glance over her shoulder. She said, "Ye can come on in now, darlin'. I have her for ye."

A tall figure appeared in the doorway behind her.

"My God," Paula said, suddenly truly frightened. "It's *you!*"

Noreen went on talking to Paula. "I know who's there. And don't think ye can fool me with that old movie trick of 'look out behind ye,' for I've seen all the American films, and... Oh."

She caught sight of the newcomer. "What the bloody hell are ye doin' here?" she cried. "Where's my...?"

Paula turned out the light. Noreen screamed. A gun fired. The sound echoed like thunder in the room.

CHAPTER SIXTEEN

WHEN AGENT CASEY SEARS got off the plane in Dublin, Superintendent Sean Creedon was waiting for him.

So was Morgan Croft.

The superintendent introduced her without explanation, then hustled Casey through customs and out the VIP exit to where an official car waited for the three of them. Morgan, gaunt and pale, said little until they were on the dual carriageway heading toward the city center.

But when she did speak, her words rocked him badly.

"My son's gone missing, Mr. Sears," she said. "He's been absent for almost two days. They found his car early this morning, abandoned on an isolated coast road. Last night, someone entered my home and committed violence against my family. My niece, Noreen Croft, is in the hospital with a bullet lodged in her spine. Paula Dixon is nowhere to be found. She disappeared in the middle of the night from her office in the most protected part of the Croft compound. Aside from Noreen's blood, there are no other signs of a struggle. She is just gone. Now, I would like to know what ye gentleman plan to be doin' about all this."

"Ma'am, I..." Casey Sears stared at the small, angry, frightened Irishwoman. "I'm sorry, but..."

"Morgan, give the lad a break, will you, m'dear?" Sean said. "He's traveled a long way to help us both. Haven't you, Mr. Sears?"

"I think I'd better hear Mrs. Croft's story from the beginning," Sears said, settling back in his seat. "From the very beginning."

Morgan obliged.

By the time she finished her recitation, they were seated in Sean Creedon's private office, drinking tea. "It's pretty clear we have two separate criminal conspiracies going on here," he said. "One for you guys, Superintendent. And one for me."

"Perhaps there *were* two conspiracies, Mr. Sears," she said, snapping out the words. "But it is also 'pretty clear' that in the person and work of Paula Dixon, those two have converged. Find her, and ye'll solve both."

"Ma'am, I'm not sure you should be in on this planning session."

"Easy, lad," Creedon said. "Don't be judging this book by the cover. Morgan Croft has forgotten more about investigation than we both know. Before she gave up her career for Liam's daddy, Michael, she was the highest ranking woman investigator in all of Ireland."

"You?" Sears stared at her. "I mean, Mrs. Croft, I'm sorry, but I had no way of knowing."

"Now, you do." Her eyes were icy blue. "Now, get on with your job, Mr. Sears. Find my daughter-in-law-to-be. Find the mother of my grandchild."

"Huh?"

"She carries my son's child. 'Tis nothing she herself knows yet, but I do. Plenty of evidence for one with eyes to see. So there are three lives at stake, lad. Get busy!''

''Yes, ma'am!'' Sears turned to Creedon. ''Here's what we have, Superintendent. Three days ago, a man left Carleton Cay and traveled to Atlanta, where, using the name and passport of one Charles Benson, he booked a seat to Shannon Airport.''

''I'll start a hunt for—''

''It's not Charles Benson you need to find, sir.''

''But you said—''

''The passport is stolen. Our target has another name.''

Creedon's eyebrows rose. ''Then what name is that, might I ask?''

''Jefferson Ebert,'' Casey said. ''He's a journalist. A *television* journalist.''

''Oh, my sweet Lord,'' Creedon moaned. ''And if we so much as touch him, he'll start to hollering about interference with the media.''

''Unless we catch him committing a felony, you're right.'' Sears glanced at Morgan Croft again. The woman's face was set in stone. ''But I don't think we're going to have too much trouble doing that.''

''I fear you're correct.''

''I'm afraid I am.''

LIAM CROFT cursed the efficiency of the Irish road patrols. He'd left his car for less than twelve hours, and it was gone—towed away, undoubtedly. He'd left a note on the windscreen, but the pouring rain had probably taken care of that.

The rain was still beating down. He hunched his shoulders against the cold, drenching wet and continued walking. Sooner or later, someone would come along and he'd take a ride. He could afford patience. Time was on his side. In spite of his temper over the loss of his car and the discomfort he now suffered, Liam was pleased. In a negative way, but still pleased.

The trip had been a success. He'd spent hours in the pub, until he felt he'd made solid contact with one young man who might have information he needed. When that individual had left, Liam had followed, tracking the youth through town, beyond the roadway—which was why he'd left his car—and into a shack located in a damp, dismal hollow near the sea.

The lad was a smuggler. Using his acting skills, Liam had convinced the youthful entrepreneur that he was a contact for an American drug dealer who wanted to expand to the Irish market. Greed had overcome caution, and the young thug had explained how the system he ran worked.

And how his connection in Dublin was none other than one Timmy Donovan. They were not running drugs yet, however. Mostly they dealt in luxury goods from the Continent as local smugglers had for the past three centuries or more. Liam had long suspected his childhood mate was into contraband dealing to compensate for the financial losses of his castle-restaurant, but had no evidence until now.

Now, he had enough to send Timmy away for a long, long time. But that was not what he was looking for. What Liam really wanted was the answer to the question of who was operating as a traitor within the family. Timmy at least was betraying no one. He'd never pretended to have any regard for the Crofts, much less loyalty to Liam. So, who had sold out to Timmy? Who had arranged for the two young bombers to get in the flat?

Who wanted *him* dead?

He slogged along, his boots splashing in the puddles, his mind working over the puzzle. His mother was the one to figure this out, given her background as a trained investigator. Or Paula, whose fine, suspicious mind would leap with joy at the justification of her doubts about Timmy.

But he was here alone, so it was his job.

Liam walked on, deep in thought.

AROUND THE TIME that her lover was thinking about Tim, Paula Dixon had a few questions of her own.

But she didn't dare ask them, even if she'd been able.

She had no idea exactly where she was. She did know for certain that she was shut in a small room, tied to a hard wooden chair and gagged with cloth and duct tape. In front of her on a rickety metal stand was a television set and tape player, turned on but with the volume off. The tape that played was looped so she had to view the same scene over and over again.

The scene was of Jefferson Ebert's late mother, Randall Ebert, declaring her abdication of candidacy for the office of district attorney.

Paula felt sick and nauseated, but with the gag in place, she couldn't give in to it. She'd die if she did. Of course, from Jefferson's point of view, that was probably all right. He lay sleeping on a narrow mattress placed in front of the one door to the room. He looked peaceful and innocent in sleep.

He was anything but.

He'd brought her here last night after shooting Noreen and flinging a smothering blanket over Paula's head to subdue her. Once blanket-bound, she had been helpless. She had heard shouts and running feet, indicating that the household had been awakened and alarmed by the shot, but no one had come to her rescue in time. A sharp needle had penetrated through thick cloth to her leg, and she'd been quickly injected with something that made her sick, groggy and faint.

For a while. She had no idea how long. She'd come to as she was being carried like a sack of potatoes into this room.

She'd learned later, as he bound her to the chair and chatted on about his skills at harassment, bomb making and now kidnapping, that he'd worn night-sight goggles so the darkness had been no deterrent to him. He'd acquired them the same place he had purchased the knowledge and tools to build the bomb—an underground press specializing in antiterrorist training for macho paramilitary types.

"I did a feature on them, don't you know," he said. "Made the nationals, too. Just a minute, thirty seconds, but it was damn good reporting. And I found out how to get even with you for what you did to Momma."

Then, he started the tape.

The damn tape!

While she'd watched, dumbfounded, he announced he was suffering from jet lag and that he would take a nap before killing her. He wanted to be alert enough to enjoy himself, he said.

Sleep on, Paula thought. Time was her friend, for a change. Then, she concentrated on what the tape showed.

She had forgotten all about the Ebert incident. Paula had been first-time candidate for the office of assistant—the one she still held, while Charlie ran for chief. Randall Ebert took on Charlie, but it didn't take long for the polls to show that one woman running for the prosecutor's office was enough for the public and the preferred woman was Paula Dixon. Ebert quit.

Two weeks later, she committed suicide. While there had been some speculation that she was severely depressed over the political reality that had downed her career, no one blamed Paula.

No one, apparently, except her son.

The loop began again. It had been running and rerunning for hours and hours, almost mesmerizing her. Paula groaned. She shut her eyes and tried to think. Tried to come up with some scheme to get out of this mess.

Not too many options. But there was one.

Someone else had been involved with Noreen. That was her only hope. When Paula had seen Jefferson and shown fear, Noreen had said she knew who was there.

She could not have known it was Jefferson.

So, who had she been expecting?

Whoever it was, Jefferson had missed him or her. While he'd bragged about shooting poor Noreen, he hadn't mentioned another victim. She was sure he would have relished telling her about more mayhem, if he'd had any further opportunities to commit some. The only hope Paula had was that Noreen's accomplice witnessed what had happened, had a guilty conscience and had the good sense to tell someone.

LIAM HEARD the big Buick before it rounded the curve of road just ahead. The tires hummed in the rainwater, and the engine growled as the driver slowed down to make the turn. Liam got out of the road, but prepared to wave at the driver for a ride.

When he saw who was at the wheel, he turned and raced away from the road into the meadow. He was leaping the first stone wall when he heard Tim Donovan call out his name.

And Paula's.

Liam stopped on the other side of the wall. If Timmy'd gone homicidal, at least he'd have some stone between them. "What about Paula?" he yelled. "If you've harmed one hair on her head, I'll hang you from your own castle wall, I swear it, Tim Donovan!"

"'Tisn't me ye need worry about, Liam." Tim held out his hands. They were empty. "Someone's kidnapped her. Shot my darlin' Noreen and made off with your woman. Right under the fine Croft noses, I might add."

"What?" Liam renegotiated the wall. He walked quickly across the wet meadow grass toward Tim. His fists clenched and unclenched as he strode forward. "What is it you're telling me? You liar! Noreen? You bastard!"

"Easy, boyo!" Tim held up his hands in surrender. "I was going to do ye evil. I admit that. But not killin'. I never intended killin'. That was all Noreen's—"

"Noreen's a child!" Liam yelled, his hands unclenched now, reaching for Tim's bull neck. "Where's Paula!"

"I won't fight ye, Liam." The big man didn't resist when Liam's hands closed on his throat. "This is too much for me," he squeaked. "My everlasting soul is sick with it." He closed his eyes. "So kill me, if ye must."

Liam stepped back. "Where is she?" He shook with rage and fear.

"Noreen's in the hospital." Tim rubbed his neck. "I have no idea where the bloody bastard who shot her took your Paula."

"But you do." Liam moved close, his face inches from Donovan's. "You do or you wouldn't have been rabbit-runnin' like this to your smuggler mate down the road, now would you?"

Tim turned paler. "You know?"

"Aye. And so will all of Dublin if you don't get your courage together and tell me. Where is Paula!"

Tim hung his head. "He took her to the castle. At least I think he did. We talked about it over some pints a day ago. He introduced himself and said he was after your woman because of an old grudge. We decided to join forces. I'd planned on hiding her for a few days to put a scare into ye, maybe blackmail ye into sellin' some land. But Noreen . . ."

"Noreen be damned!" Liam roared. "Don't you dare be blaming the child for all this. You know just what happened, or you wouldn't be running with your tail down. Now tell me, or I swear I'll tear you apart! I'll kill you now with my bare . . ."

He got no further with his threat. Timothy Donovan dropped to the soaking wet ground and started to weep. He put his face in his hands and cried like a little boy. Liam stared at him for a moment, then knelt down beside him.

"Tell me, Timmy," he said softly. "Tell me everything. Confess to me. It'll heal your soul."

"WAKE UP, Paula Dixon! It's party time!"

Paula jerked, waking with a start. She had dozed off watching that horrible tape, and thinking and . . .

Praying. Finally, praying.

Nothing had done her any good. She was still here, tied to the chair. And now Jefferson was awake, as well. He stood over her, a maniacal grin on his lean face, his long hair trailing down onto his collar, and . . .

A hangman's rope in his hands, the noose ready and knotted at the end.

"What do they say in Westerns?" he asked, waving the thing in her face. "A necktie party?" Hysterical laughter followed.

Paula shrank back against the chair. He was truly insane.

"It's how Momma died, don't you know?" he went on, the noose passing back and forth in his hands. "I found her."

Paula stared at him. For the first time, she felt something besides fear.

She felt pity.

But not for long. Jefferson set the rope down and went over to a corner where a soft-sided suitcase was stashed. He rummaged inside and took out some clothes.

"You'll have to wear this, of course," he said, holding the garments up for her inspection.

It was the suit his mother had worn when she announced she was dropping out of the race for D.A. The suit she wore on the tape. Paula growled behind the gag. Anger was now the only emotion she felt. By playing out his sick game, he was desecrating Randall Ebert's memory. She had been a decent woman and an excellent lawyer. She would be appalled at what her son intended.

Appalled at what he had already done!

"Oh." Jefferson stepped back. "I think I know what's upsetting you, dear. You're wondering why I haven't taken out my vengeance on Charlie, too?"

That surprised her. She calmed and waited. The longer he talked, the better chance she had someone would . . .

Would what? Rescue her? No one had a clue where she was or even who had her. Sears thought Charlie was the . . .

Suddenly, she understood.

"Why, I think you've got it!" Jefferson said, chortling. "I can see the light go on in your eyes. Good girl! That's right. I've framed him for your murder. You die, and Charlie spends the rest of his life in prison. I go scot-free. How's that for divine retribution? Two with one blow, as it were."

Paula shut her eyes. Jefferson might be nuts, but he was clever. Damned clever.

And the horrifying thing was, he might just manage to get away with it all.

MORGAN LEFT the two lawmen while they were still debating the best way to approach the problem of finding both Liam and Paula. She'd listened long enough. Time to do something. Tucking her purse under her arm, she went to the hospital where Noreen lay. Noreen, whose wounded body had been found in Paula's office, a handgun at her side.

Johnny Croft was in the room. His eyes were red with crying, and his thin face paler than the sheets on the bed.

"She's dyin'," he said. "Lord God help me, she's dyin', and she says she deserves it for she intended murder. What shall I do, sister?"

"Ye'll do nothing foolish, John Croft," Morgan said, addressing her brother, but regarding the face of his daughter, her niece. "Until we know the whole story, no one may judge." She took a seat beside Johnny. "What has she told ye?"

He rubbed his hands over his face. "Not much, I fear. She's so weak. Barely able to speak when she wakes."

"Tell me what she's said."

"Just babbled. About Tim Donovan. And some other man, I think." Johnny ducked his head. "Donovan was courtin' her."

"I didn't know."

"He didn't want anyone to know. Asked me, but said if ye or Liam knew, ye'd be suspicious of his motives, seein' Noreen was so young and a Croft, to boot."

"And ye weren't?"

Johnny just shrugged. Morgan sighed. Her brother was a genuine weakling. Both in body and in spirit. His wife, Noreen's mother, had died about the same time her Michael had succumbed to his heart condition. But Morgan's children were older and there were six of them. Noreen was just an infant, and she had no siblings to help raise her. The family had stepped in, of course, but no one could ever take the place of a strong parent.

So was Noreen so soured that even dying she wouldn't do the right thing? Deep inside, Morgan prayed that was not the case. She suspected that if Noreen could speak to her just for a moment, she'd open a door, bare her soul and the truth would pour out.

With luck and God's good help, that's what would happen. So Morgan settled in to wait. She took out her rosary beads and began to pray.

LIAM HAD LISTENED to Tim with horror growing in his heart. Tim, a weak man in a strong man's body, had fallen for Noreen, a strong woman in a teenage body. In tapping Noreen for his own greedy purpose, he'd unwittingly tapped into a reservoir of genuine evil.

His niece, Noreen Croft, was responsible for the attempted bombing. The attempt to kill him. Not Tim. Not some unknown enemy of Paula's. Noreen! A girl he'd watched grow up.

And never had any idea of what lurked beneath the pleasant surface. He jammed the gas pedal to the floorboard of Tim's Buick and drove as fast as he could toward Dublin.

For Tim had confessed he'd been standing in the shadows down the hall while Noreen went in to confront and kidnap Paula. He'd stood there and listened, too cowardly to help the girl. He had seen the newcomer sneak to the door. A man who had earlier proposed to them the idea of kidnapping Paula. A man they'd met several days ago, and after talking over details, had agreed to work with the day before. Tim had frozen with terror at the sight of the expression on the man's face. Had seen the stranger raise his gun...

Seen him shoot Noreen, betraying them and terrifying Tim into running for his life.

Tim had described him to Liam, described a man Liam had seen, if only in glimpses. It was enough.

He'd seen that long hair on the slight, androgynous figure running from him at Paula's house. On the driver of the red car out on the highway a day later. On the slender, long-haired Carleton Cay television newsman who had briefly stepped into the holding-cell area of the courthouse just a little while before the place blew up.

The nightmare wasn't over. It was just beginning. Noreen and Tim had run afoul of an evil much greater than themselves.

And that evil was intent on destroying Paula.

"RIGHTFULLY, we'd wait round the clock until sunrise," Jefferson said conversationally. "That's the civilized hour for executions, don't you think? A good night's sleep, then *pop,* off you go. Don't have all day to dwell on it."

Paula struggled to make her way up the long twisted staircase with weakened leg muscles that threatened to give way under her. The weakness was as much from astonishment as fear. Astonishment caused by realizing just where they were.

Tim Donovan's castle.

"I've never really given it much thought," she said, her voice a pale, raspy shadow of itself. The gag was off, but her throat felt like sandpaper. Jefferson had refused her even a drink of water, saying there was no point in wasting it on a dead person.

"Well, don't worry about it now, bitch. You don't have much time left," he snarled, his good humor vanishing. "Once you drop, that's it." He jerked on the rope around her neck, forcing her up a few more steps. "You know why I shot the little bitch, don't you?"

Paula didn't answer.

"Because she and I cooked up this part. She knew her castle-man would be too chicken to kill you, but she convinced him to hide you here until your boyfriend caved in on the land. I got lucky when I ran into the two of them in a bar. I found out she was a Croft, and we got to drinking and talking. And the rest, as they say, is history."

Paula controlled her fear with difficulty. She had to play for time. "Have you given any thought to your escape from this?" she asked. "I mean, you hang me over the edge, and half Dublin's going to see you do it."

"I know." He stopped.

She cleared her throat. "Jefferson, let's talk about this. You don't want to be punished. Not when you've gone to so much trouble to have Charlie blamed."

Her captor just stood there, staring at nothing.

"Jefferson?"

"Momma wouldn't want me to let someone else take the credit," he said softly as if he were talking only to himself. "I have to show them all. I have to do it so they can all see."

"Jefferson, no one in Dublin knew your mother. No one here gives a hoot in hell about—"

"Shut up!" He jerked viciously on the rope, choking her.

And they started upward once more.

"SIR, WE SEEM TO HAVE a situation brewing here." The officer pointed to a spot on the city map. "We've received calls this morning from the employees, saying that Donovan's Castle's closed. Locked up tight. The help are concerned. The owner was supposed to be there. Big party expected in a few hours. And given the location, I thought it might be significant.''

''Thank you, Sergeant Brady.'' Creedon studied the site. ''That's right next to the Croft estate,'' he said.

''Liam Croft's estate?'' Sears asked.

''Not his alone. It actually belongs to the clan. He's the leader.'' He indicated the extent of the estate with a circling finger. Casey whistled. ''Clan or no clan, that's a lot of urban turf to own.''

''It is. Go on,'' Creedon said, addressing the reporting officer. ''What else?''

''This, sir.'' He held out a tape. ''This was sent by messenger to RTE early today. I think you should listen to it.''

''RTE?'' Casey asked.

''National radio and telly,'' the officer explained. ''If they play the tape, it reaches the entire country.''

''Someone wants media focus,'' Casey said unhappily. ''That's not good. Not good at all.''

''Play it, then. Let's see what's on someone's mind.'' The superintendent took a small tape player out of his desk and set it up. The officer engaged the tape.

Jefferson Ebert's insane message filled the room.

''At some undetermined time today,'' his disembodied voice declared after some senseless ranting and raving, ''a murderer will pay the ultimate penalty for her crime. Paula Dixon killed my mother, Randall Ebert, and in a few hours, I shall execute her. Tell the world! Justice will be done!''

The voice went on for a few more sentences, raving again. Creedon reached over and shut it off.

''Sweet Lord,'' he said softly. ''They didn't run this on radio, did they?''

"Of course not, sir. RTE turned it over to us the moment they heard it themselves."

"Good. Then..."

"He's got her," Casey said. "Damn! He's got her! Some place public."

"Where?"

They looked at the map.

The phone on the desk rang. Creedon picked up the receiver.

Morgan Croft spoke. "I'm with my niece," she said tersely. "She's raving, but I believe ye'll find Paula Dixon at Tim Donovan's castle. That was their plan. Noreen was in league with the American as well as with Donovan. I believe your American simply used what was conveniently made available to him."

Creedon thanked her and hung up. "The castle," he said. He opened his door and signaled for his officers. "Alert every man and woman in the force," he said. "I want Donovan's castle sealed up and taken apart stone by stone."

"Yes, sir!"

"And Brady," Creedon said, "also put out a bulletin that if Liam Croft is found, he's to be detained and not told a thing about this until it's done, one way or another."

"Sir?"

"If Croft finds out, we'll have a small war on our hands," Creedon predicted. "And the Lord help anyone who's in the way. He'll likely blow the bloody castle up, looking for her. That's the last thing we need in Dublin."

"Yes, sir."

"I agree," Sears said as the officer left to convey Creedon's orders. "Croft's a loose cannon. You can't trust a man like that."

"Oh, you can trust him," Creedon said. "If it were me that crazy devil had, I'd sooner have Liam coming to my rescue as any ten other men. But it troubles me sore him doing this."

"I don't understand."

Sean Creedon rose from his chair. "Liam Croft is my friend," he said. "But more than that, Liam is important to Ireland. Mark me, Mr. Sears. Liam Croft will be one of the men who'll lead our people into the next century."

"Unless..."

"Unless he's allowed to throw his life away now. For a woman he's known less than a few months. For—"

"For a foreigner?" Sears asked. "Is that it? If Paula were Irish, would you stop him?"

"I don't know," Creedon replied. "I honestly don't know. Come on. We'd better get to the castle."

"Right!"

"But you're only an observer, Mr. Sears," Creedon warned. "Whatever happens, you can only watch. Do you understand?"

"Yes. I know. That's what I was told by my superiors."

"Then, let's go. And let's pray we get the job done before Liam surfaces. I have a helicopter waiting."

They were out the door and striding down the hallway to the elevator bank when Sergeant Brady caught up with them. "Sir," he said, breathing fast. "Two things."

"Yes, Sergeant. Go on." Creedon didn't slow his pace.

"Sir, Liam Croft's been spotted, speeding into the city in a car registered to Mr. Timothy Donovan."

Creedon stopped and swore. "There's more, sir."

"What!"

"At the airport."

"What! Spit it out, Sergeant."

"Three Americans and one Irish citizen, sir. Security reports they arrived in a private jet about an hour ago."

"So?"

"Sir, they were demanding information abut Miss Dixon and Mr. Croft and trying to charter a chopper to take them—"

"Delay them! Don't let them move."

"Sir, it's too late. They've just now taken off. They're on their way to the Croft estate." Creedon swore again and started running.

Casey Sears was right on his heels.

CHAPTER SEVENTEEN

LIAM ENTERED the city clocking over one hundred kilometers an hour. He'd taken Donovan's vehicle in exchange for giving the man a headstart on the law. Tim's big Buick shook, but it held the speed. It was good solid steel and built for American freeways. The Irish roads were eaten by the thing as it roared along. Almost immediately after he got to the city, he acquired a following of traffic-control cars. Sirens wailing, they pursued him as he left the carriageway and tore down the street toward Islandbridge.

That was all right with him. The noise of the sirens alerted other motorists and pedestrians, getting them out of his way. Once he reached his destination, the more gardai he had on the scene, the better.

As long as no one tried to stop him before he found Paula.

Before he saved . . .

Don't think. Just act. If he thought, he'd be unmanned by emotion!

He squalled around a corner and roared past the east wall of Phoenix Park. To his left stood the compound. Safe, serene, home . . .

A home from which his love had been kidnapped. Brutally forced. A reddish mist formed before his eyes.

Don't! Rage would destroy him. He needed to be cold as ice.

He needed God and all His angels to be with him right now. Now as he'd never before needed. He began to pray.

A slow sense of peace and power filled him. Liam took the next turn without racking the tires. He hurtled up the narrow street that led to the castle, slowing to a stop only when the car was almost jammed between buildings. He opened the driver-side door and squeezed out. The police were farther back, unwilling to risk their vehicles as he had. Liam ran, they followed, shouting.

He ran to the courtyard in front of the castle. The gate to the bailey was shut fast. Outside, several of Tim's employees were milling around, looking worried.

"What's on?" one of them asked Liam as he slid to a stop in front of the oaken door. "Mr. Donovan's not here, and no one can get inside."

Liam looked around, frantic again, the peace he'd felt gone. "Mr. Donovan's not coming back, either," he said. "No one else has a key?"

"Not a soul. Mr. Croft, what ... ?"

"No other way in?"

"None. It would take a bloody tank to break down that door."

"A tank? I've got one of those." Liam whirled and raced back toward the Buick. Two large gardai lads tried to slow him, but he bowled them aside as if they were made of straw. He reached the car, swung back inside and gunned the engine.

People screamed and got out of the way. The Buick lost much of its shell, doors and panels along the way, but by the time he hit the gate with it, it had enough speed to ram right through the oak. Bruised and shaken, Liam staggered out of the automotive skeleton and made his way through the splintered beams to the inner bailey.

The Buick's engine died. Sudden silence fell. From somewhere heavenward came the sound of a helicopter.

Then, people started screaming again.

Liam looked up and knew why.

TOTTIE REYNOLDS WAS in pain. Pain from her injuries, pain from exhaustion over the long plane flight from South Carolina and pain in her heart, looking down and seeing her best friend about to die.

And not being able to do one damn thing about it!

She held on to a strut and watched out of the helicopter side window. Below, not far below, Paula stood on the narrow parapet of a castle tower. Her hands were tied behind her back and around her neck was a hanging rope. Like a master holding a dog on a leash, Jefferson Ebert had the other end.

"Where's a sharpshooter when you need one?" Tottie moaned, realizing her every word could be heard by the others. They all wore headphones and mikes. Alex was piloting after practically hijacking the chopper from its regular pilot at the airfield.

"Even if you shot him," Alex said, his voice tense, "Paula might fall. He's got her right on the edge. All he needs to do is jerk that noose a little, and she's going to have to move. She'll either hang or..."

"Or fall four stories." Tottie had never felt so helpless in her life.

Tinsley said nothing. She was well beyond words at the moment.

Tobias Croft cursed, long and skillfully. "This is the sight I saw in my mind that first evening at your home, Mr. Berringer," he said. "I saw this danger. But I did not see the lass dyin'. Where's the lad? He should be with her." Then, he shouted, "Look. There!"

Tottie looked. "Oh, my God," she murmured. "My God!"

Liam Croft was standing on the floor of the tower, confronting Jefferson Ebert. He'd just come out of the trap door. He had on a vest of something shiny and held a long, thick wooden pole with a wicked metal device at the end. He was crouched into an obvious attack position. She couldn't see his expression from this far away, but Tottie was willing to bet it was fearsome.

"What in the world is he holding?" Tinsley asked, her voice tinny in Tottie's earphones. She sounded like she was going to be sick.

Tottie knew the feeling. While Liam was armed with that stick thing, Ebert had a gun. He was pointing it at Paula right now. But that could change.

"'Tis a pike," Tobias said. "A grand and ancient weapon of Irish warfare." He sounded truly proud and pleased. "He'll fair skewer the bastard. Watch, now."

Tottie stared at the scene unfolding below.

WHATEVER HAPPENED, Jefferson Ebert was a dead man! Casey Sears forced away a sense of unreality as he viewed the drama playing out below. Another helicopter hovered closer to the top of the tower than they were, keeping their police chopper at a distance. No amount of hollering had any effect on the other pilot.

Alex Berringer was at work.

So was Liam Croft. Insanely, desperately at work. He circled around, using the tip of the weapon he held to distract Ebert. Despite Casey's sure prediction that Croft was going to be shot point-blank at any moment, he had to admire the man. Facing off with only a spear or whatever that thing he held was, against a madman armed with a modern weapon took courage. Casey glanced at Sean Creedon, wanting to offer consolation on the unpreventable loss of this man the superintendent valued so highly.

Creedon was smiling! "Watch," he said. "Just you watch, Mr. Sears. And learn about the Irish fighting man."

Casey followed his colleague's advice.

PAULA FELT THE BREEZE from the river on her face, the scratchiness of the hemp rope around her neck, the alien touch of the cloth of Randall Ebert's suit on her skin. She was acutely aware of every sense in a way she had never been before.

She was also very aware that Liam was up on the tower, trying to save her. That broke her heart, because she knew he couldn't succeed. No matter what happened, Jefferson was going to push her over. He'd run the rope loosely around the iron gallows projecting from the side of the tower, but Liam had interrupted him before he could tie it securely. It didn't matter that she was in little danger of hanging, however. If she slipped, she would plunge down to the ground below and be killed.

She and her child.

Until this moment, she'd denied Noreen's claim that she carried Liam's baby. Now, moments before her own life ended, she was sure another life lived in her. Tears started in her eyes, not for herself, but for the baby. For Liam . . .

Her skin turned numb, and she quit feeling the breeze. Her hearing suddenly became her dominant sense, and she picked up every sound that was going on behind her on the tower floor. What had been a rush of white, meaningless noises took on cosmic meaning.

"I swear, you big Irish bastard," Jefferson yelled. "Come one step closer, and I'll shoot you dead where you stand and then I'll shove your lady-friend over the side."

Feet shuffled on the wood platform.

"D'ye have any idea how an Irishman kills with one of these?" Liam asked, his tone calm and conversational. He then went on to describe the damage a pike would do to its human target. "Want that for yourself, do you, boyo?" he added.

The clank of some kind of metal on metal.

"You're crazy!"

"No, I've merely joined the rest of the human race. We are a murderous lot, are we not? What's your name, laddie? I do like knowing a man's name before I rip him apart."

Jefferson shrieked in fury and fear. His gun fired.

Something went *poing.*

Paula heard the next sounds dimly, because as they happened, the rope jerked and pulled her off balance and she fell from the parapet.

But not to the ground. Nor was she hanged. Instead, to her astonishment, she landed squarely front-first on the wide t-bar of the gallows, straddling it with her legs. The breath was knocked out of her for a second, pain tore through her and her hands were still bound tightly behind her back.

But her legs were free. Using every ounce of strength she possessed, she gripped that iron bar with her thighs. The material of the suit skirt rode up, leaving her bare skin in contact with the cold, damp metal.

Giving her just the traction she needed to hold on! She shut her eyes, not daring to look down.

And did some of the most fervent praying of her life.

Liam made sure his opponent was down, then abandoned the still form and ran to the parapet. He screamed her name, but nothing came out of his mouth. His throat was almost too tight for him to breathe.

Then, he saw. She was precariously balanced not five feet below him.

"Don't move!" he yelled, tearing off the armor covering his chest. "I'm coming out to get you."

"No! Don't try it. The mortar's loose." She spoke carefully, but loudly. "You'll fall."

"It doesn't matter." He swung one leg over the edge.

And that was when the vertigo hit him.

Sweat started pouring down his face and his hands shook violently. His insides turned to jelly, and the fighting strength in his muscles faded away.

But he continued on over the side. He swung one arm out, reaching for the iron hook next to the gallows. His fingers closed around it. He shifted his weight . . .

And the hook came loose in his hand. Old, rotten mortar crumbled and spilled groundward.

Paula screamed.

He dropped the hook, held on with one hand and tried to reach for her. "I love you," he said.

"I love you," she replied.

Then, it happened. The t-bar made a grinding sound and one bolt came loose. The gibbet was about to slide away from the wall. Her weight had been too much for the old metal to support any longer.

Liam stretched out and grasped her bound wrists. He twisted the ropes firmly with his fingers. If she fell, they would fall together.

And then a voice spoke out of the sky. "Liam Croft, you silly bastard. Look up!"

Tobias! He obeyed. A rescue halter dangled from the hovering helicopter. Nearer and nearer until it hung by his face . . .

And the last bolt holding the gibbet gave way.

Liam dragged Paula to him with one arm.

With the other, he let go of the tower wall.

And as he fell with her, he grabbed at the helicopter rescue rope.

And caught it.

"Oh, my God," Casey Sears screamed. "I've never seen anything like that in my life!"

Sean Creedon whooped with joy and slapped the American on the back. "Nor are you ever likely to again. Unless you stay in Ireland!"

"Not a chance," the agent replied. "My heart couldn't stand the stress!"

"I'M GETTING real tired of ending up in hospitals every time I turn around," Paula said, wriggling impatiently under the sheet. "Can you possibly do something to get me out of here?" she asked.

Liam smiled at her. "No. Not a chance, love. You're pregnant."

"So?"

"So, you've been severely traumatized, you're with child and you're staying right here on this cot until you're given a clean bill by your doctor."

"Who happens to be one of your many cousins." Paula glared at her lover. "I bet you bribed him to keep me here."

"I'm not saying I didn't." He reached over, carefully because of his bruised arm, and brushed a lock of hair back from her pillow. "And would that be such a terrible thing, love?"

She sighed. "No, not after all the other things that have happened."

"There now. You're bein' a proper sweet bride-to-be."

"Like hell, I am," she said.

But when he leaned over and kissed her, Paula responded with all her heart. She broke off only when she heard the sound of a throat being cleared by someone standing in the doorway.

"Well, I guess we're interrupting something," Tottie Reynolds said to her companion.

"Guess so," agreed Casey Sears. "Think we ought to leave them alone and come back later."

"Come in!" Paula held out her arms, and Tottie embraced her. The two friends cried softly for a moment, then recovered their composure.

"You're looking a little rough, girl," Tottie declared. "But not too bad, considering."

"I can say the same," Paula said though tears. "Oh, Tottie, you look just fine!"

The sheriff posed. "No scars. Isn't modern medicine terrific?"

"It is."

Casey shook hands with Liam. "I got to say, man, I never saw anything like the way you took that creep out," he commented.

Liam glanced at Paula. "I did less harm than I intended," he admitted. "I was going to disembowel him."

"But you didn't," Tottie said. "You just ripped the gun out of his hand and knocked him silly. You could easily have killed, and you didn't."

"He wanted killin'," Liam said.

"He did," Casey agreed. "And you'd have done him a big favor. As it is, he's likely to spend the rest of his life in prison or an asylum." Casey Sears then went on to explain more about Jefferson Ebert. The agent had been allowed to observe when the man was interrogated by the Irish authorities.

Paula was astounded. Though Ebert had been after her for months with letters and phone calls, the escalation had begun right at the start of her relationship with Liam. Jefferson had confessed to being there when she found Liam. He had been posted up on a rise overlooking the section of the highway her Soroptimist group was cleaning. He could easily have shot her then. Ebert also revealed he had indeed been the one to dump the blood on her daybed. Liam's hand tightened on hers as Casey described the way the would-be killer told how he'd tricked Liam into chasing him and falling into the rosebushes. Since he lived just down the street, it was easy for him to run fast enough to elude capture and get out of sight quickly.

The story began to get complicated after that, Casey said. Ebert admitted to playing with Father Sheridan for months also, leading the priest on with odd confessions, then changing his tune and pretending total innocence. The father was so distraught after the explosion because he wasn't sure if he knew who the culprit was or just suspected an innocent man.

"We have backup on that from Father Sheridan himself," Casey said. "Ebert had the poor guy so confused that when the explosion happened, he actually felt he was in some way responsible."

"We need to be sure Father knows the whole truth," Paula declared. "He was a victim, too."

"Indeed he was," Casey said. "And there were plenty of others. See, Ebert waited until the bomb blast, sneaked into the courthouse by the back door and ransacked Charles Benson's office, looking for items he could use to help pin the harassment of you on the D.A."

"What?"

"Your boss and your secretary were having an affair. Easy enough to make it seem they wanted you gone."

"But why would I...?"

"Paula," Tottie said. "You were a threat to Charlie because you were likely to run for his office next election."

"I wasn't planning to. I was going to wait."

"But he didn't know that. Neither did Ebert. So, Charlie had a guilty secret that Jefferson knew about and he figured he could kill you and blame Charlie."

"Right." Casey went on. "He found enough ID to be able to leave the country as Charles Benson. With everything burning when the building finally collapsed, Charlie didn't know his passport had been stolen instead of destroyed. Ebert was particularly pleased with that coup, though he'd had no idea how handy the document would prove to be at the time."

"He must have been the person I ran into," Paula said. "The one I couldn't identify in all the smoke and confusion! Right after I went back inside to look for—" she glanced at Liam "—all my friends."

Liam just smiled.

The confession went on, detailing how angry Ebert had been when Paula left the country. How annoyed he was at the decoy. How he finally decided to take the battle to her in Ireland.

How he'd researched Liam Croft and learned of the bombing attempt arranged by Noreen. Then Casey recited a statement that Paula treasured. It showed intent and premeditation as nothing else he had said before. If she were the prosecutor, she thought, this would be her case.

"The really ironic thing is," Jefferson Ebert said, "if I'd left her alone, she'd have eventually come back home, and I could have killed her easily."

She felt like applauding. With those words, the man sank himself in a deep hole from which he would have no chance of returning.

After that, the information merged with what all of them already knew. The details of the attempt to kill Paula and Liam. The almost-suicidal chance Liam had taken in confronting a gun with no other protection than the breastplate he had worn.

"I thought bullets could go through metal like that," Casey said. "When he fired at you, I thought you were a goner."

"It's the design," Liam explained. "If he'd shot me straight on, I'd be dead. But the breastplate has a curve to it. By presenting him my torso only at an angle, I was fairly sure a shot'd deflect off the surface." He poked at his chest. "I've a hell of a bruise, though."

"Hell of a risk," Casey said.

"It didn't matter. Paula was in danger."

And that, when all was said and done, was that.

After a few more minutes of conversation, Paula sent Liam out with Casey to run down some more food. She was still starving from her almost forty-eight-hour enforced fast, she said.

She really wanted a little time alone with Tottie.

"You know I'm going to marry him," she said, when the door closed and they could speak freely.

Tottie sat down. "I figured. That means you're staying here, right?"

"Right. He can't live anywhere else. So I'll have to live here to be with him."

"Giving it all up for a man." Tottie shook her head. "Never thought I'd see the day."

"I can't go back, Tottie. Charlie, Diane, the talk that'll go on once Jefferson Ebert's story is out. You know what it'll be like. I'm not giving up a thing."

Tottie raised her eyebrows. "Seems to me you must have found something special here," she said. "Otherwise, you wouldn't be trying to *lawyer* me like this."

Paula started to reply, but Tottie cut her off. "Don't you try to tell me you wouldn't come back if there was nothing here for you. I've seen you fight and win worse battles than a little county gossip. Don't give me excuses about not wanting what you left. If you're set on staying, you must like it here more."

"All right. I confess." Paula sat up. "I love it here. I feel at ease, in spite of some of the strangeness. His family is mostly good people. I *like* them."

"Got it. Got it." Tottie raised her hands. "You found a home, finally. A place where you really fit."

Paula felt the sting of tears. "I have. You know I was never really comfortable before."

"Nobody knows it better. We grew up uncomfortable, you and I, remember?"

"I remember."

"We fought the social system, and we mostly got what we wanted."

"That's true. But, Tottie, I'm moving on."

"Good for you!" Tottie rose and gave her a hug. "And I'm damn proud you're doing it!" She sat back down. "I should tell you, your folks called. They were worried about you."

Paula looked away.

"They were! I couldn't tell them a thing. You really ought to let them know you're safe."

Paula nodded. "I know. And I will. It's just..."

"It's just time to loosen your ties and forgive," Tottie said. "You know what I'm saying?"

Paula frowned, then grinned. "I do. You're right. As soon as I get sprung from this bed, I'll call. They do need to know their only child's getting married."

"I'd love to be there when they find out it's a kind of king you're marryin'," the sheriff declared. "That should make them sit up and take notice."

"Only he's Irish, not Southern," Paula added. "That's liable to cause Momma to grow faint and Daddy to upend a few more bourbons."

They talked for a while longer. Tottie admitted to a more than casual attraction to Agent Casey Sears, but said she wasn't sure where that one would go. "I have to get back to my job," she said. "As soon as Doc Cunningham gives me the okay."

"You really weren't damaged too badly?"

"Oh, I was shook up. But I've been through bad stuff before." Tottie shrugged. "I need more time to heal, that's all."

"Speaking of healing, how's Gradon?"

"Back on the job." Tottie made a face. "Messing with everybody's mind as usual. But don't worry. Your man's cleared of that one. Gradon, it turns out, is too embarrassed to press charges."

"You're kidding."

"No, it would mean admitting an Irishman pounded him into the ground."

They both laughed again at that.

Then, Paula asked the question she'd been avoiding. "Tottie, I need to know something."

"What's that, honey?"

"Do you think Liam let Ebert live by accident?"

"Come again?"

"Was he really trying to kill and missed?"

"Nope. I see where you're going with this, but you're wrong. He knew exactly what he was doing, and don't you ever doubt it again. I've seen fights in my time, but he's magic. We were close enough to see every move. If he'd wanted to kill, Jefferson Ebert wouldn't be in custody babbling to some Irish shrink right now. He'd be in cold storage."

"Thanks. I needed to hear it. I saw him... interrogate those boys who set the bomb in the apartment. And after that, I wasn't sure what he'd do, given the right circumstances."

"He'd do what he had to, just like you or me."

"That must be why I love him."

"Lucky girl!"

"There's something else. He's terrified of heights. Petrified. I don't know how he managed to do what he did. It would be impossible for a normal man. For Liam, it was a..."

"Miracle?" a new voice asked. Tinsley entered the room. Alex and Tobias were right behind her. Tinsley came over and embraced Paula, then settled down on the edge of her bed. "I didn't know about the acrophobia. What got me was the way he caught that rescue rope with you in tow. That was some feat!"

"'Tis easy enough to explain," Tobias said. "He's Irish."

"However it happened," Paula said, "I'm grateful! Now, what about all of you? You just didn't appear by magic. Tell me how you all came to be here just in time to save us?"

"It was the phone cutting out," Tinsley said. She glanced at Tottie, who nodded. "When that happened, the two of us knew things were going sour quickly. We reached Alex on the mainland, he rushed over, got the three of us, chartered a jet and you know the rest."

"No, I don't. What about the helicopter? How...?"

"Alex bought it," Tottie said, dryly. "You know how that man likes to spend his money."

"You *bought* it?" Paula regarded Alex. "You're kidding."

"No. It was the quickest way."

"Thanks, Alex," Paula said, her eyes tearing again. "Thanks to all of you!"

Another knock on the door revealed Liam and Casey returning with armloads of food. Further serious discussion was abandoned for a time while everyone, especially Paula, feasted.

While they were enjoying the food, Morgan Croft came in.

"Noreen just died," she said.

Paula sank back on her pillow. Liam uttered a groan of sorrow. Tobias, however, looked like he was going to spit in the corner.

"She betrayed us," he growled. "For gold she would have killed this one." He pointed to Paula. "Certainly, Liam. And probably yourself," he added, addressing Morgan. "You should not mourn."

"Yes, Uncle," Morgan said. Her face was twisted with pain. "But I feel responsible. I was clan leader while she grew."

"And will ye then bear the burden of evil for her now she's with her Maker? Or will ye let it go, as it should be?"

Morgan bent her head.

"We share blame, if blame there is, Mother," Liam said, going over to her and putting his arms around her. "For I was The Croft during her teen years. However, she knew she could come to any of us if she had troubles, and she chose another path. She chose to turn against us. I'll grieve for her and pray for her soul, but I'm free of her. Now, I'm freeing you. Free yourself."

And to Paula's amazement, Morgan Croft broke down and cried.

Later, when she had recovered her emotional control, she told the group how what she'd learned from the dying young woman Noreen's last confession answered many questions.

"Her connection to the American, Mr. Ebert, was almost accidental," Morgan said. "He found out about her when he did some exploring in the underworld here in Dublin. The attempted bombing caught his attention, as you might imagine, so he went after the mind behind the deed. It did not take long for one of her lads to put him on to her as a Croft with the trust of the clan on her. A few evenings spent in the right pubs, and he found her in Timothy Donovan's poor company. From there, all he had to do was charm and beguile."

"Jefferson could do that," Tottie said. "No one ever suspected he harbored any resentment over his momma's situation. He could easily have seduced someone like your niece."

"He had a willing subject. Noreen did indeed hire those boys who set the explosives," Morgan went on. "Timothy's smuggling connections opened a whole world of criminals to her. And pretty and smart as she was, she had little difficulty recruiting and twisting them to do her bidding."

"Why did she want Liam dead?" Alex asked. "Did she really think that would make you sell land?"

Morgan plucked at the material of her skirt. "It might have." She looked at Tobias. "Without Liam, the likelihood of getting Uncle to sign the land contract was slim. And until Paula unearthed the old charter, we all believed we must have his signature or face the possibility of forfeiture."

Tobias looked puzzled. Then, comprehension spread over his wrinkled features. "Ah," he said. "So it was my name you were needin', Morgan Croft. Not myself. No wonder you sent the boy here after me. His guileful ways are deep! And so are yours, woman!"

"Don't be angry, Uncle," Liam said. "I did not tell you about the contract. I didn't force you in any way, if you will recall. I wanted you to return of your own choice."

"And so I have," Tobias replied. He folded his hands on top of his cane. "And glad I am to have done it. You're a worthy man, and Paula Dixon here will make you a worthy wife. I saw courage in you out on that bloody tower to make me proud to be a Croft for the rest of my days. Where's the bloody paper. I'll sign, if it means so much to you."

Paula concealed a smile. "They really don't need you, Tobias," she said. "Not for material things, in any event."

Everyone stared at her. Everyone but Morgan, who smiled for the first time since entering the room.

"You see," Paula said, and continued, "I went to the library at Trinity and..."

"You left the compound?" Liam asked.

"She had my company and permission," Morgan declared.

"But I told her to stay where she was safe..." He paused. "But then, you were taken from the compound, weren't you, love. Not so safe after all."

"You can't blame anyone for that," Alex said. "Ebert had an insider to help him."

"So he did," Liam said. "And I should have known..."

"Hush up, all of you. What's done's done." Tottie commanded. "I want to hear what Paula found out."

Paula continued. "I went to the library and dug through every old document I could find relating to Croft holdings. And I found out something interesting."

"What's that?" Tobias asked, intent on her every word.

"Until recently, that is, a few centuries ago, women signed for the land. So they still can. They don't need a man's signature, just the eldest woman's. The lineage started back at the beginning by the first Croft female was honored through the mother's line. It wasn't until English law truly dominated all legal proceedings that the Crofts began to put up a male front man.''

Tottie started to chuckle.

"So you see," Paula said, "Liam, if you dare marry me, I'm liable to take over the clan someday. Women rule!"

Her lover muttered something under his breath, but his smile was wide and genuine. "I'll take the chance," he said. "As soon as possible."

"Is that a proposal?" she asked.

"Why, darlin', I think I've been proposing to you since we first met."

"In a drainage ditch?" Tottie exclaimed.

"I thought she was an angel," Liam replied. "Until I smelled her."

At that, everyone erupted in laughter.

Paula's cries of "it was my perfume he meant" were lost in the merriment. Then Liam kissed her, and she protested no more.

COMING NEXT MONTH

#590 KEEPING KATIE • Patricia Keelyn
Maura Anderson had no choice. Three-year-old Katie meant the
world to her and no quirk of the justice system was going to take
her daughter away from her. So she ran...right into Alan Parks's
arms. The small-town sheriff offered her a future. But how could
she trust him when he represented the thing she feared most—the
law!

#591 TWILIGHT WHISPERS • Morgan Hayes
Claire Madden couldn't believe her good fortune when she
inherited a sprawling mansion in Maine. Not only was the house
gorgeous, but it came with its very own handyman, the irresistible
Michael Dalton. It also came with a mystery—a murder mystery—
that Michael was dead-set against her solving.

#592 BRIDGE OVER TIME • Brenda Hiatt
Kathryn Monroe wanted to make a difference. She'd spent years in
politics, but it had only left her feeling empty. She went home for a
rest, and, through some twist of fate, ended up in 1825. Here was
her opportunity to liberate the slaves...and the women. She'd
switched places with her own ancestress, Catherine Prescott. And
she wasn't sure she wanted to let Catherine's beau in on the secret.

#593 GHOST TIGER • Janice Carter
Meg Devlin's only chance of finding her father lay with
Conor Tremayne. He was the journalist who'd shot the film in
which Meg recognized the face she hadn't seen for nineteen years.
Conor seemed more than willing to help but, as their search took
them through northern Thailand, Meg had the distinct impression
the handsome reporter had his own agenda.

AVAILABLE NOW:

#586 SINGLE...WITH CHILDREN
Connie Bennett

#587 DANCE OF DECEPTION
Catherine Judd

#588 LUCK OF THE IRISH
Sharon Brondos

#589 CANDY KISSES
Muriel Jensen

Take 4 bestselling love stories FREE

Plus get a FREE surprise gift!

HARLEQUIN®

Don't miss these Harlequin favorites by some of our most distinguished authors!
And now, you can receive a discount by ordering two or more titles!

HT#25409	THE NIGHT IN SHINING ARMOR by JoAnn Ross	$2.99	☐
HT#25471	LOVESTORM by JoAnn Ross	$2.99	☐
HP#11463	THE WEDDING by Emma Darcy	$2.89	☐
HP#11592	THE LAST GRAND PASSION by Emma Darcy	$2.99	☐
HR#03188	DOUBLY DELICIOUS by Emma Goldrick	$2.89	☐
HR#03248	SAFE IN MY HEART by Leigh Michaels	$2.89	☐
HS#70464	CHILDREN OF THE HEART by Sally Garrett	$3.25	☐
HS#70524	STRING OF MIRACLES by Sally Garrett	$3.39	☐
HS#70500	THE SILENCE OF MIDNIGHT by Karen Young	$3.39	☐
HI#22178	SCHOOL FOR SPIES by Vickie York	$2.79	☐
HI#22212	DANGEROUS VINTAGE by Laura Pender	$2.89	☐
HI#22219	TORCH JOB by Patricia Rosemoor	$2.89	☐
HAR#16459	MACKENZIE'S BABY by Anne McAllister	$3.39	☐
HAR#16466	A COWBOY FOR CHRISTMAS by Anne McAllister	$3.39	☐
HAR#16462	THE PIRATE AND HIS LADY by Margaret St. George	$3.39	☐
HAR#16477	THE LAST REAL MAN by Rebecca Flanders	$3.39	☐
HH#28704	A CORNER OF HEAVEN by Theresa Michaels	$3.99	☐
HH#28707	LIGHT ON THE MOUNTAIN by Maura Seger	$3.99	☐

Harlequin Promotional Titles

#83247	YESTERDAY COMES TOMORROW by Rebecca Flanders	$4.99	☐
#83257	MY VALENTINE 1993	$4.99	☐
	(short-story collection featuring Anne Stuart, Judith Arnold, Anne McAllister, Linda Randall Wisdom)		

(limited quantities available on certain titles)

	AMOUNT	$
DEDUCT:	**10% DISCOUNT FOR 2+ BOOKS**	$
ADD:	**POSTAGE & HANDLING**	$
	($1.00 for one book, 50¢ for each additional)	
	APPLICABLE TAXES*	$ _____
	TOTAL PAYABLE	$ _____
	(check or money order—please do not send cash)	

To order, complete this form and send it, along with a check or money order for the total above, payable to Harlequin Books, to: **In the U.S.:** 3010 Walden Avenue, P.O. Box 9047, Buffalo, NY 14269-9047; **In Canada:** P.O. Box 613, Fort Erie, Ontario, L2A 5X3.

Name: _____

Address: _____ City: _____

State/Prov.: _____ Zip/Postal Code: _____

*New York residents remit applicable sales taxes.
Canadian residents remit applicable GST and provincial taxes.

HBACK-JM

HARLEQUIN®

COMING SOON TO
A STORE NEAR YOU...

THE MAIN
ATTRACTION

By *New York Times* Bestselling Author

This March, look for THE MAIN ATTRACTION by popular
author Jayne Ann Krentz.

Ten years ago, Filomena Cromwell had left her small town
in shame. Now she is back determined to get her sweet,
sweet revenge....

Soon she has her ex-fiancé, who cheated on her with
another woman, chasing her all over town. And he isn't
the only one. Filomena lets Trent Ravinder catch her.

Can she control the fireworks she's set into motion?

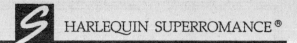

HARLEQUIN SUPERROMANCE ®

CATCH THE FEVER OF
SPRING BREAK WITH
HARLEQUIN
SUPERROMANCE!!

SAVE 30¢

ON YOUR NEXT PURCHASE OF ANY
HARLEQUIN SUPERROMANCE NOVEL

To the Dealer: Harlequin Books will pay the face
value of this coupon plus 11¢ handling upon presen-
tation of this coupon by your customer toward the
purchase of the product specified above. Any other
use constitutes fraud. Coupon is nonassignable, void
if taxed, prohibited or restricted by law. Consumer
must pay any government taxes. GST is included in
the value of the coupon.

LIMIT ONE COUPON PER PURCHASE. VALID ONLY
ON HARLEQUIN SUPERROMANCE NOVELS IN
CANADA. Mail to: Harlequin Superromance, P.O. Box
3000, Saint John, New Brunswick E2L 4L3

Coupons redeemable at retail outlets only.

OFFER EXPIRES JUNE 30, 1994

52600861

SRSB:CDA

$\mathcal{S}$ HARLEQUIN SUPERROMANCE ®

SUPERROMANTIC WEEKEND SWEEPSTAKES
OFFICIAL RULES—NO PURCHASE NECESSARY

To enter, complete an Official Entry Form or 3" x 5" card by hand-printing "Superromantic Weekend" and your name and address and mail it to: Superromantic Weekend Sweepstakes, P.O. Box 9076, Buffalo, NY 14269-9076 or Superromantic Weekend Sweepstakes, P.O. Box 637, Fort Erie, Ontario L2A 5X3. Limit: One entry per envelope. Entries must be sent via First Class Mail and be received no later than 7/15/94. No liability is assumed for lost, late or misdirected mail.

One prize, that of a 3-day/2-night trip (any days based on space and availability) for 2 to Scottsdale, Arizona, will be awarded in a random drawing (to be conducted no later than 8/31/94) from amongst all eligible entries received. Prize includes round-trip air transportation from commercial airport nearest winner's residence, accommodations at Marriott's Camelback Inn and $1,000.00 spending money. Approximate prize value, which will vary dependent upon winner's residence: $3,000.00 U.S. Winner selection is under the supervision of D.L. Blair, Inc., an independent judging organization, whose decisions are final. Travelers must sign and return a release of liability prior to traveling. Trip must be taken by 9/15/95 and is subject to airline schedules and accommodations availability.

Sweepstakes offer is open only to residents of the U.S. (except Puerto Rico) and Canada who are 18 years of age or older, except employees and immediate family members of Harlequin Enterprises, Ltd., its affiliates, subsidiaries, and all agencies, entities and persons connected with the use, marketing or conduct of this sweepstakes. All federal, state, provincial, municipal and local laws apply.

Offer void wherever prohibited by law. Taxes and/or duties are the sole responsibility of the winners. Any litigation within the province of Quebec respecting the conduct and awarding of prize may be submitted to the Regie des loteries et courses du Quebec. Prize will be awarded; winner will be notified by mail. No substitution of prize is permitted. Odds of winning are dependent upon the number of eligible entries received.

Potential winner must sign and return an Affidavit of Eligibility within 30 days of notification. In the event of noncompliance within this time period, prize may be awarded to an alternate winner. Prize notification returned as undeliverable may result in the awarding of prize to an alternate winner. By acceptance of their prize, winner consents to use of their name, photograph or likeness for purposes of advertising, trade and promotion on behalf of Harlequin Enterprises, Ltd., without further compensation, unless prohibited by law. A Canadian winner must correctly answer an arithmetical skill-testing question in order to be awarded the prize.

For the name of winner (available after 9/30/94), send a separate stamped, self-addressed envelope to: Superromantic Weekend Sweepstakes Winner, P.O. Box 4200, Blair, NE 68009.

SRW-RULES